fishing
for bacon

NeWest Press

by michael davie

Library and Archives Canada Cataloguing in Publication
Davie, Michael, 1970-
    Fishing for bacon / Michael Davie.
(Nunatak fiction)
ISBN-13: 978-1-897126-37-0.-- ISBN-10: 1-897126-37-9
    I. Title. II. Series.
PS8607.A83F58 2009   C813'.6   C2008-907094-1

Editor for the Board: Suzette Mayr
Cover and interior design: Natalie Olsen
Cover illustration: Natalie Olsen
Author photo: René Michaud

 Canada Council Conseil des Arts
for the Arts du Canada   Canadian Patrimoine
Heritage canadien   Alberta Foundation for the Arts   edmonton arts council

NeWest Press acknowledges the support of the Canada Council for the Arts, the Alberta Foundation for the Arts, and the Edmonton Arts Council for our publishing program. We also acknowledge the financial support of the Government of Canada through the Book Publishing Industry Development Program (BPIDP).

NEWEST PRESS

201.8540.109 Street
Edmonton, Alberta T6G 1E6
780.432.9427
newestpress.com

No bison were harmed in the making of this book.
We are committed to protecting the environment and to the responsible use of natural resources. The text paper used for printing this book is acid-free, 100% old growth forest-free (100% post-consumer recycled), processed chlorine-free, and printed with vegetable based, low VOC inks. These inks are transported in reusable drums, saving landfill space.

2 3 4 5 12 11 10
printed and bound in Canada

To Ben, Spencer, and Jo, who are each currently fishing for Bacon.

1. ● **When I was ten** my father left and so my mother gave me a fishing rod. Not a new rod or even a fly rod, but a green and brown second-hand spincasting rod, the kind with the closed-face reel and thumb-button trigger. Said she got it at a garage sale. I frowned at it and asked for a fly rod instead – a new one. But my mother rolled her tongue around the inside of her clenched lips and said I sounded just like my father. She said he liked new things too, and if I wanted to play with new things I could just walk right out that same fucking door he did. I wanted a new fly rod, but I sure didn't want to walk out that same fucking door my father did. I didn't even know which fucking door he'd walked out, the front or back.

Robert Redford never made a movie about *spincasting*. And if he did, you can bet your tackle box Brad Pitt wouldn't star in it. Spincasting's got none of the grace or romance of the fly-fishing cast. Fly-fishermen sneer and say that spincasting's like drinking port from a coffee mug. Even still, it can be a difficult skill to master – especially at ten. In those first few weeks of learning, I snagged my shirt, my hair, my ear. Occasionally I'd hook people fishing next to me. Once I even tangled my line around my shoes and floundered into the river. Eventually I harmonized the snap of my wrist and the thumb-button release with the forward acceleration of the rod – at least enough to hit water. I figured out that spincasting is all about timing.

Since then I spend most days fishing. Fishing is the only thing worth spending time on, living along the Crowsnest River in a tiny old mining town with no mines where the streets have no sidewalks except for the few old slabs lining Main Street with weeds busting out of the cracks. For four years I clubbed out a lure with that stiff green and brown second-hand spincasting rod, snapping my wrist, casting out, reeling back in. And though I never caught a single fish, I eventually stopped snagging shrubbery, overcasting the river, and balling up my line inside the closed-face reel. Instead I started sailing lures across the river where they'd plop into the water just under the opposite bank, often within a couple feet of my aim. I was ripening into a master caster. At least until I turned fourteen.

At fourteen my casting hiccuped and wobbled worse than when I first started. I began hooking branches twenty feet up on the other side of the river. Then my voice began to whir and screech like the drag on my fishing line. I had to carry my tackle box in front of me to hide the crotch under my waders that rose more often than a brookie in a mayfly hatch.

At school we had a whole two-week course about whatever had infested my body, but I never made it past ten minutes of a single class. Every time Mrs. Jorgensen enunciated "ejaculatory gland" or "testicles" or "gonadotropins" through her long, wooden-looking teeth, I'd either throw up a bowl's worth of that morning's Count Chocula, or all the blood would slide out of my head and my body would slip down out of my desk and onto the sparkled linoleum.

Mrs. Jorgensen said I'd figure it all out if I just reviewed her handouts. The handouts had cross-sectional diagrams that looked like the discards from a gutted whitefish, and medical terminology that rolled my eyes into the back of my head. I wrapped up rocks in all her handouts and sank them in the Crowsnest River.

I found out what was happening to me from overhearing kids talk in the schoolyard, but I didn't get the whole picture. My mother said what was happening was happening because I wouldn't eat her rutabaga. But Grandma Magic Can, who lived with us, told me to nevermind. To just relax. My body, she said, was getting ready for love.

My body spent the next three years getting ready for love and, no matter how relaxed I fought to remain or how much rutabaga I forced down my shaking throat, my casting wouldn't recover.

Three quarters through my seventeenth year, I couldn't wait for my body anymore. I was ready to be ready – ready to figure out what love was all about.

As with spincasting, I had to discover what love was all about on my own. My mother didn't really feel one way or the other about fishing, but she sure as shooting knew what she felt about love. A fat-assed, dirty-bum lie, she called it. The line of her mouth would crinkle and her top lip would beak out over her bottom one. You're better off on your own, she'd lecture, often when I wasn't even in the room. Since my father left, my mother has only had two rules:

1. Keep quiet when her soaps are on.
2. Stay the hell away from girls.

Girls turn boys into men; her coffee breath filled the air. And men are pigs. You're better off odd than a pig. But Grandma Magic Can said my mother was full of shit and that I wasn't so odd, but I was sure as hell's bells gonna need a girl in my life. The problem, she said, was there weren't any good ones left. We needed to get me a catalogue, she said. Then we could order me one. Between them, I wasn't sure who to believe. Then I remembered Kenny Rogers singing something about there being "someone for everyone," and both my mother *and* grandmother always say that Kenny Rogers sure as shit knows how things are. So I decided to believe him.

Seemed simple enough. To figure out what love was all about, I just needed to find my *someone*.

Looking back now, I've finally figured out what both spincasting and love are all about – and surprised to learn it's the same thing. Timing.

My name's Bacon Sobelowski. I have bad timing.

2. ● As far back as I can remember, I've

had bad timing. I only ever dropped and shattered a glass of milk during the climax of *Guiding Light*. As a child I only bounced up onto my parents' bed on the Saturday mornings my father was fighting a "fucking brain-melting headache." And diarrhea only attacked on hot stuffy summer days while I was buckled into the front passenger seat of my mother's Lancer.

My bad timing began at conception. Which occurred shortly before my father left on the first of his "just need a little me-time" away periods. That one lasted a year. Grandma Magic Can has explained that I was the result of an unwanted pregnancy in an unwanted woman whose troubles were compounded with an unwanted premature birth that struck one morning while my mother was frying up breakfast. Grandma Magic Can said she wrestled my mother into the back of the car and charged to the hospital. The whole time my mother kicked at the back of Grandma's headrest and squealed for the only thing she really wanted out of the whole sordid mess: her breakfast. I've been told that, during the birth, my mother shrieked at the doctor, "Bacon!"

and at each nurse, "Bacon! Bacon!" She barked at a housekeeper, "Bacon!" and at the housekeeper's mop, "Bacon!" She even questioned an IV stand, "Bacon?" Afterward, when a nurse informed my mother that I was a boy, she curled up around her pillow and sighed, "Bacon." When the nurse asked her if she had a name for Baby Boy Sobelowski, my mother stared at the cold, grey wall and snivelled, "Bacon." The exhausted hospital staff must have obliged because they labelled my crib accordingly: Bacon Sobelowski. My mother, I suppose, just never got around to changing it.

3 • Bellevue seems like an easy place to find

something – your someone or otherwise. There just aren't a whole lot of places to look. But on the flip side ... there just aren't a whole lot of places to look.

Bellevue sits timid, just off the Crowsnest Trail highway, not pushing up against the road but not far off in defiance either. Each day, cars, trucks, and trains speed past, and, I guess, so does time. Grandma says Bellevue doesn't have the resources you might find in a city or other more modern towns. Bellevue. It's pretty much been left to fend for itself.

The wind blows harder in Bellevue, like it recognizes the vulnerability of the town. The strong gusts scuffle your hair, shove you as you walk, pick up the winter's dust and gravel and hurl them at you. And as if casting wasn't enough of a challenge, that old Bellevue wind will snatch up any lure under three quarters of an ounce and chuck it right back at your face. It blows nearly every day in Bellevue. The few days it doesn't, the wind's really only resting around a corner. On those days people move quietly around the still town, careful not to wake it.

To start the search for my someone I quickly determined that only six girls in my grade twelve class were single. Three of them were pregnant, two already had children, and one was at home battling mononucleosis. We'd all been at the same school for several years now, and none of them had ever spoken to me much more than to occasionally tell me, "Hey, Bacon, Bell called looking for his palsy." I never really knew what that meant, but Mrs. Jorgensen sometimes scolded them and assured me that I had a normal face, I didn't have Bell's palsy, and told me not to pay them any heed. In any case, it seemed a long shot that one of *those* girls was my someone.

Then, one Tuesday morning, Mrs. Jorgensen's lips curled out and her long, wooden-looking teeth chomped and chattered, telling us that a new student would be joining us tomorrow. She — *the new student was a she!* — moved to Bellevue from Medicine Hat. A new girl! The timing seemed too good to ignore. I wondered immediately if she might be my someone.

I could hardly wait for the next day to come, to see what the new student looked like. Would her voice be the whispering lap of a creek bank or as raspy and loud as a raven's gripe? Would she be pregnant? How thick would her hands be? My mother always said women retain water the same way they retain facts, and you can tell how smart a woman is by how meaty her hands are. My mother's thick, fleshy hands always looked so strange on her otherwise small, brittle frame.

At dinner that night I couldn't finish my chili, partly because of the anxiety of imagining what the new girl looked like and partly because my mother made that particular night's chili with rutabaga instead of beans, and with cubes of leftover ham steak instead of ground beef.

That night I lay in bed in my basement room, gazing at the brown bath towel tacked over the small window. The wind jabbed at the towel, flicking the loose corners up against the spongy, water-stained ceiling tiles. Then the wind would turn and swirl and begin tugging at the towel, sucking it back up flat against the frayed screen. Each time the towel lifted, I half expected to see the new girl revealed behind it, perhaps a peek at her sneakers miraculously walking past my basement window.

How would I know she was the one? My *someone?* Would my casting recover? I barely slept that night, partly because I couldn't stop wondering about the new student and partly because my stomach rumbled from the little bit of chili I'd managed to eat.

When morning came I shot out of the house early, hurrying to the bus stop. But a massive tremor in my stomach forced me to spin around and race back faster than I'd left. I spent the morning on the toilet and the afternoon in bed, sipping Tang to rehydrate. My mother was working evening shifts that week, so she spent the day at home with me. I managed virtual silence in my bedroom, but I knew my feet were shuffling to the bathroom too loudly when she wrenched the volume up even louder on *Guiding Light* and *One Life to Live*. I didn't sleep much better that night. Bad timing never leaves my side.

Finally, on Friday morning, I slogged out of the house and watched the bus jolt to a stop like it did every morning, as though ramming the rear end of a car. Rollie Dawson heaved open the door and thrust up his chin in a half nod, a toothpick drifting across his mouth.

"You seen the new girl?" Rollie said through clenched teeth. I paused on the first step and shook my head. "Humph," Rollie hiccuped. "Honest to Christ, boy." He plucked the toothpick from his mouth, glanced back over a shoulder, and whispered, "If the life givers gave that girl anything, they gave her legs." He tapped the toothpick at the air as if to say that's a fact, then tossed it back in his mouth.

I stepped down the aisle and peeked from seat to seat, half expecting to see Marilyn Monroe's legs stretching out into the aisle, a soft set of hands pushing down on a wind-blown skirt.

Then I spotted her. The new kid! Her eyes turned, gazing out the window. I slid into the seat across from her and pretended to read my social studies text, unable at first to even pop a glance her way. When I finally snuck a peek, I saw how right Rollie was about the life givers. They'd given Sara Mulligan miraculously long, creamy butterscotch legs. Legs stretching out from under jean cut-offs. I immediately thanked the life givers for giving us such a warm March. Those legs were perfect. Her shorts had several tears in them and were doodled with black marker scribbles, including a star drawn in a circle and a rough sketch of a fist with its middle finger extended. When she turned from the window, I noticed the life givers had given Sara Mulligan something else. Moles. A dozen of them. All across her face. It took most of the bus ride, peeking up from my social studies text and the story of Archduke Franz Ferdinand's assassination to count them all, but I spotted an even dozen.

Sara didn't make a lot of friends at first. None at all, in fact. I could imagine how difficult it must have been to move to a new town with just a few months left in the senior year, not to mention with kids calling her "Holy Moley" behind her back and saying her face was Braille for "butt ugly." Nobody ever ridiculed those legs, though.

I don't know if any of the kids really believed Sara was butt ugly. She wasn't. Being a new kid in our school and her unusual moles just made her an easy target. But underneath those moles, around those moles, and even in those moles, lay beauty. Beauty hid in her sharp features, her pointed nose, the barbed cut of her eyes. Sara's beauty was a hard, jagged beauty, the kind you might catch flashing in the cobbled texture of asphalt, or in the sparkling glint of metal on a fillet knife.

I spent the first few weeks after Sara arrived cooking up reasons to stroll by her locker. With beautiful precision, she punctured the dotted outline of a circled star design into her locker door, using only the sharp end of a pencil compass.

The first time Sara Mulligan spoke to me I farted. It was at a campfire party along the Crowsnest River. Nobody ever actually invited me to any of the campfire parties, but I'd hear about them and walk the river in my old pair of hip waders, knee-deep in the water, half-heartedly fishing but squinting to see what I could see. What I saw that night were several kids laughing, others pushing down small trees, and most of them taking turns jumping over the campfire. About every third or fourth jumper stumbled and collapsed into the fire. He'd roll away, brush himself off, and laughter would echo over the water; then the next kid would go. Several metres away from it all, Sara Mulligan sat alone on a picnic table next to the river. I guessed she hadn't been invited either. Dusk had just barely begun to settle in with the sun sinking into the river, the water aflame all around me, Sara's moley face silhouetted against the fiery setting sun.

I nearly tipped over in the water right then because Sara Mulligan turned and waved.

I spun from her sight so quickly I splashed the tip of my rod into the river. Then I yanked it up and heaved out a clunky cast that splashed even more, the lure sinking just a few feet in front of me. I bent a glance back toward Sara.

"Hey," she called, her open hand waving me forward. "C'mere."

My stomach ducked, my legs wobbled, my lungs paused, my body gave a shiver, and that's when I farted. As though my butt had seen her wave and blurted out, "Who's that?"

At that very moment I noticed a fish, not eight feet away, cruising the swirl I'd just been fishing. A good-sized rainbow, though oddly it didn't have the face of a trout. It had my mother's face: her aspirin pallor, her sleepy eyes, her tiny, tent-shaped mouth.

I turned back to Sara who was leaning back on the picnic table, stretching out her legs—long as spaghetti.

The trout with my mother's face shot bubbles from its mouth and, as those bubbles reached the water's surface and burst, I could hear the echoes of my mother's caw: "Stay the hell away from girls." The trout drifted toward me, almost brushing against my waders, drifted up the river, drifted out of sight.

I knew I should follow the fish with my mother's face, head upstream and around the corner, but my feet in the cold rubber boots of my waders wouldn't move. I could barely hold my grip on the spincasting rod; my cheeks burned as though I were leaning into the campfire with the others. When I looked back toward Sara I suddenly knew exactly what Kenny Rogers meant when he sang, *I was soft inside, there was something going on.* Ah-ah.

"C'mere!" Sara frowned, waving harder.

I made myself stumble over.

Sara's eyes pushed from her face, reaching out at me. "How come you're not sitting at the campfire?" she asked firmly, almost suspiciously.

My mouth opened and closed several times, trying to find a word. I sneezed on her chest.

Sara cut me off before anything else left my mouth, brushed her T-shirt off, and said, "You weren't invited, were you?"

17

I shook my head and wiped my nose.

Her grey alloy glare aimed at me like a pistol barrel. "So, why you here?"

I looked over toward the group gathered around the campfire, down at my hip waders, then back at Sara. I couldn't believe I was having a conversation with her!

"If you weren't invited, I don't understand why you'd – " she paused, and a kink in her lip rose on one side, lifting her mouth into something like a smile. "Unless ... are you *spying* on me?"

My eyes stretched open. "No, of course not!" I said. "No, no."

She studied me. "I see you, you know. Walking by my locker. Looking for me. That's the kind of thing *stalkers* do."

"Oh, no, no." I shook my head. "I'm not a stalker."

"What then?" She lifted her chin. "Just a little creepy?"

"*Creepy*? No, I'm not – "

"Let's walk." She nodded down river.

"What?"

"Come on." She hopped off the picnic table and motioned for me to follow her downstream.

I couldn't look at any part of her, not her eyes, not her moles, not even her legs. I kept my glance pinned to the ground, terri-fied of each shuffle-step in those wet and squeaking waders, certain my tensed feet would fail and I'd collapse into the dirt.

"Do you not sleep or something?" she asked.

"I sleep fine," I said.

"Your eyes always look sleepy."

"Everybody says that," I replied without lifting my head. "That's just the way I look. I don't have Bell's palsy either."

"You walk funny too, you know," Sara said. "Like you're try-ing to kick your boots off or something." I couldn't help but lift my eyes to the glide of her own stride, her legs so graceful and smooth. In my peripheral, I could see her hand swaying beside her as she walked. I imagined that hand brushing against mine. Her soft, thick hands – smart hands. My boot caught a root in the path. I lurched forward but was able to catch the scruffy branch of a limber pine before falling. Sara kept walking as if I wasn't there.

Just around the river's first bend Sara turned, knocked the green and brown second-hand spincasting rod with the thumb-button trigger from my hand, heaved herself onto me, knocking us both over, and plunged her tongue into my mouth.

Behind us the river thrashed over rocks and sweepers. I could hear in the midst of the rapids a distinctive splashing, not of water over rock but of a fish flipping and slapping. The splashing grew louder and more frenzied but was soon drowned out by the choking gurgle of the rapids.

Sara's tongue rooted all around my mouth, sweeping over regions my own tongue had not yet found. Unsure of my role, I stretched my mouth open as wide as it would allow, diligently holding that position, trying to remain calm. I imagined I was at the dentist – that helped me keep still.

Sara pulled up her knees, driving one into my side. It seemed strangely deliberate. She then pushed a thumb into my eye, sat herself up, and, through my blurred vision, I saw her throw off her shirt.

The river sounded suddenly more distant, softer, like tiny shearing scissors – the sharp splashing was gone. I could hear the shuffling of leaves and the heavy, unrhythmic stamps of what, through the dusk and my watering eye, I could just make out to be a severely intoxicated girl. Kelsey Westerfield, I guessed. She must have stumbled from the campfire. She wandered right close and actually stepped over us. I'm not sure if she'd even seen us. Though I desperately needed to swallow, I continued holding my mouth wide.

A hollow clang sounded off to our side. Another. Two more, and then a sharp shattering. Empty beer bottles were hurled over from the campfire, crashing into some designated heap not far from where we lay. It seemed we'd settled in the empties pile. I feared a can or bottle might hit us. A drunken Kelsey Westerfield was now down on one knee, unsteadily propping her head against an aspen. She threw up.

My shirt tore when Sara tugged it over my head. She had a terrible time freeing me of my hip waders, lifting me off the ground with each heave until one of the shoulder straps snapped, whipping back and flogging me across the forehead. The waders finally gave, peeling off and sending Sara stumbling onto her back. Left in my shorts, my legs revealed themselves thin, clammy, and pale. Sara hurled the waders into the river with a grunt, and I watched them float off with the current. Throughout it all I held my mouth open, never sure when she'd need to put her tongue back in again.

Sara pounced over me. I tried to cross my ankles, certain my mother-faced fish was watching, but Sara pried them apart, tore off my shorts and then finally my underwear. I felt much of my blood leave my head, rushing down my torso. Sara straddled me on her knees, glaring down, clawing at my chest and shaking me by the shoulders. She screamed for me and at me, and, for whatever reason, even drove her elbow into my head.

Although it was an unusually warm March, it was cold without clothes on, the ground noticeably damp. Sara adjusted her nakedness over me. I shut my eyes and imagined myself in the warmth of my dentist's office. But then I imagined the kids at the campfire sitting in other dental chairs trying to hold in their giggles while Sara – dressed as a dental assistant – moved from one to the other, standing over them, flossing their teeth and whispering about mine. Was there something wrong with my teeth? What was wrong with my teeth? Word spread to the waiting room where people exchanged knowing glances and restrained smiles over their *Maclean's* or *Equinox* magazines. The dentist pushed a mirror over my face and I saw little baby teeth all pale yellow, like the tiny niblets of corn I sometimes pierce with a hook for bait. Two of the tiny teeth simply rolled right out of my mouth, unable to last through the cleaning.

I kept my hands still, too frightened to know where to put them. I wanted to lift a hand to Sara's skin but I heard my dentist's voice, "You put your hand *where*? Bacon! You don't do *that* when you're doing *that*." What was *that*? I wondered. I certainly didn't want to do *that*.

I opened one eye, hoping to spot a misshapen nipple on Sara or something hidden and odd that I could threaten to tell if she laughed about me with others. But her nipples were perfect, as rosy as the inside of a gill.

Sara pushed down all the way over me, and then lifted herself up slightly. The ground began surging below me, rising and falling. I felt so dizzy my head began listing to one side. She pushed herself down once more and I ejaculated. The wind brushed through the trees with a sad wheezing sound, like air seeping from a malleted trout.

When I opened my eyes, Sara was still sitting on top of me, woofing and heaving, nearly unable to catch her breath. She bared her teeth and growled in one of the most intimidating spectacles I've ever seen. I couldn't tell if she'd found something enjoyable in what had happened or if she was furious.

As I shrank inside her, she settled her breathing, scrubbed her knuckles hard over my hair, and exhaled, "We should go over to that campfire." The campfire? Why would we go there? What did she want from the campfire? But wait—she said *we*. She wanted *we* to go!

Sara peeled herself from me and stood glaring down at my thin, pasty nakedness. I had to smile at my dumb luck: who would've found their someone in a campfire empties pile?

As we approached the campfire, the others stared, tilting their heads in toward each other, whispering. Sara locked my arm around hers and pulled us up next to the fire.

"Got any more of those?" Sara said to Amy Russell, nodding at the Kokanee in her hand and at the cooler beneath her. Amy blinked and gaped around, then stood up, opened the cooler, and handed Sara a beer.

Three guys from my shop class, who had never spoken to me before, leaned in around me, nudging in between Sara and me, giggling and whispering, asking if I'd just "popped her cherry." Sara and Amy Russell laughed about something. I strained to hear more but couldn't. Did I pop Sara's cherry? I wasn't sure how to respond. I was pretty sure I knew what that meant but it seemed to me more like Sara had picked the fruit herself and hurled it at me like a scud missile. I didn't want to explain that it was me who felt like I'd had something popped, it was me who was having trouble walking and, after the way the whole thing unfolded, it was me who almost worried that somehow *I* might

21

conceive. I just shrugged. One of them pushed my shoulder and nodded, another handed me a beer, and they all smiled and laughed and asked me what I thought of the Flames' chances for the playoffs.

All night I talked to people I'd never talked to before. Every now and then Sara would eyeball me through the crowd and lift her bottle just slightly in my direction. At one point she slid up next to me, pushed her tongue back in my mouth – right there in front of everybody. When she pulled it back out, a corner of her mouth curled up and she whispered, "There won't be any more of these we don't get invited to."

She was right.

4. ● At school, kids now nodded at me in the halls,

sat next to me on the bus. The guys in shop class included me in talk of who puked on what last weekend or why Fords sucked or why they rocked. I'd nod and laugh or shake my head if that's what they were doing. One day one of them took me aside, turned his face a little sideways, squinted, and quietly asked if I knew why Sara moved here. I shook my head. He sneered like he'd just proved something and walked away. "Why do you ask?" I called after him. He turned back, smiled widely, but didn't answer.

Sara never seemed to bother much with anyone at school other than me. Girls now talked to her, but not much. Nobody, though, called her Holy Moley anymore. Secretly, I was relieved she didn't make friends. I worried about what she might say to others about what we did, how we did it, if I'd done it correctly.

During the weeks that followed I didn't get much of a chance to test if my casting had recovered. Sara and I were seeing a lot of each other. At noon I'd grab my lunch from my locker and, more often than not, she'd come by and lead me over to some part of the yard where we'd eat together. After school she'd sometimes intercept me on my way to the bus to instruct me her parents wouldn't be home until later and so we'd be going back to her house. While my enthusiasm for fishing continued, it was my time with Sara Mulligan that taught me that the fishing rod – no matter how gratifying – comes second.

It took until June, just three weeks from graduation, before I actually asked Sara if she was my someone. I guessed she was. She seemed to be. But I needed to know for sure. That afternoon Sara and I lay cupped together under a blanket, still undressed, in the glow of her basement TV. Her small breasts pressed warm against my back. That's when I finally asked her.

"Am I your *what*?" her voice soured.

"My someone," I answered. "You know, like in the Kenny Rogers song. There's someone for everyone ..."

"I'll be honest, Bacon," she said with hard eyes, "I don't listen to Kenny Rogers. And neither should you."

"My mother says he sure as shit knows what's what." On TV a farm supplies commercial flashed across the screen. The Lethbridge station said the weather was up next.

"Listen Bacon," Sara said. "We're just trying to make the short time we have left in this stupid school tolerable. Having sex and having it known that we're having sex keeps us off the bottom of the food chain." She had one arm tucked under my head while her free hand drew circles in my hair, just above an ear. Even through her gentle touch I could still feel the strength of her hard fingers, like the graphite dowels of a fishing rod.

"Does that mean you're not my someone?"

"I don't know, Bacon." She sat up a little. "Why are you so worked up about it?"

"I don't know," I shrugged. "A frog in a well."

"A frog in a *what*?"

"A frog in a well," I said. "Grandma Magic Can says it every time I learn something new. 'Frog in a well,' she'll say, and her smile wrinkles up her whole face. Then again, she smokes weeds – that might be what's wrinkling up her face."

"Your grandmother smokes *pot*?" Sara frowned with disbelief.

"No, not pots – *weeds*."

"Bacon," Sara dropped her head and laughed, "weed *is* pot. Same thing. It's all ganja, mon."

23

"Yeah, I know. But I meant *weeds*. Grandma picks thistle, quack grass, chickweed. Whatever she finds along the river. She dries it in the oven, dices it up, uses an old Fanta can as a pipe. Calls it *magic can*."

"*What*?" Sara's thin, crisp hair shook with her head. "Are you kidding me?"

"No," I said. "She says Kenny Rogers does it."

"Kenny Rogers does not!"

"Trust me, Grandma Magic Can would know." I turned to watch the Lethbridge weatherman on TV. He had a spooned chin and a moustache that kept getting sucked into his tiny hidden mouth, tripping up his words: "Tomorrow Medicine High should reach a hat of twelve, er, I mean Medicine *Hat* should reach – no it's Lethbridge that'll be twelve, Medicine Hat will … well, heck, I'm not really sure what Medicine Hat will be …"

"So what does it mean?" Sara asked.

"The magic can?"

"No! The frog in the well."

"Oh," I said. "Sorry. Grandma Magic Can likes to speak in proverbs. Korean proverbs. My grandfather was in the Korean War. I guess he came home from Korea with a book of translated proverbs and a son. Grandma Magic Can adopted the book but not the son. She sent Grandpa and the child back to Korea." I paused to imagine my grandfather up and moving to a totally different country, different culture. I'd never been out of the Crowsnest Pass. I wondered if he told anybody in Korea why he'd moved there. Or did he keep it secret? I thought about Sara moving from Medicine Hat.

"I never met him," I said. "My grandfather, I mean. At least with my father I got to know him for a few years before he left. Mom says all men leave." I saw Sara's jaw clench and instantly regretted what I'd said. "Anyway, Grandma never explains the proverbs. She says I'm a smart boy and I'll figure them out."

"What do you *think* it means?" Sara asked.

"Well," I rolled onto my back, gazing at the ceiling tiles – they had spotted holes and worm-like markings just like a brook trout. "I always pictured a tiny frog living his whole life in a small, dark well, then one day taking a giant leap, hopping right out, seeing something completely new for the first time. Imagine how excited that frog would be. That's how I felt when I learned to spincast."

"That's cool." Sara lifted my chin with a curled finger. "So then what new thing did the frog learn about this time?"

"Love," I said.

In an instant Sara drove a fist into my ear. I stuffed my head inside the crook of my elbow and waited for the humming to stop.

She glared at the TV and stuffed a thumb between her teeth. Her mouth looked caught between wanting to smile and wanting to strip the flesh from her thumb.

"Don't ever lie to me, Bacon."

"OK." I rubbed my ear, unsure of what had just happened.

"Never."

"I never have," I said.

"Nevermind that, you cocksucker," she said. "Just don't ever do it."

"OK."

She pulled my hand up near her chest, squeezing it in her graphite dowels so hard I felt my blood thumping to break through where she gripped. Her eyes glossed over, and for a moment I thought she might cry. That or eat my hand.

The weatherman dropped his pointing stick and resorted to his short, stubby finger, which barely poked free from his jacket sleeve. In fact, it looked more like a nipple stabbing at each little town dot on the map, as though hoping one dot would form a mouth to take it in. "Heavy rain's expected for the Pincher Creek area tomorrow—no, wait ... that's not 'til Thursday. And darnit anyway, where's Pincher Creek gone on this map?"

"Know what I think your granny's proverb means?" Sara said.

"What?" I squinted through the pain in my ear.

"I think it means she thinks you live a sheltered life." Sara slid one of those remarkable legs over top of me. "Let's scronk again."

I lay disoriented from the stinging waves in my ear and the jumpiness I felt whenever I was with Sara. So many new feelings, each one like stepping into a crumbling riverbank, spilling murkiness into the water and sending a sudden shift in the current.

"How come we never protect ourselves?" I asked.

"Protect ourselves?" she chuckled. "From what?"

"You know ... I mean why don't we use contraceptives." I shivered at the sound of the word. It sounded too much like medical terminology.

"*Contraceptives*?" Her frosty eyes narrowed. "Bacon, I don't believe in contraceptives."

"You don't?"

"No." She pulled an arm out from under my neck, dropping my head.

"But they're real," I said. "I've seen them. My father kept some in a shoe box —"

"No, Bacon," Sara shut her dark eyes briefly and sighed. "I mean I don't *use* them."

I wiggled around to face her but found I had to lower my glance to her less intimidating breasts. "You don't use them? Do ... do you mean you *can't* get pregnant?"

She sneered. "I'm sure I'm perfectly capable of getting pregnant."

"Oh," I said to her rosy nipples. "Then isn't this dangerous?"

She made a face like I'd just crapped her blanket. "Of course! That's the point. We're rolling the dice each time we scronk — it's exciting as hell."

"Exciting?"

"It's wild!"

"I don't know, Sara, maybe we should —"

"Hey," she snapped, "if protection is really that important to you, Bacon, we just won't have sex. Nothing's safer than abstinence. Just say you don't want to have sex anymore. Go ahead."

Over her shoulder I could see the Lethbridge weatherman had recovered his pointing stick and was tapping it, not toward one of the sunny faces or a rain cloud — but instead to a round cartoon pig's head that had suddenly appeared on the map, just overtop of where Bellevue should be. The stumpy index finger of the weatherman's other hand was thrust out toward the camera, wagging back and forth slowly, threateningly. And the weatherman didn't have his face anymore, but my mother's face instead, as pale as the underside of a jackfish.

"When does your dad get home?" I asked.

"Don't worry about him." She wagged her lower end over me teasingly. "He's a pussycat. No, check that—he's just a pussy. He'll worry about what I tell him to worry about. He's not even my real father. He *adopted* me."

"Oh," I said, craning my neck to check the stairs. "But that doesn't mean he wouldn't still prefer we not lay naked on his basement carpet."

She eased her blood-warm body on top of my frozen carcass. "It's not safe," Sara whispered mockingly. "We're unprotected. Just tell me no."

I flinched as I heard the door upstairs. Footsteps sounded above us. "Will he come down?"

"I told you not to worry about him."

Sara's warmth swathed over me. My body quivered. We finished before the weatherman.

Sara pawed the blanket over me like she was covering a kill. She pressed her lips right up against my ear and whispered, "Here's hoping my period comes."

My stomach shifted, dropping a little. "Are you my someone, Sara?"

She chuckled at that. "I'll tell you what," she said. "We'll test it."

I looked up at her through half-closed eyes. "How do we test it?"

"Leave that to me. I'll let you know."

The top of the stairs creaked. I felt my eyes widen.

"Goddamnit, Bacon," Sara hissed. "This is the third time I've told you not to worry about him." I tried to lift myself but her hand pressed down on my chest with such firmness I swore I felt the basement floor give beneath me. Her moles turned brown-red, reached and glared like a dozen tiny angry eyes.

"Sorry," I said.

"Now, my *sister*, on the other hand," Sara said, softening, almost giggling, "well, she'd shred your dink like a carrot."

"*What*—" I tried to squirm free from her grip.

"What's going on down here," a sandpaper voice I guessed could only belong to her sister called down. She appeared bent over on the staircase with a fist clenching a cheese grater like a club.

"Holy shit," Sara laughed. "It *is* her. You better run—"

27

I returned home to my mother scrubbing a penny over a scratch-and-win, and Grandma Magic Can smoking knapweed from her Fanta can. They asked if the wind had died down outside and I confirmed it had. I also confirmed that yes, the sky was still clear. Neither of them asked about—maybe they didn't notice—the shredding marks across my forehead; or where the rest of my clothes were; or why I wore my T-shirt as though it were pants, my legs stretching out each arm hole, both hands clenching fistfuls of fabric to keep the shirt from falling away.

Sara never took me back to her house again. She said her sister was a little protective and "uneven." Sara and I still hooked up two or three times a week, and I waited anxiously for whatever her test was going to be to see if I was her someone. I'd never know when she was going to approach me and when she did she'd take me down to a heavily treed patch along the river, or take my hand and lead me underneath the stairs by the drama room. Every three weeks or so I wouldn't see much of her at all for several days, except to overhear her swear at everything and everyone. My stomach would pinch and twist and burn, but then she'd get her period and she'd laugh at how close we came that time, and she'd scream, "Wild!" Soon enough we'd be heading back down to the river and the whole process would start all over again.

5. After four months of dating, three days after my last high-school final, Sara took my hand, quite firmly, from across the table at the Pure Country Restaurant and Lounge and said, "Bacon, we have to get out of this shithole."

"But you love the beef dip here."

"No, not this *restaurant*." She frowned. "I mean Bellevue. The Crowsnest Pass. This whole shitty dump." She waved her hand around as though trying to sweep away everything in sight.

"You think Bellevue's a dump?"

"Of course." Her eyes sprung open wider as she pushed back her chair. "Don't you?"

"I don't know," I said. "I guess maybe I don't know what to compare it to."

Sara leaned over her plate. "Bacon, Bellevue sucks. It's not even that this town *is* a dump so much as it *got* dumped. It's like life broke up with Bellevue and moved on. Years ago. Bellevue's old and alone. There's nothing left to do here but buy the town a colostomy bag and bring it a dog or a cat to pet now and then."

She plunged her beef dip into her au jus like she was crushing out a cigarette, stuffing it into the little glass bowl, twisting it down under her thumb. When she hoisted it back out, it barely resembled a sandwich: crumpled and twisted, bleeding au jus down her hand, a thumbprint embedded deep in the bread. "High school's done," she said. "Everybody else is going to be applying to universities and colleges, moving on. I'm sure as hell not going to get left here." She tore loose a strip of sandwich with her teeth. "Not that we need to go to some stupid brain-fuck school, but at least get to someplace with a heartbeat. With culture. Bellevue's got no culture. Calgary. Now that's a city. Calgary would be wild."

"Calgary?" I said. "You just got here a few months ago."

"Wasn't my choice," she snarled. "Not that I cared if we left Medicine Hat. But I sure as hell wouldn't have picked this place. My ass-faced father figured there'd be less trouble for me in a smaller town. Like the Hat wasn't small enough already."

"Calgary. Calgary." I couldn't stop saying the word. It couldn't be more than two and a half hours from Bellevue, but it may as well have been Pluto. "*Calgary,*" I said again, this time as though it were some newly discovered species of trout.

"Wouldn't it be great?"

"I'll bet it would be." I plucked a string of onion from my beef dip and set it on my plate. "Maybe we'll end up there one day."

"No, no, no. Not *one day*, Bacon. *Now.*"

"Now?" I reached for a napkin.

"Right now. Today. Finish your beef dip and we'll go." Sara clenched her fork, not in her fingers but in her fist.

29

"We can't just go to Calgary," I said. "We're not even packed."

"We don't need much. Just stuff a backpack with some clothes and we'll bolt." She jabbed toward the door with her fork.

"What would our parents say?"

"Parents?" She laughed, curling her tongue to hold in a French fry. "My dad will be fine with it because that's what I'll tell him to be. You don't even know where your dad is. And no offense, Bacon, but I'm not sure your mother would even notice if you ever came home again."

Beef dip shifted in my stomach. Sara was right about my father; I had no idea where he was. My mother told me she had been nothing more than a courtesy car in his "perennial partner exchange program." His choice of companion, she said, was inversely related to his birthday. Every third birthday my father traded in his old model – that's what my mother said he called it – for a newer one. And the newer model was always five years younger than the current one. "They lose half their value the minute you drive them off the lot," my father used to say. On his thirty-fifth birthday, my mother was twenty-nine, I was eight, and my father stepped out to test drive a twenty-four-year-old waitress. He came back again a few months later, but at thirty-nine he took a ride with a twenty-two-year-old tour guide. Never returned to the show room. When he turned forty-two we heard he'd put an offer down on a twenty-year-old front desk clerk from the Black Nugget Motor Inn in Sparwood. I guessed he'd be turning forty-five soon and thankfully he wasn't around to meet my eighteen-year-old someone.

"How would we *get* to Calgary?" I asked.

"Well, now that's the thing." Sara pushed her plate aside. Her grizzly eyes and the anxious gape of her mouth startled me. I could feel my cheeks fill with a salmony flush. "We'll need your mom's car."

"My *mom's* car?"

"You get her car," Sara said. "I'll go pack, and we'll meet back here."

"I can't take my mom's car."

"Of course you can." Her sharp eyes tugged at me and I knew right then that I had better put my beef dip down. "It's not hard.

You get the keys, you open the door, you start the fucking thing up, and you drive here. Then we go to Calgary."

I watched a stray strip of beef slide down the side of my au jus glass, sinking further into the heavy brown juice, then disappear. "Why don't we take your dad's car?"

"Oh, that's a good idea," she sneered. "Or we could take *my* car. Or why don't we just build a car? Or better yet, how about we take the shut-the-fuck-up car?" She leaned in on one elbow. "If I could get my *dad's* car, assface, I'd have taken it already. He hides the keys."

Sara stood, stuffing an arm into her coat. "Finish up so we can go."

A third of a beef dip still sat on my plate. Grandma Magic Can always said I never speak my mind. I was never good at that. If she'd been there, she would've said, "Rice eaten in haste chokes like a fist in the throat." But she wasn't. So I said, "I don't have a driver's licence."

"You what?" Sara stopped.

"I don't have a driver's licence."

"Bacon — "

"I don't have one."

"Bacon, look at me."

I slid my glance up to her face. Her moles were eyes, glaring down at me. Her face turned the red of gums.

"I've seen you drive."

"But I don't have a licence."

Sara sat back down with her coat half on, her eyes threatening to burst. "Bacon, you wouldn't drive without one." She inhaled through closed teeth. "Now answer me honestly. Do you have a driver's licence?"

I poked the top bun off my beef dip with a fork. "Well ... I have a learner's permit," I said. "I've only ever driven with my grand-mother."

Her mouth turned up at the corners into something that was anything but a smile. "So you *can* drive."

I nodded.

"That was it, Bacon," she frowned. Her face tightened. "That was the test."

"The test?" I saw her rolling the chili pepper dispenser in her palm just moments before I felt it strike the side of my head, just above the ear.

I covered my head with both hands and curled over the table. The lid scraped as she unscrewed it from the jar. "Let me see," she said, tugging gently on my wrist. "Let me see!" I opened my shaking hands from over my head. One hand was stained with a small smear of blood. "It cut the skin a little," she said. "It's not a big gash or anything. Heads bleed more than they should." Then she slapped a handful of chili peppers onto the cut and scrubbed them in with the heel of her palm. I leapt back out of my chair, but she caught me by the hair and pulled me back down, pushing my head to the table. "That was pretty close to a lie, Bacon," she snarled. "That bit about you not having a driver's licence. Not a total lie and that's why we're still talking. But, it was *deceitful*. You have a learner's permit. You can drive with an adult in the car. I'm eighteen. That's an adult. Right?"

"Right." I squirmed, trying to free my head.

"I warned you not to lie to me, Bacon." She released my hair. Her fingers traced gently over my forehead. All background noise disappeared at that moment, everything turned still. Ranchers dining beside us sat perfectly silent, staring. Even the air the fan above sent down seemed to slow and pause.

"Guess I'm not your someone." She glared at the cutlery on her plate as though willing it to bend. "You wouldn't deceive your someone."

I tried to blink away the blotches from my eyes, to regain clear focus. "You cut me," I said.

Sara's eyes glassed over. Her lips wrung into a tiny tight dot until they almost disappeared. She sat staring down at her cutlery for what seemed like an hour. "Bacon –" she started with a whisper, but then put the back of her fist to her mouth. Neither of us said anything more for several minutes.

I don't know why Sara hit me. I didn't like it but I liked the awkwardness of the moment a whole lot less. I wished I could recall some kind of appropriate proverb to help ease the tension but instead I said, "That test wasn't fair."

Sara covered her face with her fists and shook a little. Her mouth finally cracked open in a crescent slit and her voice broke as she said, "Just answer this, Bacon. Do you want to go to Calgary with me?"

I didn't know anything about Calgary. But I wanted us both to stop feeling bad. "OK," I said.

She didn't look up. "Will you meet me here at ten?"

"Yes," I said.

"Promise me."

"I promise." Under the table my knees rocked back and forth. "Do I need to get my mother's car?"

Sara's jaw clenched, her lips turned white. She glared down at something in her water glass, maybe the reflection in it. Then her jaw released, her lips loosened, and very silently she nodded.

I had no idea how I was going to get my mother's car or what my mother would do if I took it to Calgary. It was a terrible idea. Still, I heard myself tell Sara, "OK."

I struggled home through a shoving wind, slipped into the house, and tiptoed across the kitchen. Grandma Magic Can stood on a small footstool, bent over the sink, washing her hair. I grabbed the Lancer keys from the junk drawer and snuck downstairs to my bedroom. My mother would return from bingo in less than fifteen minutes, so I quickly stuffed three pairs of underwear, four T-shirts, a pair of cords, Fresh Surf scented Speed Stick, my toothbrush, a half tube of Colgate, and my small, clear plastic tackle box into a daypack. I grabbed my spincasting rod and scurried out to my mother's Lancer. The wind slapped the door shut behind me.

I started the engine, clenched the gearshift, but couldn't bring myself to pull it down into reverse. I stared ahead at the green and yellow corrugated panels of the carport, tracing down one of the cracks that led to a small hole where the plastic wall had cracked and chipped away. The car shivered as it idled.

"Calgary," I said, hoping it would suddenly make sense spoken aloud. Did people fish in Calgary? If they did, I'd bet my tackle nobody spincast. I didn't understand why we needed to go to Calgary. But I did understand that tender love was blind;

I remembered Kenny Rogers singing so. He also said love required a dedication. Maybe that's what I needed. Dedication. Ah-ah.

The porch light flickered on and Grandma Magic Can appeared at the door, a towel wrapped tightly around her small tomato head. She must've heard the engine. She pushed open the screen door; I jerked the car into reverse and stomped on the gas pedal. The Lancer lurched, hurling down the driveway. *Thud!* A dull thump echoed inside the car. I hammered the brakes with both feet and spun around to see the back windshield covered with what appeared to be an ass. An upside-down ass. A torso sprawled chest-up on the trunk, legs shooting up over the roof. The ass – a strangely familiar ass – came to rest, pinched up against the windshield. The square shape, the black acid wash jeans, the thin, tubular thighs. It was my mother's ass.

Grandma Magic Can hurried down the driveway, clutching the towel to her head with one hand and covering her mouth with the other. I jumped out of the car and helped my mother off the back of the Lancer. Bingo daubers spilled across the driveway, rolled down and collected in piles next to the curb.

"For the love of Christ!" my mother cried. "What the hell happened?"

Grandma Magic Can pushed her into the back seat and ordered me to drive to the hospital.

"Hospital?" my mother said, lifting a hand to her ruffled hair. "Good God, I'm fine. Just tell me what happened...."

I spun the Lancer onto the highway; the hospital was six kilometres away in Blairmore. The little round clock taped to the dashboard said 9:37. Sara! I tried peeling off the highway at the turn to the Pure Country Restaurant and Lounge, but Grandma Magic Can cried, "Where're you going?" She thrust the wheel back toward the highway. "Lord lifting Jesus, Bacon, don't you know where the bloody hospital is?"

"Sorry."

"I don't need to go to the goddamned hospital," my mother said.

"I need to go to the Pure Country Restaurant and Lounge," I said.

"We're *going* to the hospital." Grandma Magic Can slapped the dashboard with her open hand.

Again, it was my timing. Five seconds earlier and I don't back the Lancer into my mother. I drive past her as she's walking along the sidewalk. At worst she might have lifted her I-didn't-win-at-bingo scowl my way. Fifteen seconds earlier and she probably doesn't even see me leave. But my timing was what it was, what it's always been, and so I drove my mother to the hospital, rushing past the Pure Country Restaurant and Lounge. I squinted into the rearview mirror, hoping to catch a glimpse of Sara in the growing dusk.

We reached the hospital at 9:46. I had eleven minutes to get to Sara. After my mother was admitted and led away by a nurse, I made a move for the door.

"Bacon," Grandma Magic Can called. "Oh, good idea. You move the car out of the tow-away zone and I'll meet you in the cafeteria. I *love* the chicken fingers here. We'll get some for your mom, too." She turned and waddled away, the towel still wrapped around her wet hair.

I could feel Sara's cold stare of impatience pushing my glance down to the floor. I called the Pure Country Restaurant and Lounge from a payphone and asked them to check for her. The bartender said they were too busy and hung up. My stomach cramped, sick with angst. What could I do? I moved the car and hurried back into the cafeteria, pacing around the table, unable to sit still while we waited.

The doctor released my mother at 10:47, confirming her claim that she was in fact fine. "Diagnosis," she said, "sore ass." She waved away the chicken fingers. "I told you we didn't need to come. All we accomplished here was giving Dr. Poke-and-Prod a free boo at my ass."

"Oh, for God's sake." Grandma threw a crumpled napkin over her plate. "Your ass was hit by a car. He has to look at it."

"Well of course you wouldn't doubt *him* — he's a *doctor*." My mother made quote signs with her fingers when she said "doctor". "Stuff a pig's nutsack in a lab coat, it's still a pig's nutsack."

"Can we go to the Pure Country?" I said.

"Why the hell is everybody hungry?" my mother snapped. "It's almost eleven at night for Christ's sake. Just get me home. And try not to hit anybody on the way."

After getting my mother safely inside the house, I sprinted over to the Pure Country Restaurant and Lounge. Warren, one of the cooks, was hauling out a bag of garbage to the dumpster. I asked if he'd seen Sara. He couldn't hear me over the wind, so I asked louder and he nodded that he had. She'd been loitering around out front for nearly an hour, he said, waving the bag of garbage at the sidewalk. Said she popped back in, glanced around smiling — at least he thought it was a smile — then left. Just kind of strolled slowly down the highway.

That's the night Sara Mulligan left Bellevue.

6. I once heard someone say fishing is the Prozac

of the sportsmen. You cast out the blues and reel in a rainbow. The day after Sara left, my dose came in a tear-shaped orange and black Kamlooper spoon with a treble hook. Barbs pinched back, of course. First lure I ever had. Still have it. I squeezed open the swivel at the end of my line, hooked on that rusted old Kamlooper, and trudged down to the river they call the Crow.

The smooth stretches of thigh-high water on the Crowsnest River are filled with fly-fishermen, spitting and smoking and waving their nine-foot rods for all creation to see. Passing by them, I shielded my collapsed green and brown spincasting rod from view with my slightly turned shoulder, and I kept up high on the rocky ledge away from the banks. I hesitated to spook their trout and preferred to sneak past the straying eyes of those fly-fishermen. If they spotted my rod their eyes would drop down to my closed-face reel with the thumb-button trigger and, though their mouths might have held hard, they wouldn't have been able to wipe the smirk from their eyes.

I fished a shallow, murky stretch of river further up the bend. Tight rows of splintered and discoloured pines crowded out any view of Turtle Mountain. No deep pools could be found on this stretch, and most fish that passed through did so quickly, hurrying on to deeper, clearer spots. Fewer fish, but fewer fly-fishermen.

Dense shrubs, high grass, and willow thickets overhung the bank. I pushed in as deep as I could stand; branch thorns scratched blood from my cheeks, my feet sunk to the ankles in a gurgling, boggy patch, water filled my tennis shoes — a pair I was forced to sacrifice since Sara had hurled away my waders — aphids massed across my shirt, the seething whir of horseflies and mosquitoes stuffed my ears. I thrust my rod through a tiny break in the thick branches, angling the rod cautiously down toward the water, like the delicate tweezers in the game of Operation, careful not to snag the hook on any twigs, limbs, or leaves. With only a few inches of wiggle room, the best cast I could hope for was a flick of the wrist, no more than you'd give a finger snap. I called this "fencing-jab casting," and I loved that it was as un-fly-fishing as a cast could be. At best I could only ever hope for about four feet of actual cast. Of course, if the method ever caught a fish, I'd have no idea how to pull the thing back through the mesh of thickets.

I had no clue what drew Sara to the city. Muggers and thieves and burglars and frauds lived in cities. Suddenly I wished I'd gotten her a whistle or bear spray. I rubbed at the spot on my head where the chili pepper dispenser had hit, still swollen and scab-crusted. Then again, I thought, maybe Calgary needed the bear spray.

I wondered if my father had also been drawn to the city. If that's where he ended up. I remembered fishing with him once, I think I was six. I never had a rod back then; I'd just follow alongside and watch. That day I'd peed in the river while he cast. He waited until I finished then let the tip of his rod drop and splash in front of him. He raked a row of yellow teeth over his bottom lip and told me we should move further upstream. I asked why and he said, "Well, first off I don't like fishing in piss. Second off, once you go mess a fishing hole up, it's spoiled. Got to move on or pack it in." He glared down at me for a moment then tousled my hair with his thick hand. My head nearly bobbled right off my neck. "But that's OK," he said, "because there's always more upstream."

He took three giant strides up the river, stopped, turned, and gazed somewhere past me. Then he chuckled. "Hell, there's always more downstream, too. There's just always more, son."

I also recalled my father pushing his breakfast aside one morning, just him and me at the table. His fork hadn't even touched an Eggo. "If you get sick of waffles," he said, "don't eat 'em. You know?" I nodded because he'd wanted me to, but I wasn't sick of waffles at all. Especially Eggos. "Evolution didn't work out in a way so we'd have no choice but to eat waffles all fucking week." I nodded again, but it was only the second day we'd had waffles. "Hell, if I felt like it I'd go have a peanut butter and jelly sandwich for breakfast." His tone dared me to deny him. "Or fish and chips, for Christ's sake. A fucking cheeseburger." I couldn't pry my eyes off his cooling Eggo. "There just ain't enough breakfasts," he sighed. A few days later he embarked on the last of his "just need a little me-time" away periods. He never returned.

I spent the rest of that afternoon wondering about Sara and throwing out dozens of fencing-jab casts into the murky water. But no matter how many casts I threw out, I never did reel in a rainbow.

7. I felt that summer approaching the way you feel a teacher's eyes heading down the row, bearing down on you, looking to call on you for an explanation from a chapter you didn't read the night before.

No school. No job. No driver's licence. No Sara. No plans. Life overtook me while I stumbled around figuring out what love was all about.

Whenever I get confused, Grandma Magic Can pushes her glasses up her nose, lifts her chin, and says, "Don't drink kimchi soup before the rice arrives." I think that means do tasks in order. My mother always says do the easiest task first, if it takes long enough you might forget about the hard ones. The task that seemed easy enough was getting a driver's licence. So I did. Got it on the fourth try.

The next easiest task on my list was a job. So I got one. The Super Stop Confectionary hired me to sell gas, propane, fishing licences, lures, Juice Newton cassette tapes, packets of powdered sugar doughnuts, and king-sized Kit Kats. The Super Stop also served as the local Greyhound bus terminal, which meant I served as a counter agent and occasional baggage handler. Three times a day a Greyhound belched in with a swirl of exhaust and dust and carried people off to Fort Macleod, Claresholm, Calgary, Red Deer, and Edmonton. Every bus that stopped swallowed up and hauled away more people than it dumped out. Usually nobody got off. People disappeared into Greyhounds the whole time I worked at the Super Stop. The math didn't add up. After a while there shouldn't have been anybody left in Bellevue.

Four days after getting the job, on July 3, I turned eighteen. Grandma Magic Can met me after my shift and took me to the Legion. She said I was a man now and she wanted to buy me my first beer. We clinked glasses and I sipped at the pee-like liquid. I decided against mentioning I'd sampled beer before. When I was eight my father shared his Pilsner with me. I'd try to find all the rabbits on his can and for every rabbit I found he'd squeeze open my mouth with his big hand and pour in a plop of beer. The taste was like shoe juice – but I loved trying to find all those rabbits. I found fifteen.

Sara drank Pilsner, too. And rye. She sometimes snuck a flask of Wild Turkey to school. She'd pull it out at lunch, in the far end of the field where we'd pass it between us. I'd try to swallow a little now and then, but usually I'd just squeeze my face tight and only pretend the smoky liquid was scalding down my throat.

Grandma Magic Can finished two beers to my one, and then ordered us each another. Instead of shoe juice, the beer tasted faintly like Sara Mulligan. Like wet winter mittens. And that taste had a weight to it, it pressed down on my tongue as though it were tasting me.

"Drink up," Grandma said, flapping an arm off the bar. She lifted a shaking glass to her mouth and finished her last swallow.

"Best get ourselves home to your mother," she added. "And don't mention anything about the beer." As I stood, my view of the leather stools, the stacks of plastic cups, the wood-panelled walls, the cracked red Exit sign above the door, all jerked like a nudged film projector. Grandma gingerly lifted herself from her stool and stretched a toe down to the floor like she was getting into a bath. I reached across the bar, gripped tight onto the keg tap to hold myself still, refocused, and then we waddled our way home.

My mother had brought a bucket of KFC from Blairmore and had my third favourite cake sitting on the table: McCain Deep 'n Delicious. Chocolate. She said she didn't know where the god-damned candles got to but that if I could blow out her smoke I'd get three wishes instead of one. Her cigarette blinked and winked but I wasn't able to extinguish its red glare.

After dinner, Grandma Magic Can went to the bathroom and my mother cracked open a beer, telling me to finish it quickly before Grandma came back out.

"Eighteen," my mother said, arms folded, leaning up against the fridge. She exhaled a beery breath and gazed up at the copper frying pan clock hanging from the wall. "Eighteen years ago ..." Her monotone voice trailed off. Her eyes veered into that familiar detached, drooping stare, the kind that made her look so bored and tired that you worried if someone walked up and swung a splintered fence plank at her face whether or not she could even be bothered to duck.

My mother's beer – Club beer – tasted like Sara too, but this time, instead of sipping, I took on full mouthfuls and swashed the beer over my tongue, tasting it thoroughly. It warmed as Sara had warmed. I had no idea why she had to get to Calgary with such immediacy. Or why she'd want to leave without me. As I forced the beer down, something deep in my stomach fought to push it back up. But the rising disturbance in my throat regurgitated not beer, but words.

"What do you do when you can't understand – " I snapped my mouth closed with a hiccup. I smothered and swallowed down a belch, hoping the words would go with it. One of my mother's eyebrows lifted, and the other frowned. I dearly wished I hadn't said anything, but now I had to finish out of awkwardness. "When you can't ... you know ... seem to figure out why somebody did something?"

"Pfff!" She turned and dumped dishes in the sink. "That depends," she said. "If you're my age you let it whittle out another crack in your face and flip on the news. If you're your age, you thank Christ you're only eighteen and life's a big joke. Either way, nothing to figure out." Just then the toilet flushed. My mother spun and hissed, "*Down it.*" I took a giant glug. She wrenched the can from me and winged it below the sink. "You want to come to bingo tonight, Bacon?" she asked in an isn't-everything-dandy voice as Grandma emerged, straightening her skirt. "You can use the hammer dauber." My body kept tilting to one side, drifting away from my head. Even if I were interested, I wouldn't be able to blob bingo numbers with any swiftness or accuracy. I'd learned long ago that bingo was a game of ruthless and unforgiving pace. I told them I was tired and just wanted to watch TV.

After they left, I pulled on a light jacket and stepped outside into the evening air. I meandered down toward the highway, circled around the free campground, and headed over to the giant crow's nest — a crude thirty-foot sculpture of a mother crow in a nest with her gaping-mouthed young.

Apparently small, dumpy townships require a monstrosity to attract tourists. A giant crow, the world's biggest truck, a gigantic piggy bank, a massive Easter egg, mammoth perogies. When Bellevue's giant crow's nest didn't bring in the hundreds of expected tourists, the town built a new attraction next to it, right in the shadow of the mother crow. Since bigger didn't work out better, the town went with smaller. They built the miniature six-seat Wayside Chapel — the littlest church. They put in tiny pews, a tiny podium, and topped it with a tiny pointed steeple. So small it's barely visible to the passing motorists, which would seem to complicate its function of attracting tourists.

I stood staring at the empty church. Empty campground. The un-mowed grass where no families stood snapping pictures under the giant crow. I ducked down and stepped inside the chapel, scrunched down into one of the tiny seats, my knees near my chest, banging one of them on the pew in front. The knock echoed up over me like a fleeing bird, vanishing up through the ceiling, up inside the steeple. I imagined the tiny chapel hosting a marriage. A tiny bride, a small groom, a teeny pastor, and maybe three or four short relatives. Just a small wedding, they'd call it. Who would ever guess a tiny chapel could offer so much. Nobody driving past the town, holding out for cathedrals, or passing through to bigger cities. Nobody who left Bellevue behind.

From its thirty-foot perch the mother crow watches semi-trailers and cars and buses speed past. She quietly observes our little town. She's watched people leave and never come back and she knows why.

I shuffled up past the Moose Mountain Grill and down Main Street, past the real estate agency, which was for sale, and the renovations store, which was being renovated, and then down to the old Bellevue Inn that I'd never been in. I asked the desk clerk for a room, the tavern, to be specific.

I squinted through a haze of smoke and drifting dust; my sinuses stuffed immediately and the heavy air leaned into me as I walked. The stale smell of cigarettes mixed with a moist stench that reminded me of boiled hot dogs, flooded basement, and banana farts. The walls were covered with shelves holding softball and billiards trophies, fibreglass trout moulds, and a taxidermy cow-pie fastened to a plaque that read "Bellevue Inn Bullshit Award." Standing shunned off to the side stood an old shuffleboard table that clearly wouldn't require sprinkled sand to help the pucks slide – knuckle-deep dust covered the table. Patrons clearly preferred the two pool tables, the felt scratched and worn like skinned knees.

Elderly ladies with bloodshot cheeks babbled at tables where elderly men in flat-billed trucker caps nodded silently. The few younger men and women sitting with them – probably their sons and daughters – yawned and smiled. Each group circled a thin aluminum ashtray like a campfire, heaping with butts instead of logs. I couldn't hear any of the conversations because of an old Billy Squier song – *Stroke! Stroke!* – that drowned out everything except the clang and whirl of the vLTs.

Finding an empty table, I ordered *myself* a beer for the first time. I imagined Sara sitting on a similar vinyl chair in a tavern in Calgary, though in Calgary it wouldn't be a tavern, it would be a club. And it would be *wild*. Sara threw back shooter after shooter, downing six to my one beer. *Stroke! Stroke!*

I ordered a second and a third, but none of the beers tasted much like Sara anymore. My gaze dropped to the carpet splattered with grease and gum and other dark stains I couldn't identify. A lone French fry lay under my table, abandoned by some callous diner, forgotten and passed over by even the carpet sweeper. I wondered if it'd still be there tomorrow. After dumping a crumpled ten and three toonies on the bar I wandered home, but not before strolling all the way down to the river and pausing at the spot where Sara and I first scronked. I pushed my boot at the pine needles, wishing to kick up a ghost, or maybe hoping some imprint of our time together would still exist.

A Canada Goose flew overhead, its long neck bent forward while it stared down at me, honking like a crazed clown. The Canada Goose is my mother's favourite animal. She says that's because if I wandered anywhere near one, the goose would attack with righteous fury to keep me away from chicks. When I suggested that geese don't have chicks, they have goslings, my mother hissed that geese could snap bones so I best just keep an eye out and stay the hell away from chicks.

I hurried home after the goose made a second pass.

8. I never enjoyed working at the Super

Stop. People always rushed in and rushed out, passing through Bellevue on their ways to somewhere else. Some of the somewhere elses I'd heard of, some I hadn't. But you could bet your last bobber that those somewhere elses were all somewhere else I'd never been. We'd never gone much of anywhere as a family. We tented up in the hills a few times, hauled our empties over to the bottle depot in Frank, and Grandma Magic Can and I gobbled up free samples of turkey jerky at the Sunday country market in Coleman. But we'd never left the Crowsnest Pass.

One day a tall woman who smelled like wet wool strode into the Super Stop to purchase gas for her minivan. She also bought a Lou Bega air freshener, and a 3 Musketeers bar.

"Where are you headed?" I asked.

"Fernie." She smiled into her purse, fumbling for a credit card.

"That's in BC," I said.

"It sure is," she nodded, not looking up.

"Where you coming from?"

She handed me her credit card suspiciously and said, "Calgary."

I didn't take it right away. Instead I scowled and asked, "Why *Fernie*?" Which was a strange response because I'd have loved to see Fernie.

"Well, if you must know, we're going camping." She wagged the credit card and tapped it on the glass counter. I glared while I took it. "You sure do ask a lot of questions," she added, even though I'd only asked three.

"There's camping here, you know," I said, snapping open a plastic bag. "Over there by the big Crowsnest. It's *free*."

She peered over at the empty sites. "Mmm," she said. "I guess it would be."

"We also have fishing," I said. "Way better than Fernie."

"Super." Her mouth pulled into a flattened smile, "If we ever decide to go *fishing* we'll come straight down here to ... what is this place?"

"Bellevue," I said.

"Bellevue," she nodded.

I returned her card and, with my other hand in the small bag under the counter, I pinched my thumb into her 3 Musketeers bar. Then I did it three more times until the bar was flattened.

"You should work for the Chamber, kid," she said.

I nodded but never thanked her for stopping at the Super Stop. I didn't thank anybody that day.

When I got home my mother was plopping hamburgers onto the barbecue. My mother's hamburgers are just like regular hamburgers except instead of patties she rolls them into spheres, about the size of a racquetball. Often just as rubbery. Her burger-balls are jammed with onion shards that look like dozens of yanked out fingernails and usually cause the burger-ball to crumble apart. Those fortuitous burger-balls that do hold together rarely survive the bunning. Normal patties lay flat and flush, but burger-balls roll between the buns and frequently shoot out from the pinch of the bread. Grandma Magic Can once asked my mother why she couldn't just press the hamburger into patties. My mother's back straightened and she blew a sigh from her nose. She said that her hamburgers save a step. She flapped a dismissive hand, two fingers loosely clamped on a cigarette. This ain't the Moose Mountain Grill, she said. You want fancy patties, *you* flatten them.

I picked at a few crumbles of burger-ball but managed to force down little more than a couple bites. I hadn't eaten much of my mother's dinners since Sara left. I'd been skipping breakfast, too.

As usual, after dinner, Grandma Magic Can and my mother – arms full of daubers and trolls and grocery checkout magazines – scurried off to bingo. Again, I hit the tavern. The fifth straight night.

I'd brought enough money for five beers. After finishing the fourth, I shut my eyes, rested my forehead on the lip of the bottle I held firmly to the table in both hands, and tried to hold the world still. My ears filled with the gravelly *whoosh* of scooped ice from behind the bar, the tap of pool balls, the rev of a motorcycle outside. It struck me that if Sara had truly been my someone, she wouldn't have just up and left. Someones don't leave their some-ones. Clearly, I thought as my forehead slipped from the bottle and thumped on the table, Sara wasn't my someone. Or else she was but didn't believe it. Or didn't fully realize it. Only two things could be true: a) Sara Mulligan was not my someone or 2) Sara was still my someone and didn't realize it. Or else c) she was my someone and realized it, but it was just bad timing.

I propped up two cardboard coasters into a tent, then toppled it with a swing of my bottle, cursing myself for not getting answers from Sara before she left.

I wondered if maybe she was testing me. Maybe she needed me

to prove I was *her* someone. And instead, I sat drinking in a bar. Making coaster tents.

I hoped another beer would make the questions stop. It did. But the walk home wore off the distraction and, as soon as I stumbled into our house, the questions started up again. Collapsing into the sleepy tweed embrace of our couch, I spotted the magic can on the side table.

I picked up the old Fanta can, a small pinch of leafy weeds still piled over the tiny holes Grandma had carefully poked in a flattened side. I flickered on the little blue lighter and brushed the flame over the crispy leaf shards, just as I'd seen her do so many times before.

The smoke tasted like insulation, which I'd mistakenly tried when I was five (I'd thought the walls of our unfinished laundry room were being stuffed with cotton candy). The smoke from the weeds scraped my throat just as the insulation had, and I coughed and coughed until my stomach wrenched as though rammed by one of Sara's knees.

When I caught my breath again and opened my eyes, I saw every one of Sara's moles staring down at me, bobbing and hovering around my face, and suddenly I was back lying by the river next to Sara. I watched her lift herself on top of me, hands pressing down on my chest, her glassy, firm gaze not letting go of my wide eyes, even as hers closed. I felt my head surging and lapping like the river water beside us, while at the same time I still sat on the couch, and I must've unzipped my jeans because I could feel my cold hand warming against myself. My head snapped and bobbled as Sara shook me, her fingers threatening to rip through my skin. I swallowed the warm taste of her honeycomb breath and clutched myself tighter, stronger – gripping like she would've. The string-art owl hanging on the wall and the brass lamp and the TV and all the living room furniture blurred and shuffled over each other like cards. The owl swallowed the lamp, the TV morphed with the clock, the clock said it was twelve-thirty and that meant Letterman was on. I fumbled for the remote with my free hand, switched on the power. Paul Schaffer sniggered as Letterman told some joke about George Bush and Bob Barker going to Vegas. The studio audience hooted and laughed. Were they laughing at me? I hated them. And what was I thinking about before that? Oh, yeah — Sara. I tightened the loosening grip on myself and struggled to focus on her sweet, moley face, to block out the studio audience's laughter. Sara rolled over me, waves cresting over each other. I stretched for the remote with one clumsy hand, desperately trying to squeeze with the other hand — a hand nearly too tired to go on. Finally I reached the power button, and the laughing disappeared. My heavy eyes shut from the blurred walls around me. My hand slowed as the fingers of my mind slipped, losing their grasp on the ledge of my focus. My task still unfinished. That's probably when I fell asleep.

The next morning I woke with sinuses filled with cement, a head full of battery acid, and eyes pierced by invisible hooks. The whole room smelled like feet. I opened a sore eye to Grandma Magic Can standing across the room looking over at me with a strong, backward lean, clinging to a tub of laundry and making a face like she'd just eaten a bad sunflower seed. I'd woken in the living room, still collapsed on the couch, my jeans swirled around one ankle, my left hand asleep, numb, and prickling. And still wrapped loosely around my penis. The now flaccid penis lay retreated into my hand like a frightened fingerling. It appeared sleep had taken me before Sara's ghost could.

Grandma Magic Can glared down at my right hand, which lay locked in a numb but firm grip around the Fanta can. I sat frighteningly still as she dumped the laundry down, marched over, bent down, and peeled each finger free from the magic can. She stomped away but stopped at the door to turn back and shake the can at me wildly.

I waited for some proverb about finishing what you start. But Grandma Magic Can, it seemed, had no Korean wisdom for that moment.

I would've rather been the audience to a table of sneering fly-fishermen boasting on about the twenty-four-inch rainbows they landed than lug myself to the Super Stop that morning. My brain felt like it was bleeding. Behind the counter I drifted off to sleep and stayed that way until the wind blew open the door and two tiny elderly ladies – the Barrow sisters – scampered in. Even on their toes they barely came to my chest and that's including the two inches of thin, rollered white hair on each of their heads. Same style.

As they always do, the Barrow sisters marvelled with delight and surprise at every object they passed. "Ooh," one said to the candy rack. "Mmm," the other said to the sunglasses display. "My," they both said to shelf of motor oil.

The sisters, into their early eighties, still worked reception together at the mine tour. They'd never worked a shift apart. Each of them bought a large bag of Tostitos, a litre of Dr Pepper, and a Calgary newspaper. Why wouldn't they buy the local weekly, the *Crowsnest Pass Promoter*? I just knew they'd be disappearing into a Greyhound. As I packed up their snacks, I slipped a local paper into each bag. Consider it a breadcrumb trail, I thought. Sure enough, they took their bags outside and sat in the wind waiting for the 1:40 PM to Calgary.

When the bus arrived they climbed on, but then the shorter of the short ladies stopped, shuffled back across the parking lot, and pushed open the Super Stop door. "Ohh," she said. "You put these in our bags by mistake." She wagged the local newspapers at me.

"That's OK," I said. "You keep them."

Her mouth tugged down on one side, almost right off her chin. "We don't want them." She dumped it on the counter and scuttled back out to the bus. "Mmm," she said to the door chime.

I clenched the paper for a moment then snatched up several more from the wire stand, tromped out to the bus, and banged on the door. When the driver opened up I handed him the stack of local papers and said he could distribute them. Free of charge. He began to object but I hurried back into the store.

I'd barely gotten behind the counter when the driver shot in with a wailing gust of dirt and litter. He dropped the papers on the counter. "Thanks anyway."

I lunged out from behind the counter but he was too quick. "It's a great paper!" I called after him. Scooping up the entire stack from the rack, I ran out to hurl them at the idling bus. But then I stopped. The now howling wind scattered several pages from my hands; I had to kick back a leg to keep from blowing over. Standing there, panting through my teeth, I thought about how my shift would soon end and I'd go home again and my mother would invite me to bingo and I'd say no and go to the tavern instead and then the next morning I'd come to work hungover and buses would sweep up more folks and I'd slip more papers into more people's bags and they'd bring them back and dump them at my feet and by day's end Bellevue would be short another few souls.

Go to the temple and lock the gate, go to the temple and lock the gate, Grandma Magic Can always mutters when she's doing laundry or dishes or dicing weeds or immersed in some other tedious routine.

I tried to imagine what Kenny Rogers would do with so much restlessness fighting in his head, and I figured he'd probably work it out in a song or at least take someone else's song and make a hit out of it, which wouldn't be any good to anybody trying to figure something out based on Kenny Rogers' ideals. So instead I put the papers back in the rack, issued myself a ticket, locked the door to the Super Stop, and got on the bus.

A turkey farmer with a collapsed nostril sitting next to me introduced himself. I told him I was Bacon Sobelowski and I was going to figure out if Sara Mulligan was my someone.

9. After nearly three hours on the bus, I

spotted Calgary in the distance. Its cobbled profile clumped atop the smooth prairie horizon like acne on a cheek.

It's hard to tell exactly at what point you've entered Calgary. Road signs, streetlights, and houses creep toward the highway long before you even realize you might be in a city. Soon, more houses and lights and signs sneak up and crowd around until you're engulfed by thick clusters of housing projects, half-built bridges, massive dirt mounds, new community direction signs, and parking lots the size of lakes – filled with people spilling out of their cars, streaming into giant chain stores you see in commercials on TV. I pressed my forehead up against the large bus window, taking everything in. I had to admit, Calgary would be something when it was finished.

We passed a huddle of salmon-coloured houses. They'd thrown up a wall around themselves, a clear separation from an even larger troop of liver-coloured houses next to them. The salmon-coloured houses painted their wall the same salmon colour, I suppose to show the liver-coloured houses just whose wall it was. The liver-coloured houses had done the same. Crowds of smelt-coloured houses and bruise-coloured houses divided themselves by smelt-coloured walls and bruise-coloured walls. Then we passed more liver-coloured houses. I wondered if those liver-coloured houses were allies of the other liver-coloured houses.

At the Greyhound station the bus sneezed to a stop. I took a tentative step off, unsure of the asphalt. A soft breeze tugged gingerly and smelled of oil and salt and wet cardboard. The noon sun brushed across my neck, sparkled in the tiny pebbles of broken glass across the parking lot.

This was the city of Sara.

I found a payphone outside the depot, but the phone book must have somehow caught fire; the book's pages were charred down to the binding. Inside, I approached a round lady in a Greyhound golf shirt and asked for a phone book. She chewed hard on her grape gum, waddled over to the ticket counter, tugged open a drawer, lifted out a phone book, and heaved it onto the counter without saying a word.

When I thanked her, she rubbed the back of a thick finger under her nose and sniffled. I fumbled through the pages to the M's. My finger traced over plenty of Mulligans but none that started with Sara. I looked for misspellings: Muligan and Mulligon and Molligan. Nothing. Then I flipped back to the Mulligans again. Still nothing.

"Get off at the wrong city?" the round lady smirked, seeming to gain a lift from her sarcasm.

I tried directory assistance for new listings. Nothing.

"Everything all right?" the lady asked, her smirk fading a touch.

"I never even thought she might not have a phone." I flipped through the M's again, glanced around the station as though hoping Sara might somehow be there, then fumbled through my wallet. Twenty-seven dollars and fifty cents. "When's the next bus back to Bellevue?"

The round lady's grin flattened to a pencil line as she ran a finger down the schedule. "Not 'til tomorrow morning, dear."

A stream of people poured into the station, unloading from a newly arrived bus. I watched as each person broke from the line to embrace their husband or wife or friend or son or daughter or parent or their someone who'd come to meet them. Then, as abruptly as they'd arrived, they all left in their newly reunited groups.

A man in blue coveralls wheeled a trolley of brown-paper-wrapped packages across the grey cement floor. Somewhere in the back a phone rang. I surveyed the station and rubbed a wrist over an itch on my ear.

10. Two major traffic arteries straddled the Greyhound station. Lines of cars whirred by on either side, veering and honking. A train squealed past, shuddering under the weight of massive crates stacked on top of other massive crates. I flinched when the train's angry horn bellowed at me. Power line towers lined the tracks like giant outlaws, their metal arms spread, cocked, ready to draw. My heart hammered like I'd just ran the whole way from Bellevue. I checked the destination marquees of all the buses, hoping the round lady had been mistaken and one of them was headed back to the Crowsnest Pass. None were. Across one of the frantic roadways I spotted a river and immediately darted through a small break in traffic, nearly getting clipped by a speeding ice cream truck.

After shuffling down the steep embankment, I pinched off my shoes and socks and stepped into the cool water. The smooth stones of the river's bottom caressed softly on my feet. My breathing slowed into deep, steady breaths, soothed by the water's slow drift and the familiar, sweet, weedy river smell.

It appeared ludicrous to think I could find Sara in that strange and monstrous city. But I reminded myself that you don't eat kimchi soup before the rice arrives. First, I needed to eat. Then, a place to crash. After that I'd look for Sara.

A few scattered leaves, a couple of twigs, and a crushed Slurpee cup floated past me, riding the slow rush of water headed toward the towering cluster of buildings downtown. I followed it all, tentatively swishing through ankle-deep water, just a few steps from the gravelly bank.

Rivers were quiet places, but the roar of traffic just up the bank sounded like an air force battle in a war movie. I worried about stepping on a mine.

A few feet to the left, the bottom dropped off and I spotted a brown trout glaring up at the noise above. Fly-fishermen curse browns for being persnickety. Pickiest trout of all. Not me. I admire them. In fact, they're my favourite fish. Some trout bite at everything tossed their way. Not browns. One day a brown might only eat grasshoppers, the next day he'll only eat caddis flies. Sometimes he'll snub the entire insect world and decide to eat other browns. All I know is browns decide what to bite and that's too bad for the fly-fishermen if it's something they're not using.

After twenty minutes of slogging down the river, I'd found myself smack downtown. I scrambled up the bank and sloshed around barefoot over the grass and gravel, waiting for the sun to return some of the colour the cold water had taken from my tired feet. Then I slid my socks and shoes back on and injected myself into the dark gut of the city.

Speed was everywhere in Calgary. Cars sprinting out in front of cars trying to sprint out in front of other cars. People on bikes did the same. Those who walked, walked like others drove. You'd think someone had just hollered "last call" at Rum Runner Days. Crosswalks had timers. Every store name seemed to start with *Fast* or *Speedy* or *Quick* or *Kwik*, and every second business offered a drive-through. The whole city swarmed.

People hurled toward me like asteroids. If I couldn't dodge them, they clipped off my shoulder and carried on, even veering off the sidewalks, stepping onto the streets just to get ahead of the next person. One man, a lanky fellow with random patchy tufts of beard that looked like pubic hair, tromped faster than any of them. His shirt, little more than a mechanic's rag, flapped at its tears. A frayed toque clung loosely to his head. He walked hunched over, as though enduring food poisoning, and stomped instead of stepped, mumbling while he moved. When he neared closer to me I jumped out of his way and then almost cried out for help when he whirled and glared at me. His head darted in every direction, his eyelids fluttered like a moth. He babbled in my direction, then stomped off.

I squeezed my way through the crowd and into a high rise to escape the street.

An escalator carried my tired feet up to a food court on the second floor. First thing's first, I needed to get fed. I understood at that moment why Sara had said Bellevue had no culture. The Calgary food court had everything you could imagine: raw fish sashimi, frijoles, broiled scampi, lemongrass tofu, minestrone soup, calamari. Surprisingly, none of the places had beef dips. So I went to A&W. A&W didn't have beef dips either, but it did have Double Teen Burgers with bacon and cheese. My mother used to bring some home from Blairmore sometimes. With a big fat bag of onion rings and root beer, of course.

The pale, freckle-faced man at the till said, "What would you like?" I peered up at the menu above his ruffled red hair. Eight brightly lit panels with dozens of different options. Papa Burgers, Mama Burgers, Chubby Chicken, macaroni salads, chocolate chunk cookies. They even had breakfast. Funny, I'd never been *inside* an A&W before. I'd just eat whatever my mother brought home. I looked up at the menu and back down at the freckle-faced man. I could only shrug.

"Want a minute?" he asked. For a moment I thought maybe a "minute" was some kind of burger or side dish, so I shrugged again.

"Can you tell me if you're at least hungry?"

"Yes," I felt my face flush.

"Great start," he said in a voice as flat as the drive to Calgary.

"It's a big menu," I said gazing at the eight-panel menu.

"Chop 'er down," he yawned. "You just got to chop 'er down. Feel like beef or chicken? If you feel like chicken, just look at the chicken menu. If you want beef, ignore the chicken menu."

Despite his impatience, I liked his thinking. It was a huge menu, but he'd chopped 'er down to two things. The menu seemed smaller. "I only know the Double Teen Burger with bacon and cheese," I said.

"Super. One Chubby Chicken Burger it is."

"Chicken burger?"

"Yeah," he sighed. "It's the closest till button to my finger. That's three-forty-nine."

"I see. Can I have onion rings, too?"

"Well, now that you ask, I'm obliged."

"And also a root beer?"

"That'll go nicely. Six-fifty-nine."

As he filled my tray, I thought of something I'd always wondered every time my mother brought home a brown, grease-stained bag of bacon double cheeseburgers with cheese. So I asked him, "What does A and W stand for?"

"'Amburgers and woot beer," he said, passing me the tray. "Next!"

I carried my tray through the rows of tables and the jumbled smells of dozens of different countries, and found a table in the corner by a window. The rumble of so many conversations roared like Lundbreck Falls.

The A&W had slathered and soaked the sandwich in so much mayo I could've drunk the chicken through a straw. I'd never order another one. I knew then that I didn't like Chubby Chicken Burgers. My mouth turned up into a bit of a smile because that was something I didn't know before. But the hard *clomp* of boots interrupted my brief smile. I turned to see that same tall, dirty man I'd seen earlier on the sidewalk, now winding around the tables, stomping as though stepping on spiders — headed directly toward me. His olive-pit eyes zeroed in on mine. If the window could open I might have jumped out.

The dirty man stopped just short of barrelling into me. He stood leaning over my head, glaring down, mumbling sounds that didn't make sense. Then he threw his arms in the air, clearly distraught.

He collapsed into the seat across from me, shaking the table and sending me lurching forward, almost spilling my woot beer.

I sat face to face with him, afraid to put another onion ring in my mouth. He began swaying in his seat with the rhythm of a rocking chair, his hands fondling at the pubic-like hair on his chin, fingers working like a spider's legs, his mouth twitching and rambling out strange moans. He smelled like an outhouse in August.

Every now and then his voice would spike on one syllable—almost like a yelp—and everybody around us would jump. People at other tables frowned and slid sideways glances at the man, or lifted their trays and moved.

I had no idea what he wanted, but I reached the wet chicken burger across the table as a peace offering. He shook his head wildly and waved the sandwich away, almost knocking it from my hand. I guess he'd tasted one before. I pointed to the onion rings and he barked out something incoherent.

Still unsure about what the man wanted, I opted for a long shot and asked, "Any chance you know Sara Mulligan?" He gripped his head in his hands like he was fighting a migraine.

I finished my onion rings, slowly slid out of the seat, and carried my tray over to the garbage. A cleaning man held the swinging trash door for me.

"Don't let him frighten you," the cleaner said, nodding toward the dirty man. "He's harmless."

I dumped out my tray and thanked the cleaner.

"Most people just avoid him," he said. "Everybody figures he's just some crazy homeless guy."

"Isn't he?"

"Who's to say?" the cleaner said. "Probably homeless. But crazy? I don't know. You a doctor?"

"No."

"Me neither. Everybody assumes he's speaking gibberish. How do we know? Maybe he just speaks a language we don't."

I liked the cleaner's thinking. It didn't make me any less terrified of the dirty man, but I liked that thinking.

"Maybe he's just lost his way," the cleaner continued, leaning against the garbage, arms folded, gazing at the man. "Maybe he just needs to get home. Maybe he doesn't seem so crazy at home."

All the other people had cleared out of the corner and found new tables further away. I glanced over to the dirty man rocking in his food court bench, then back at the cleaner. "You'd make a good brown trout," I told him.

"Thank you," he said.

11. Outside, a lady sat propped up against
a shopping cart stuffed with pop cans, a lawn chair, a sleeping bag, a sofa cushion, three walking canes, and a Fisher Price parking garage. Her mouth held only four front teeth, and her dirty blonde hair might have been just blonde underneath the dirt. She sat corralling up tobacco from an impressive heap of discarded cigarette butts, then rolled it all up with great speed inside new papers and into new cigarettes. "Spare some change, hon?" she gummed.

I told her I needed my money for a place to stay.

"Well, if you're counting your pennies," she coughed, "you'd do best to lodge down by the river. Get under the lip of a bridge right where it meets the grass. Good cover from the elements."

I counted thirty new rolled cigarettes in her pile. "You sure smoke a lot."

"I don't smoke at all." She pushed a knuckle against her right nostril and blew hard out the left. "I sell to the others. A gal's got to make a buck. Look, if you don't fancy the bridge idea, then you best keep moving. You don't want a hotel around here, Sleepy. You'll pay out your pooper downtown."

She was right about my pooper. Every hotel I found charged over two hundred dollars a night. Some more than four hundred! My feet burned but I kept walking, headed south where the buildings flattened out, seeking a less pooper-punishing place for the night. After checking a dozen hotels, I worried the search might take me all the way back to Bellevue.

I thought about calling home, but if Grandma answered she'd end up asking why I was in Calgary, I'd end up explaining, then she'd tell my mother, and my mother would scold me for coming all the way to Calgary for a girl.

The burn in my feet climbed into my shins as I continued checking every hotel I could find. I wandered under a bridge, down several more blocks, then stumbled onto a street with a string of pubs and bars. A heavy, bald man guarding the door to the Swig and Swine eyeballed me as I passed. His thick, heavy belly sloped down hard over his belt and reminded me of the crumbled mountainside at Frank Slide. He snarled in my direction and growled, "G'won in."

"Pardon me?" I said, unable to keep from peering at his avalanching stomach.

"G'won in," he said again.

"What's in there?" I asked, hoping he didn't think I meant his stomach.

"Do it now, man," he said. "There's no cover. It'll be ten bucks after seven. Best bar in town."

"Why's it the best?" I asked.

"Because it's *wild*."

"It's *wild*?"

"Yeah." He nudged up his T-shirt to scratch the soft blonde hair of his sloping belly. "Wild."

"Do you know Sara Mulligan?"

He shook his head. "Maybe she's in there."

I looked in toward the dark bar but could see nothing. "She just might be," I said, and stepped in.

The stagnant air of the bar smelled like pond scum. Before my eyes could adjust to the dark interior, my ears filled up with a crackling scream. "Bacon fucking Sobelowski!"

I whirled to see Brent Tufford, a short, twitchy guy who sat in front of me in social studies class. He never so much as borrowed a pencil from me, but now he came staggering toward me, grinning away, arms thrown open, strands of sweaty, rust-tinted hair clinging to his brow, his drifting eyes red and clammy.

"Bacon fucking Sobelowski!" he cried again, his face spotty and flushed. He explained that he just registered for school. "University's where it's at," he hollered like I was underwater. Spittle struck my face. "You should see the women!"

I told him I was looking for Sara Mulligan and he laughed and said Sara was at university.

"At *university*?" I said. "The University of Calgary?"

He laughed again and stretched a heavy arm around me, his face pushed right up against mine. "Not *the* Sara Mulligan. *Hundreds* of Sara Mulligans. Man, all the Saras you'd ever need." Then he threw his hand up in the air and motioned me to slap it with mine. I did. "Yah!" he screamed, and shoved his way back into the crowd, chuckling and shaking his head. "Bacon fucking Sobelowski!"

If I could run into Brent Tufford in Calgary, it suddenly seemed plausible I could find Sara. Circling the room, I asked every third person if they knew her. Nobody did. I approached two women in the corner who looked much older than everyone else in the bar. One had a small, square face with a heavy brow pressing down on her small eyes; the other was sitting so upright her back curved inward like a bending popsicle stick, ready to snap. That one had a shiny forehead and dark hair wrenched back. I asked if they knew Sara Mulligan and the one with small eyes asked if she *should* know Sara Mulligan. The shiny-foreheaded lady asked what I wanted from this Sara Mulligan person. I told them I'd come up from Bellevue and needed to ask Sara if she was my someone. I mentioned the Kenny Rogers song and how Grandma Magic Can and my mother always said he sure as shit knew how things were. The one with the small eyes rolled those small eyes and muttered, "Whack job." The one with the shiny forehead nudged the other and said, "No, that's sweet."

A waitress swiped a rag over their table and shiny-forehead ordered me a beer and them two more of whatever they'd been drinking. Their empty glasses had cucumber slices as garnish.

"My name's Karla," shiny-forehead said. I shook her hand.

"I don't have a name," small-eyes said, prying something from her teeth with a straw.

"I'm Bacon Sobelowski," I said.

"Of course you are," small-eyes said, fanning her face with the menu tent card. "You're more *her* market." She tipped her head toward Karla then slid off the stool and swaggered over to where Brent Tufford and two other guys I didn't know were playing pool.

"The universe must've sent you." Karla smiled.

"What do you mean?" I asked.

"Nothing." She pulled out the now empty stool beside her and motioned me to sit. "Are you a student, Bacon Sobelowski?"

"I was," I said, easing onto the stool. "High school, I mean. I just graduated."

"Perfect." She wiggled in her seat. "So a bachelor's degree is next? Best years of your life."

I shrugged. "Is everybody here a student?"

"We're not," Karla said, pointing her chin toward her no-name friend chalking up a cue.

"Are you teachers?"

"Heaven's no." Karla seemed to find that funny. "I'm a real estate agent. I specialize in finding post-secondary students places to live."

"Don't they have dorms for that?"

"They have dorms for some students." She pinched something free from her eyelash. "But other students require perquisites those dorms don't provide. At least not for those students." Only a few seconds fell between each song, when we didn't have to yell at each other. "Have you received your acceptance yet?" she asked.

"Acceptance?"

"Yes, to the university."

"Oh." I fondled a button on my shirt. "I haven't actually applied yet. I don't know for sure if I'll – "

"You *have* to apply!" She slapped a hand on the table.

"I do?"

"Of course you do. If nothing else to keep your options open."

"I guess so," I said, slouching a little.

"What do your parents think of your disinterest?"

"We've never really talked about school."

"But they don't mind you coming to a bar at six o'clock on a Wednesday?"

"They don't know I'm at a bar," I said. "They don't even know I'm in Calgary." Strangely, I could swear I saw her smile at this.

"What does your father do, Bacon?"

"I don't know," I shrugged. "Before he left us he drove a truck. When he worked." The waitress delivered our drinks. I took a quick, deep pull from my beer that felt so awkward and unnatural I almost coughed it all back up.

"Well," Karla said, "do you want to end up doing the exact same thing your father does?"

"I don't want to end up doing anything my father does."

Karla's eyes narrowed in a way I couldn't decide looked sad or satisfied. "Synergy," she whispered.

"What?"

"That's why you found me." She folded her arms on the table. "Synergy."

"I don't under —"

"Do it tomorrow. Promise?"

"Do *what*?"

"Register." She gripped my wrist with unexpected strength. "Promise me you'll register."

"Well ... ok," I said, though I wasn't sure how I'd go about registering. I imagined tuition would be more than the twenty dollars I had on me or the eighty dollars I had in the bank. Karla released my wrist and nodded her pleasure.

"What's that?" I asked, looking down at her drink, eager to change the subject.

"Gin," she said. "I drink gin to keep me slim. And not just any gin." She wagged a finger. "Hendrick's. Imported from Scotland. *Must* be garnished with a cucumber. It's made with coriander, juniper, citrus peel, cucumber, and rose petals. Each ingredient alters the taste in a totally different way, but the combination of it all works jointly. *That* is synergy." She lifted the glass up between us. "Rose petals — imagine!" She tilted the glass toward me. I took a sip from the lipstick-stained straw. The drink tasted like Rug Doctor, but I didn't mind because it reminded me of clean carpets and spring.

I told Karla all about Sara and Bellevue and how I closed the Super Stop and just up and got on the bus and Karla laughed and shook her head and said, "Bacon, I exist for people like you."

I also told her about how Sara up and left for Calgary and I'd not heard from her since. Karla nodded the whole time and smiled sympathetically, as though she expected just that.

"You know," she said, "Calgary's a pretty big city to find a person without an address. I mean, I hope you find her and all, but maybe the universe needs to *bring* her to you."

"The *universe*?"

"Oh, yes." She dropped her hands flat on the table as though it needed to be held still. "If you ask something of the universe, it always answers. Just not always the way you expect. See, you might not find Sara, but she might be brought to you. Or you might be taken to her. Or perhaps something else entirely." Karla pointed a cautious finger at me. "Keep your eyes open."

"I will," I said, backing away from her finger.

"Have you got a place to stay while you're here?"

"Shit!" I jumped nearly toppling our drinks. "I almost forgot. I gotta go ... I need to find a hotel." I glanced around the bar as though expecting to see a check-in desk. "Do you know any cheap hotels?"

"And then some," she laughed. "Relax. Sit down." Her hand wrapped lightly around my forearm. "This is super-synergy. I own several places, Bacon, and you're more than welcome to stay at one of them."

"You have more than one?"

"Three condos and two houses. One of the houses I live in, the rest are revenue properties. One condo is nearby. Just over in Eau Claire. And it's currently vacant. Fully furnished. Sitting there all alone. You need a place – and I have an empty one. Synergy! See, the universe is already conversing."

It was a generous offer, but I couldn't accept. My mother would've had what Grandma calls a conniption fit. If it were a male stranger who offered the empty condo, my mother would call that sweet, blessed fortune. But to my mother, girls who were strangers needed to be stayed away from even more than familiar girls. I centred my beer back on its coaster and frowned.

"Oh, don't worry, Bacon. You've obviously got a good heart and that deserves to be rewarded." She squeezed a smile. "I'll even pick you up tomorrow and take you to the university to apply."

My stomach flinched. I couldn't stay at a stranger's empty condo — especially a female's. But it was also getting late, and I didn't have money for a hotel. I pulled free the coaster from under my beer and read both sides, perhaps hoping it offered advice. It all felt like a terrible idea but, at the same time, Karla was as close to a normal person as I'd seen in Calgary. We talked a little longer; she had two more Hendrick's, I had two more beers, then we wandered to her condo.

The lobby inside Karla's condo building had marble floors and ceilings high enough to cast in. She had to punch a code in a keypad just to get in the first set of doors. Her place overlooked the Bow River and the city that sprawled for miles.

"This is amazing," I said.

"Thank you," she beamed. "It's a great location." But I hadn't meant the location. It was a lousy location. Far too many buildings around.

She had a tiny stereo the size of a fly box, a fireplace operated by remote control, and a bookshelf crammed with *People* magazines and hardcovers on soups and souls and myths of this and harnessing that.

"Well, I'm wiped," she said. "If you don't mind, I'm going to crash. Help yourself to anything."

"You're staying here too?"

"Yes," she chuckled. "Is that OK?"

"Well, sure, of course. I just ... I thought you had a house...."

"I do, but I'm tired and don't want to drive all the way across town."

"Oh," I said. Only seeing one bedroom, I took the couch and reminded myself I was saving two hundred dollars on a hotel.

"What are you doing?" she said.

"I'm sorry." I jumped from the couch like I'd broken something. "I was just ... going to lie down."

"Don't be silly," she said. "The bed's a king size."

My stomach clenched.

"Come on." She motioned me over.

I gaped at the bedroom like I'd stumbled across a mountain lion. The couch, I told her, would be fine.

"It's not even a couch, Bacon." She flapped a hand at it. "It's a love seat."

"A love seat?" Suddenly I didn't even want to stand next to it. "I'll be fine on the floor," I said.

"Sweet Earth," she chuckled, "you're not allergic to sleeping next to a woman, are you?" The word "woman" suddenly made me feel as woozy as if she'd said "gonadotropins" or "rectus femoris." "Woman" was a word for my mother or grandmother. "How old are you, Bacon?"

"I'm eighteen." I wanted to ask her the same.

"What kind of eighteen-year-old guy is still scared of women?"

That word again. "I'm not scared of—" I had to reach for the bookshelf to steady myself.

Karla pulled the covers back on one corner, leaned against the thick bevelled trim of the doorway, smiled, and, making a graceful summoning wave of her hand, said, "Come freely. Go safely...."

I stood hesitant for several moments before deciding it would be OK if I slept in my clothes. I wouldn't so much as untuck my shirt. In any case, if I didn't lie down soon, I'd fall down.

The bedroom was filled with pink lacy doilies. All the frames on the walls held pictures of Karla. Pictures of her in the mountains, playing tennis, a picture of her in a bikini standing beside a Welcome to Florida sign, a framed picture of her in front of the Eiffel Tower, and even a picture of her stuffed into a Montreal snow globe. She had black-and-white fuzzy pictures too, and in those pictures she wore nothing at all, though she kept her back turned.

Karla obviously didn't share my need to sleep fully clothed because she came out of the bathroom in thin, pink, lacy underwear that looked just like the doilies. When I stepped back, she laughed and asked if I'd ever seen a negligee before. She pulled out a camera from her handbag, threw her arm around me, held the camera out, and snapped a picture. She giggled, shut off the lights, and in the sudden darkness she said, "Bacon, you gotta be thinking ... right about now ... you're a long way from home."

12. In the dark, uncomfortable stillness I lay

stiff and clenched. My feet throbbed from the long day of walking. I found it strange Karla bothered to even throw on the thin, pink, lacy underwear. It covered little of anything, and I heard her wiggle it off herself before she reached the bed anyway. The covers ruffled and I felt the mattress shift as she slid her shiny forehead onto my pillow. Her breath spread warm and itchy against my neck, each exhale stretching up over my chin, reaching for my drying mouth – which felt so awkward lying there lifeless and stupidly open.

Karla inched her hand onto my chest and whispered, "What does Sara look like?"

"Pardon me?"

"This Sara," she said. "What does she look like?"

I described Sara's narrow face, her long, perfect legs – even her moles. Then Karla asked if I remembered what Sara smelled like. I said I did. "Try to imagine that smell," Karla whispered. I did.

Karla's fingers traced over the bridge of my nose. A tingle webbed out across my face. I knew she shouldn't be touching my face but I couldn't seem to lift an arm or turn my head. It was her place; she kindly let me stay. I was terrified of looking ungrateful. As long as I didn't touch back, I decided it would be OK. Her finger followed softly around the curl of my nostril and down and across my lips.

Heavy laughter and shouting echoed up from the street below and continued all night. The whole city of Calgary was laughing at me. I thought of going to the window to see if any of the laughing people were Sara.

Karla rolled herself on top of me, her back to my chest, her head stretched back and tucked in beside mine. She lifted my hands to her face. "This is Sara's face," she said. But it wasn't. Sara had moles. I missed those moles. And Sara didn't have a forehead that shone. Karla moved my hands down to her neck. I tried to envision the tanned stretch of darker skin that ran up Sara's neck; I put my face up against it, hoping to see the tiny hairs I remembered glistening from my kisses. Karla slid my hands onto her chest and said to imagine it was Sara's. But Karla's breasts were large and heavy, slumping over the sides of her body. Her nipples weren't round like Sara's; they were squished and egg-shaped. Even without much light I could see they were darker – the colour of over-broiled cheese. Karla pushed her lips up against my ear and whispered, "The universe is answering, Bacon. Call me Sara."

Her lips moved across my cheek, slid onto my mouth. She tasted like coffee and bologna and a green Aero bar.

I tried to burrow myself deeper into the bed, hoping Karla, on top of me, wouldn't feel the erection that had forced itself up. It felt like my first boner, the awkward, alarming, tickly kind of boner you get before you even know what a boner is. Karla noticed it. And as soon as she did, she turned, slid a hand down, and grasped it. I was close to passing out. I tried to roll over to keep her from unfastening my jeans, but she tugged me back by a belt loop, jerked the zipper open. I worried she'd laugh at such a young, pale penis. I tried to imagine she was a doctor, doctors need to look at penises, all ages of penises. I imagined I had a terrible virus that caused blistering and broken skin on my young penis, and every time the doctor moved it to examine closer, the lesions opened wider and the skin ripped apart and it sent a jolt of terrible pain up my whole body. The pain should've been all I could focus on. It wasn't. I ejaculated.

Karla lay next to me, kissing my neck in the darkness, still holding my withering penis. "Synergy," she whispered. I pretended to drift asleep, but didn't sleep a second. I would've slept better under the bridge. I heard Karla shuffling, and a clamour from her night stand. Her cheek pushed up against mine and I was instantly blinded by a brilliant flash. The flash of her camera. Karla nestled her face next to my shoulder, threw an arm across my chest. The orange skin on her forearm looked loose, even in the dark.

13. In the morning Karla took me to a

breakfast diner and ordered us both coffee, even though I don't drink coffee. But exhausted enough, I drank it.

The sharp, deep lines on the waiter's cheeks made his whole face appear to cave in on itself. He kept brushing back the long, thin, blonde-grey hair from his high forehead to see where he poured. Karla called him Tom but not because his name was Tom. She said he looked like Tom Petty. Only older. Maybe Tom Petty's father, she laughed. I didn't know what Tom Petty looked like. I just knew he sang. Tom Petty the waiter never sang, or even spoke for that matter. He just glared at your plate or waved the coffee pot or nodded questioningly at the empty cream containers on people's tables. Karla asked him to take a picture of us with her camera and he nodded. He never even said, "Say cheese." He just snapped the shot and set the camera down. My lack of sleep caught up to me then, because I decided that if Karla took one more picture of me, I'd have enough to say for me and Tom Petty. The waiter, I mean.

"After breakfast we'll shimmy on straight over to the university," Karla said, pulling the crusts off my toast even though I usually eat them. I was too tired to protest. Reaching for a napkin, I stopped to gaze at my reflection in the dulled chrome dispenser. "And if we get you all registered," she sang, "I'll take us out for dinner tonight to celebrate. What do you think?"

I had no idea what to think. I felt about as jumbled up as the packets of jams and jellies stuffed in the wire preservatives holder. I pushed a fork prong slowly through the foil lid of a marmalade packet. A thin orange swirl oozed out.

"You not hungry, Bacon?"

I rolled my shoe over a stray sausage on the linoleum beneath our table, then swept it under my seat. "I want to find my someone," I said.

"Oh, Bacon." She pouted sympathetically. "I know it's harder for you. Especially while other guys your age will go through a dozen someones at university." She wiped the corners of her mouth with a paper napkin. "I've no doubt someday down the road you'll find a someone all on your own – oh, just a sec." She reached a hand out at Tom Petty. "My large grapefruit juice – which by the way was exquisite – had five ice cubes in it. That kept it nicely chilled, but also made it mostly ice. Not much juice. You'll be able to take something off for that, won't you?" Tom Petty shook his pot, swirled the coffee around in a lazy motion. "Maybe just charge for a small." Karla nodded and thanked him before he could answer. She turned back to me. "But I'll tell you this, Bacon, you don't want to wait. To go through your age without a someone ... well, that just wouldn't be right. You don't get those years back. But that's why you found me. The universe pointed you to me."

I looked at her with concern. "Are you saying ... *you're* my someone?"

"Not exactly." She twisted her spoon deep in a yogurt parfait glass. "*I'm* not your someone but I can *be* your someone. That's what I was last night. And that's who I can be again tonight. I'll be any someone you want, any night you need. Except Tuesdays and Thursdays, I've got aqua Pilates."

"I don't understand –"

"Just think of me as the great equalizer." She closed her mouth over a spoonful of yogurt. "So you won't have to end up sapped of energy from four years of snotty university bitches who won't give you the time of day. I, on the other hand, love your sleepy face. And your funny, ruffled hair." She reached out and stabbed a hand through my hair. "You'll never have to feel inadequate with me. It's a perfect setup. You get an education, a place to live," she leaned forward across the table, "and the most feral social life a boy could ever dream of."

I found my hands clutching at my knees under the table. "Why would you do all that?"

"I like you, Bacon." Karla licked the tip of her finger, pressed it down on a toast crumb and lifted it to her tongue. "I really do. You're sweet. I'm doing this for you. For your future. And of course occupancy. Got to keep the properties full." She chuckled then lurched forward. "But what's important right now is that I need an answer from you."

"What answer?"

"I need to know if you're interested." She folded her arms and cocked her head to show her seriousness. "Do you want my condo?"

"Your condo?"

"Do you want to live there during your studies? It comes completely furnished, includes five appliances, and offers all you need to know about love just a phone call away. That's me."

My mother would say all I need to know about love is that it's a load of peanut-packed shit. Kenny Rogers never wrote anything about universities or high-rise condos or real estate agents who specialize in students.

"I just need a yes or no, Bacon." She flipped over an open palm. "Whatever you decide."

"Karla, I don't think I could ever afford your—"

"Don't be silly," she laughed into her water glass, spitting out an ice cube. "I'll help you afford it."

Across the room, Tom Petty swept several hash browns off a table with his hand. They tumbled and scattered across the floor. I excused myself, motioning to the bathroom. I squeezed out only a few drops from a bladder that felt as tight and empty as my stomach. I waited for more pee to come, but none did and I wondered if maybe the hollow ache I felt was a line Kenny Rogers forgot to add in somewhere between knowing when to walk away and when to run.

Sara said Calgary would be wild. That the big city was where it's at. But that morning in that diner in Calgary, I decided I wasn't a city guy. At least not a Calgary guy. In fact, I wasn't sure I'd need to see much more of Calgary ever again.

When I came back out, instead of returning to our table, I stepped around the far booths as Karla analyzed the bill, hurried past Tom Petty, and scurried out the door. I ran on blistered feet upstream along the river, all the way to the Greyhound station. Shortly after, the morning bus to Bellevue hauled me away.

14.

When the bus finally reached the Crowsnest Pass, it continued speeding down the highway instead of turning off for the Super Stop. We sped right past the free campground, the giant crow, the tiny six-seat Wayside Chapel, and right past Bellevue. I scurried to the front and told the driver I needed to get out.

"Bus doesn't stop in Bellevue no more," he said.

"But I have a ticket for Bellevue." I wagged the evidence at him.

"You have a ticket for Blairmore." He lifted his sunglasses and rubbed his eyes.

"But it says Bellevue," I said, checking the ticket again.

"Blairmore's the new Bellevue," he yawned. "They merged the two stops as of today. Not enough traffic to justify both."

"But Blairmore's six kilometres away."

"Exactly," he chuckled, sipping coffee from the lid-cup of his thermos. "Besides, nobody ever gets off at Bellevue."

The giant crow disappeared around the bend behind us, its large, white eyes watching us pass.

I trekked the hour and a half back to Bellevue through the blasting wind that kicked and shoved, looking for a fight. By the time I reached home, my feet had been sanded down to bone.

I could've slept for three days.

Stepping inside, I heard my mother call, "Is that you?"

"Yeah," I uttered with what felt like my last ounce of energy.

"Bacon, come sit down." I could hear my mother thrashing away, deep inside the hall closet.

"You want me to sit in the closet?"

"What?" Three hangers clanged as they fell from the rack. "No. The kitchen. Go sit in the kitchen. We need to talk." She kicked out a pair of black pumps I'd never seen before. Even with creases across the leather toe, the straps squashed flat, and a corner of the left heel chipped, the shoes struck me as swanky. My mother hadn't sported anything beyond water-stained Brooks runners since before my father left.

69

I dragged myself up the three steps to the kitchen and collapsed in a chair, gazing into the upholstery pattern between my legs. Tiny silvery stars in a mint-vinyl galaxy. Sleep was setting in just as my mother turned the corner with a long, dark coat strung across a shoulder, a black pleather handbag stuffed under an arm, and a fist clasped around the straps of her crinkled black pumps. Her wrenched glare found my face – not quite my eyes, but my face to be sure. That was unusual. My mother doesn't bother to look people in the face. Suddenly I had the anxious feeling she was on to me. That she knew I never made it home last night. That I hadn't called. Exhausted and frightened of what she'd say, I also felt strangely thrilled. Had she gone downstairs to check on me? Maybe she'd even waited up.

My mother stood with her free hand supporting herself on the back of a chair, grimacing for a few moments as though irritated by having to interrupt her closet rooting.

"I thought of coming down to tell you this earlier," she said, "but I didn't want to wake you. You're up now so I'll tell you."

She switched her weight to the other leg. "Bacon." She paused a moment. "Your grandfather's left us."

And then just like that, the thrill disappeared and left only exhaustion again. "I know," I sighed, tugging a sock down to peek at my bleeding, blistered, crusted feet. "He left before I was born."

"What? No, no. Not left *this* place." She wiggled her fingers, each one pointing at a different room of the house. "I mean he's left *this* place – *this world.* The guy's dead."

Out on the living room couch, Grandma Magic Can poked a knitting needle at the crumble of leaves on her Fanta can.

"Oh," I said, realizing I'd never really known much about him. "How did it happen?"

"Nothing special." My mother dumped the jacket and handbag onto the table. She spun and fumbled through a drawer. "Went to bed alive, woke up dead."

"He *woke up* dead?"

"Well no, I guess he wouldn't have woken up. Went to bed alive and ... I don't know, what would you call it? *Slept in* dead?"

In the living room, Grandma's turned-in lips sucked up a lungful of smoke.

"Wow," I said, fighting the slumber glazing over me. "Passed suddenly in his sleep," I said softly to myself.

"Well, I don't know how *sudden* it was." My mother plucked a small stack of bills from under the cutlery tray and stuffed them into her purse. "Sonovabitch was seventy-eight. Doesn't seem all that sudden to me. That death was damn near eighty years in the making."

Grandma coughed up something between a belch and a gag.

I traced my finger over the mint and silver vinyl of the chair, trying to imagine my grandfather's face in the starry pattern. "I didn't know you kept in touch with him."

"We didn't," Grandma muttered from the living room.

"Some executor from Korea called this morning," my mother said, scuttling around the kitchen. She tucked in each chair, nudged the coffee maker a quarter of an inch to the left, unplugged the toaster, moved the coffee maker back, refolded the dishtowel and draped it over the oven door handle. "If buddy hadn't called," she wiped the table with three big loops of a dishrag, "might be we never would've known." She paused, folded her arms, and leaned back against the counter. "When your grandfather came back from Korea packing more than just a few memories," she started into the story I'd heard her tell my father, and anyone who'd listen, three dozen times before, "Grandma kicked his sorry ass — and that love child's — right back to Asia." She nodded proudly, wrung out the rag, and folded it over the faucet. I'd always noticed Grandma wince every time my mother told the story. "Never heard from him again."

"He called," Grandma said.

"What?" My mother took a step into the living room. "You never told me —"

"Nothing to tell. I never bothered answering those rings."

"You never bothered answering — well, then, Jesus Christ, how the hell do you know it was him?"

"It was him." Grandma wiped the knitting needle clean on her sweats.

"Right." My mother rolled her eyes and turned back to me. "Anyway, the funeral's in two days. We're leaving this afternoon."

"Where you going?" I yawned, rubbing my heel over the lip of the chair's crocheted leg sock.

"Korea."

"Korea?"

"Of course." My mother scribbled away at some list on a pad. "That's where the sonovabitch's been living for the last forty-seven years. No sense in shipping the corpse the hell over here."

"Korea?" I said again. It seemed too far away to be real. I was too exhausted to even imagine.

"We had to pull out the Bonanza money I won last year to pay for the tickets." She fixed her eyes on me like I was the one who'd died. "That was earmarked for a car." She returned to her list. "Anyway, we'll need you to drive us up to the airport."

"Drive you? What? Which airport?"

"Calgary, of course," she tsked and frowned. On the table, between the wet swipes of my mother's rag, I saw toast crumbs she'd missed, laying there like fallen rock. "Where the hell else would we fly out of? Are there trans-pacific flights I don't know about departing out of the Henderson barn in Cowley? Jesus, Bacon."

The withering lilac bush out back poked its twigs at the kitchen window in the slapping wind. I felt a sudden fold in my stomach, my feet throbbed, my head wobbled on its neck.

"You'll need to pick us up, too. Costs damn near more than the goddamned flight to leave a car in the airport for a week. And the parking bastards don't offer no bereavement discount neither. So, get yourself ready, we'll leave in an hour."

She marched down the hall to her room. I heard her heave the suitcases out of the closet and slap them onto the bed. She could've stuffed me full of clothes too if I could've only slapped down on that bed for a moment.

Grandma Magic Can smiled absently at an old print on the wall we'd picked up together years ago from the market in Coleman. A lone cowboy-fisherman fighting a large thrashing trout. In the image you could see the fish had just snapped the line.

That old cowboy must've enjoyed one heck of a fight for whatever time he kept the big trout hooked. Snow covered mountains faded off in the background and ice still clung along the water's edge. I don't know who the artist was but scribbled small in the bottom corner was 1498/1500. I always thought that was pretty cool—we got the third last one.

I wondered if Grandma Magic Can ever dreamt she'd end up living out her life with her daughter. Maybe that's what happens to people who don't find their someone.

She relit the shards of weeds with a lighter, inhaled sharply.

"I'm sorry," I said, propping myself up against the wall between the living room and kitchen. "About Grandpa."

Her scrunched-up face and thrust-out chest meant she was holding in a lungful of smoke. She turned only partly way toward me, paused, then blew out the smoke. Waved it all away with her knitting needle.

15. It struck me, on our way to Calgary, that a possible reason we'd never left the Crowsnest Pass as a family was my mother's car. A fourteen-year-old Dodge Lancer. As soon as you got it up over eighty, it trembled like a wet cat. Get it up closer to a hundred and you'd think the thing was trying to mix paint. You couldn't place a hand on the exterior without touching rust. A good-sized hole corroded out of the floorboard underneath the driver's seat where exhaust seeped in. Too long in that car and you'd go funny-headed and start to see the road through fish eyes.

Already beyond drowsy, those fumes made it impossible to concentrate. I rolled down my window, leaning my head out for a blast of air.

"Hey!" Grandma called from the back seat. "Let's keep those windows up."

My mother threw her a scowl.

Grandma tugged her shawl over her shoulder defensively. "An old lady gets cold, you know."

"Right," my mother sniffed. "It's twenty-five degrees out. You can get yourself a glue stick for the plane. For now the rest of us need some fresh air."

I signalled and passed a huge green combine taking up most of the road. The farmer's old cowboy hat reminded me of the print in our living room.

"Grandma," I said, peeking into the rearview mirror, "how come you never remarried?"

She coughed out a sandpaper laugh. "Heavens, once is enough."

"Did you ever date again?"

She cranked out another chuckle. "Lord, no! No barn dances or rodeo bashes for me."

"Didn't you want to find your someone?"

"Your *someone*?" my mother piped in. "What the hell do you mean *your someone*? There's no *someone*. There's pigs and whores and those smart enough to stick to themselves. That's all there is."

"That's not what Kenny Rogers says," I braved.

"The hell you know about Kenny Rogers?" my mother spat.

"In that song." I gripped the wheel with both hands. "You know ... *there's someone for everyone.*"

My mother sat stumped for a second, glaring at the dashboard, then snarled. "You mean *Tommy*? Pfff." She waved a hand at the air. "Yeah, Tommy found his someone all right. And what did it get the little coward? A broken Becky and three outlaws too many in her hoo hoo. The world's chock full of Gatlin boys, Bacon."

"But, the point of the song—" I started.

"The point," my mother said, "is that Kenny, bless his goddamned heart of gold, never wrote the stupid song. Some buttholes named Roger Bowling and Billy Ed Wheeler did. Kenny just lent his sweet pipes to churn an otherwise ass-wiping sheet of music into a goddamned piece of art." She lifted an arm over the headrest and hiked herself around to face the back seat. "After sending Grandpa packing, your Grandma here was wise enough not to waste any time looking for any more trouble. Am I right?"

Grandma shuffled herself in the seat, reached for her frizzy curls, and tapped them down as if they'd blow away. "I suppose after losing an ox, one repairs the barn." She turned toward the window. "That way no more cows get out." She pulled out a crumpled tissue from under her sweater sleeve, rubbed it under her nose, and tucked the tissue ball back up her sleeve. "Of course, then the lost one can't get back in either...."

"Yeah, well, if the lost cow ate cud in some other barn," my mother said, "then that sonovabitch cow can go freeze in a ditch." She unravelled a Discman from a plastic grocery bag, stuffed the cassette adapter into the stereo and flipped open the lid with her fingernail. "Your Grandma's better off," she sneered. "Besides, it's not exactly the deepest pool of talent in our parts."

In the mirror I saw Grandma Magic Can nod slightly, staring out at the passing prairie.

We passed a sign that read Claresholm 1 km. Halfway to Calgary.

"Brought the *Duets*," my mother announced, fumbling through the cds in a plastic grocery bag. "And *21 Number Ones*. Kenny can't be expected to field this funeral solo. Sheena and Dolly are going to have to pitch in."

I tipped my head back out the window, fighting to stay awake. "How come you guys are even going to this funeral?" I asked.

"That man was your grandfather," my mother spat.

"I know," I said. "I just meant you don't seem to have really liked him."

"His mischief aside," my mother poked at her cuticles with a house key, "he stuffed his sperm in a woman – that woman back there – who womaned your mother – me – who birthed a child – *you*. So just have a little respect."

"Sorry," I said. "I didn't mean – "

"Oh for Christ's sake," Grandma Magic Can said, "the man was an asshole."

My mother jerked and twisted herself to face the back seat. "Then why the hell are we going all the way to goddamned Korea?" Just then Dolly's voice lifted gently through the three working speakers.

"Sometimes you got to go to assholes' funerals, too," Grandma said. "And not because he was your father or my husband or

Bacon's grandfather, that don't mean beans. That's not why we're going. I don't expect you'd remember love from a rat fart, Lydia, but you could quietly attend the funeral of a man we both once loved. However briefly." She folded her arms.

I focused on the road not daring to look at my mother. But I couldn't help sneaking a peek at Grandma Magic Can in the mirror. Her face flushed and tight.

"You take what morsel you're tossed and eat the damned thing up," Grandma continued. "That crumb might be miserably small and turn rotten, but don't ever go forgetting how good it once tasted."

"Christ," my mother said.

We entered Claresholm just as Kenny entered the stage to join Dolly. "Stop at the 7-Eleven, Bacon," Grandma said. "I need a pee and a corn dog."

We all did.

16. At the Departures gate, my mother

yanked her luggage off my shoulder and said, "For Christ's sake, don't forget to pick us up." She pushed a hundred dollars into my hand. "For gas and stuff." She threw one arm half around me and leaned in a little. "There're meat pies in the freezer and some cans of Chunky in the cupboard." She glanced behind at Grandma Magic Can checking the Departures screen, then said under her coffee breath, "There's beer in the bottom fridge shelf. Help yourself. Just leave a couple for when I get back."

Grandma waddled over and hugged me. I felt her hand slip into my back pocket. "That's two hundred dollars," she whispered. "If you feel like it, stick around Calgary for a bit. Have some fun. Otherwise I put some beer in the fridge back home. Just don't tell your mother."

I watched them disappear through the Departures gate, and then there I was alone in Calgary. Again.

17.

Since Sara first mentioned the idea of Calgary back at the Pure Country Restaurant and Lounge, I'd always pictured it as *her* city. When I'd watch the Calgary channels on TV, I'd think of her. When someone bought a *Calgary Sun* at the Super Stop, I'd think of her. I'd often imagine a spot on Calgary's Bow River similar to that turbulent bend on the Crow where we'd first come together, water rushing over rocks, bubbling over banks. A shaded spot where the dark soil and damp leaves feel cool against a naked backside. A place where we could gaze at the city's skyline and Sara could whisper all the wild things she'd found in Calgary. But now, as I gripped tightly on the wheel of my mother's coughing Lancer, shaking down the Deerfoot, and as I peeked over at the towering hoodoos of cold, coarse concrete and dusty glass, the city had somehow attached itself to Karla's face. I heard Karla whispering in the gritty Calgary air that slithered in through the Lancer's vents. I smelled Karla's breath as I pulled into the traffic that clogged Memorial Drive. And I felt the weight of Karla's heavy, sagging breasts as I stepped passed the elaborate stone work, the flower landscaping, the grand pillars, the arched entranceway, and buzzed her condo.

"Hello?"

"It's me, Bacon," I said to the intercom.

"Bacon!"

"Sorry I left the breakfast diner."

"What happened? I sent the waiter into the bathroom to look for you."

"Tom Petty the waiter?"

"What? Oh, yes, Tom Petty."

"I didn't think you'd be here," I said. "I thought you'd be at your house."

"No, I'm here, I'm in the middle of showing the place. Give me a sec, I'll be right down."

I propped myself up against a gravelly planter and fought to keep my heavy head from rolling off my shoulders.

77

After a few moments, a young guy about my age, one hand clamped to his head to keep his red ball cap from flying off, scrambled out the door, tripping over himself trying to get out. "They don't rent places like *that* in Saskatchewan," he said, then fled across the parking lot, down the street, and out of sight.

Karla appeared a few minutes later. "Sorry to make you wait." She pushed her lips into my cheek. "Just had a viewing," she sang. "This place is going to get snatched up quick."

"Guy in the red cap?"

"Yes," she smiled. "That was him."

"He didn't seem all that interested."

Her smile fluttered a little. "That's because he's a moron."

I uncrossed my numbing legs and stood free from the planter.

"But he'll be back." She tugged her purse further up her shoulder.

I tried to catch a last glimpse of the frightened kid, but he had disappeared behind a building. "How do you know?"

"I know," she said sharply, fumbling for something in her purse she didn't find. "Trust me, he'll come back. About a month or so into first semester. Dying to get in. Willing to pay anything. But he won't get in."

"He won't?" I stifled a yawn, my mind unable to calculate how long it had been since I last slept.

"No, he won't, Bacon."

"Why not?"

"Because *you'll* be living here."

My glance dropped down to a lone ant climbing up the planter. "Karla, I'm not sure I want—"

"*I'm* sure. You're here, aren't you? You left this morning—much like young Trevor just did—and you came back. Just like Trevor will. But you came back first. So you get the place." The ant paused on a sticky-looking stain along the planter's surface. I checked for more of his colony but he was the only one.

"Look at you, Bacon." Karla reached up and held my face. "Your eyes look even sleepier than usual. They're redder than a fresh fifty-dollar bill."

I pulled back from her hands and refocused my heavy eyes. I couldn't even recall what we'd just been talking about or how I'd gotten there. I flicked away the ant I'd been watching, sending him hurling across the sidewalk. "I need to look for Sara."

Karla clutched her purse with both hands. "Well," she sighed, "if the universe wants you to, you'll find her."

"If I *look* hard enough, I'll find her."

Karla adjusted the pink scrunchie that pinched her hair back. "Sure," she said. "Nothing's impossible. But it's a big city, Bacon."

"I know. You said that before. But I've been thinking about that." I squinted from the sun behind her. "I just need to chop 'er down."

"Chop it down?"

"Yeah. Sara likes her places wild. So we just look in wild places. Ignore the rest. That's how I'll find her."

"Bacon," she waved away a fly, "there are a lot of places in Calgary I'd call wild."

"Yeah, but I'll bet there are a lot more you wouldn't."

"True," she said hesitantly.

"So see, now the city doesn't seem so big."

She glanced around as though checking if the city had actually shrunk.

"You could take me to some of those places," I said, even though the only place I really wanted to find right then was a place to sleep.

Karla nodded slightly, her smile as thin as fishing line. "I could. I could drive you around," she said. "On one condition."

I felt myself slip back against the planter. "What condition?"

"We go by the university first and get you registered."

"University? Karla, I don't –"

"No deal then."

"It's just that I have no idea what I'd take –"

"Take business. That's what everybody takes when they don't know what to take."

"I know nothing about business."

"Of course, that's why you'll go to school."

"Why is my education so important to you?"

"Do you want to work at the Super Stop the rest of your life?"

"I don't think I work there at all anymore," I yawned.

"You want to end up like your father? Bacon, this is your

chance to set yourself on the path of opportunity. To throw yourself out there, right onto an energy wave. Or, it's your moment to get left behind. You have two choices."

A discarded apple sat perched on one of the planter's corners, rotting. "I don't know if I'm smart enough for —"

"The universe says you are. That's why you're here. That's why we met. It's synergy." She threw her palms out to emphasize how easy it all was. "What's it going to be?"

"I don't know, Karla."

"I do. But this is a decision you have to make."

"Maybe I should wait a year —"

"No! That's absurd. Waste of a year."

"I don't know if I'm ready for —"

"Yes, you are."

"Aren't there any other options?"

"No. None that don't flout the universe."

"So I just go apply? Just like that?"

"Like I said, that's your call."

I poked a little hole in the planter soil with my finger, then covered it back up. I wished I could plant myself away and sleep. "Maybe you're right," I shrugged. "I don't have any other plans."

"Excellent. You're making a wise decision, Bacon. We'll apply at the college too. In case you're not smart enough for university."

We tore off in Karla's car, a sporty vehicle as red as fresh blood and every bit as shiny as her forehead. The top even came down and we drove with it that way, ripping through Calgary, the wind slapping our hair. "You have a great car," I told her.

"It's OK." Her tightly wrenched hair stayed gripped back, even in the wind.

"What is it?"

"Mustang convertible."

"I don't know much about cars," I said. "It looks brand new."

"Oh, God no," she laughed. "It's over a year old."

Karla paid my registration fees. Said I could pay her back. I told her I had no idea where I'd get the money. She turned her shiny forehead to me, the left side of her mouth grinning high. "I do," she said. "I do."

18. Finally noticing my eyes – they'd

been shut since we left the university – Karla suggested we delay our Sara search a day or two. Too done in, I couldn't even nod. And even though I'd packed nothing more than a fishing rod, hoping to test a creek or two on the way home, I accepted her assumption that I'd spend the night.

She drove us back to her condo and promised to make anything in the world I wanted for dinner and then put me to bed. I said I wanted beef dip. She didn't have any beef so she made us a bean and lentil salad. "Something a little more summery," she gushed. "It's important to eat in harmony with the seasons."

The gloss and sheen of her pink toaster, pink microwave, and pink blender kept me from slipping into sleep right there at the table.

"Tell me about your parents," she said, dumping a scoopful of bean salad onto my plate.

"My mother?" I yawned. "Not much to tell. Works at a laundromat. Plays bingo."

"What about your dad?"

"Left when I was ten." The bean salad sloshed wet and oily in my mouth, the soppy texture of fish eggs. "My mother repaired the barn and thinks my father's a cow who should freeze in a ditch. She also thinks he's a pig."

"Wow," Karla chuckled. "He must suffer from multiple anthropomorphism disorder."

"My mother thinks all men are pigs." Karla's dining room was separated from the living room by a bookshelf stuffed full of long-titled books that my tired eyes strained to read: *Look Like a Celebrity Beauty Guide, You Have to Say I'm Wealthy: We're Married, The Idiot's Guide to Tax Evasion.*

"I guess your folks just weren't meant to be." Karla buttered herself a heavy slice of some kind of four-hundred-and-seventy-three-grain bread. It seemed much more like a fall or winter food to me.

"Maybe," I said. "Who knows."

"I do." Karla lowered the bread just before she bit. "If they were right for each other, he wouldn't have left. Or she wouldn't have driven him away. Whichever."

"He left," I said. "For a much younger tour guide. My mother called her a 'who-er' guide. She said the who-er guide didn't have a bus to who-er guide on, so she got people like my father to ride *her* instead."

"Was the tour guide his — what do you call it? — his *someone*?"

"My father had a lot of someones."

"No." Karla stuffed her mouth full of bread and shook her head. "You can have a lot of *somebodies*, but you only have *one* someone. And no matter how many somebodies you have, your someone will still be your someone."

"How do you know a *somebody* from a *someone*?"

She threw me a sideways glance. "Your someone doesn't leave."

I stopped chewing. "Karla, you don't think Sara's my someone, do you?"

"That's not for me to say." She poured herself a glass of wine. "I just know you're not going to find some unlisted girl in a city of a million bodies. And if you do, you'll just get your heart broken because she doesn't love you."

"How can you know that?"

"I'm sorry, Bacon," Karla said, her voice muffled by a mouthful of beans, "but she wouldn't have left you in Bellevue. She would've called. Or e-mailed. Something. But that's OK. No two people think of each other the same way. Even those who love each other love each other differently. For different reasons. Different degrees. And it's OK to love somebody who doesn't love you back. Sometimes the fantasy's better." Her words were sharp, her voice so matter-of-fact, yet gentle.

"Girls can be very manipulative, Bacon," she frowned. "It's not that there's anything wrong with you — oh dear, I have to be careful how I say this — but a guy like you should always *question* what a girl like that wants from you."

I felt my shoulders sink and my lips slip apart. "You think she *wanted* something from me?"

"I have no idea." Karla waved a fork dismissively. "Who knows with us women? But on the flip side, Bacon, there may also have been confusion on what exactly you felt."

"What do you mean, *what I felt*?"

"Sure, Sara left you. But *you* let her go."

"She left without me—"

"Ever think of her when you're not horny?"

"Of course!"

"Sure you do." She jumped to her feet with a sharp smirk, walked her plate to the sink.

I set my fork across the plate. Whatever appetite I'd had fled. "I'm really tired," I said.

She sighed and smiled a someday-you'll-get-it smile. "OK then, let's hit the hay."

My eyes wandered to the large, pink ceramic bowl on the counter behind Karla. A solitary glistening apple sat in the bowl. "This time," I said, "I'll sleep on the love seat."

Karla grinned. "Oh? Is that why you came back and buzzed me? To sleep on my love seat?"

"I just think it might be best—"

"For the love of body, mind, and soul, you're a guy! This is what guys do. You have an obligation to yourself." She pulled me up by the arm and steered me toward her room. "People will think there's something wrong with you. You have a lot to learn about being a man, Bacon. You can't sit waiting for a woman to grab you by the throat each time. You're already eighteen! Now pull up some mattress, kid." She flapped a hand at the bed. "I'll give you the best sleep you've ever had." Then she disappeared into the bathroom.

When she returned she was wearing doily underwear again. "Oh, before I forget," she said, pushing some kind of form into my hands, "sign this."

Again, I could see straight through the thin, silky material of her underwear. The dark, oval nipples on her heavy breasts. "What am I sign—"

"Student loan application." She perched herself on the edge of the bed. "I filled everything out for you. I know how to squeeze out the max on these things. Done dozens of them."

"Twenty-seven thousand dollars?" I gasped and sank down beside her.

"Isn't it wonderful?"

"Wonderful? That would take forever to pay back!"

"Pay it back?" She shook her scowling face like I'd wet myself. "You don't *pay back* student loans, Bacon. You *default* on them. Anybody who knows anything knows that much."

I scratched my elbow and frowned heavily. "But that would ruin my credit rating."

"Only for seven years. It'll take you seven years to get out of school and settled. By then you'll have met your someone. If you want a car or house you just buy it in her name. It's perfect. Trust me, I know this business."

"Karla, I'm not even sure I want to go back to school – "

"Oh, for the love of all things divine. Not this again." One of her legs crossed over the other, revealing red flushes on the skin of her thigh and a coffee-stain birthmark the size of a potato chip. "Bacon, this is just an application, it still needs to be approved."

"But twenty-seven thousand dollars?"

"Tuition and books cost a lot. Plus, of course, this place." Karla plopped her head on my shoulder; a fat breast slid its heft onto my arm. "Look, the government *wants* to help. You *need* the help. It's synergy."

I was so beyond tired I couldn't tell if I was awake anymore. The whole day felt like a dream. I gazed at her glossy-lipped smile, her wine-stained teeth. I watched the little cracks in the yellow skin around her lips tighten as she squeezed them together and leaned in on me. Her crinkly lips wormed across my cheek, down over my neck. "Sign it," she whispered, "and then we'll see if we can get a little further this time."

I dropped the pen without signing, shut my eyes from it all, and hoped for some interruption to save me from myself. Then it came to me. A familiar, momentum-breaking worry that broke off Karla's kiss like a snapped fishing line. "Shouldn't we use protection?" I said.

"Protection?" Her eyelids twitched.

"Contraceptives," I said. "A condom."

"I know what they are. I have actually seen one before," she snickered.

"Me too. My dad kept some in a shoebox. Anyway, I just think it's best we be safe." Distraction or not, it doesn't take a lot to make a baby—I'd learned that much in sex-ed class. A little dab will do. Mrs. Jorgensen used to shake a yardstick, warning us not to get trapped in a life we didn't choose.

"I'm sorry," Karla giggled. "I don't mean to laugh. I just haven't used one in years. I can assure you I'm clean, and I need no assuring that you are. Still, it's very responsible of you, Bacon. By all means throw one on."

"Thank you," I said. "Do you have one?"

"*Me?*" she laughed again. "Lord, no." She glanced around the room. "You should carry your own if you're so concerned. Check the end table. Who knows what one of the tenants left behind."

In the drawer was a package of Caffedrine caplets, a bottle of Sleep Ease, some kind of lotion, and sure enough a condom in a blue package. It must have been there a while. The sides were torn, the corners dog-eared, and the whole package had collapsed and shrivelled enough that you could see a faded ring outline of the condom.

Being the first condom I'd ever used, it took several minutes to chafe the dry latex over my skin. Approaching Karla, I kept one hand down around my penis, pinching the condom so it didn't slip off. She guided me into her reclined body, and her hand slid along my hip and around to my backside where her thumb, unexpectedly, wormed its way into my anus. My back seized and I turned as taut and hard as a frozen fillet. Terribly uncomfortable, I was just about to ask her if she realized the location of her thumb, and what I should—or was expected to—do next. But then, just as suddenly, I ejaculated.

I withdrew, as did Karla's thumb, then straightened myself and peeked down at her startled face. My erection quickly faded. A sudden wave of fear crept over me as I saw Mrs. Jorgensen shaking her yardstick, lecturing: "Sometimes condoms leak...."

I whirled and ran to the bathroom—not her en-suite, but the

main bathroom off the living room. The condom, still clinging to my now soft penis, hung like a teardrop. As I sprinted across the living room it swung from side to side, hurling my penis, slapping it up against the skin on either side of my groin. It was like a small, sweaty arm reaching all around for high-fives. I locked the door to the bathroom and carefully peeled off the condom.

"Bacon, are you all right?" Karla called. I could hear her shuffle out of bed.

"Yeah."

"What are you doing?" The bathroom door creaked as she leaned against it. "What's the matter?"

"Nothing," I said. "I have to pee."

I fastened the condom around the faucet like you would a water balloon, clamping it secure with my thumb and finger. I figured I'd fill the condom with water and, as it expanded, check for signs of dew or any trace of moisture leak. I needed certainty. But as I eased the tap on and water began to pour, the condom didn't expand at all. In fact, the water ran right through, flowing freely out the crusted end of the condom that must have exploded. I let out a squeak.

"Are you sure you're OK?" Karla patted the door.

Some noise fell out of my mouth that sounded something like, "Umamban." I lifted the condom eye-level and watched several soaked latex shards dribble into the sink.

"Bacon, honey?" Karla knocked. "Open the door!"

My eyes dropped from the sight of the crumpled rubber down to my wilted penis--a penis that no longer looked as it should. The shrivelled shaft was the same, but the head was now my mother's head, her pasty complexion, her tight frown. "Pigs!" is all she said.

"Bacon, please!" Karla rapped.

I yanked open the door, hoisted the blown-out condom right up to her eyes and said, "You might be pregnant."

Karla stumbled back, swatting at the air. "Jesus, Bacon!" she screamed. "Get that thing out of my face!"

"The end gave out," I said, my voice breaking. "It's all inside you."

Karla laughed so hard she collapsed to her knees. When she

finally caught her breath, she covered her face with her hand and said, "I told you not to even bother, Bacon. I'm fixed."

"You're what?"

"I'm tied." She clenched her mid-section. "I can't get pregnant."

"Oh," I said, gaping at the condom. "You can't?"

"Throw that damn thing out." She laughed harder and snapped a picture of me.

I ditched the condom in the bathroom garbage and zombied over to the bed. I was asleep before I'd finished lying down.

That night I dreamt I was walking with my spincasting rod, headed toward a sprawling, sparkling green lake. A lake so large you couldn't see the opposite shore — if there even was one. On the path, just a few metres from the bank, I found a jackfish. Its tail had crisped in the sun, its eyes plucked out by gulls, its stomach torn open, entrails stretched out across the path. I peeled the jackfish from the mudded path and pierced its pale lips onto the rusted hook of my Kamlooper. The jackfish dangled from the end of the line on my green and brown spincasting rod, twisting slowly in the faint breeze.

19. ● I slept straight through until two

o'clock the next afternoon. Karla left a note on her pillow saying she needed to get home but would be back later that night to help me look for Sara. She'd also left the student loan application on the bedside table with a pink sticky note reminding me to sign it. I didn't.

Brushing my teeth at the sink, I began to think Karla might be right, that maybe Sara had wanted something from me. God knows what. I ran my hand through the neglected hedge of hair on my head and all its fugitive tufts. I'd never really had a hairstyle or even known how to keep it. I pulled up the folded skin of my eyelids and watched them sink back down. They really were droopy. I suppose I'd just gotten used to them. I studied my shoulders, thin and narrow, my chest, shapeless and bald like a little boy's. It'd been foolish to think Sara had ever been attracted to me.

Karla didn't believe Sara was my someone. But she did think it was ok to *pretend* Sara was my someone so long as I pretended Karla was Sara when I did. But if Sara was my someone only when Karla was pretending to be Sara, wouldn't that make Karla my someone? And if Karla was my someone, why did she want me to imagine she was Sara?

I'd never felt more unsure about things in my life and I'd spent my life remarkably unsure.

I considered holing up in Karla's condo until she returned, seeing as how Calgary's ferocious pace, crammed streets, and peculiar people left me feeling like I'd just tumbled into the boiling eddies of class-five rapids. But the condo's pink appliances, with their shade of aroused flesh, left me feeling no less uneasy. The city, on the other hand, possessed one grand redeeming feature that every city, town, and hamlet on the planet should possess: a river.

In desperate need of the calm soothing of a river, I grabbed my green and brown second-hand spincasting rod with the closed-face reel and thumb-button trigger from the Lancer. Karla's condo was only a blessed few steps from the mighty Bow River.

I came upon a narrow section of the Bow, a manufactured lagoon of calm, shallow water nestled in between the bank and an artificial island. A paved pathway, clogged with bikers and joggers and sweatered dogs and baby strollers, snuggled right up to the river for as far I could see.

My first cast brought in a clump of weeds the size of a lettuce head. The back swing of my second cast slapped a passing rollerblader in the chin. Fortunately, the hook didn't take. My third cast hit water but brought several fluttering and squawking ducks paddling toward me, not the least bit shy in my presence. In fact, they seemed strangely drawn to me. Worried they'd frighten away any nearby fish, I stepped back up the bank and headed farther up the river. I found a good spot between two large cottonwoods and shuffled down to the river's edge. Again, just before I cast, several ducks paddled toward me. I moved upstream, but they followed. I switched back downstream. They followed. Every step I made, the ducks paddled after. Every cast, they chased. When I simply stopped casting, the ducks waddled ashore, circling me, quacking, and poking their bills around my feet. Calgary, I decided, had stupid ducks.

"Shoo!" I hissed. "Scoot! Get back in the water." I hugged my spincasting rod tightly, fearing they might snatch it.

I tried to ignore the mallards, pecking so close they occasionally caught the toe of one of my tennis shoes, but with every cast more swarmed. Soon, a dozen gulls joined, then six widgeons, and three grebes. Some quacked, some shrieked, but they all fluttered and splashed and chased. Some nipped at my laces, one caught a pinch of my sock.

Then the mess of waterfowl parted, clearing a path for a large Canada Goose – my mother's favourite animal. The large beast glided down from the sky, landed with a stumble, caught its footing, and scuttled directly for me. Its bill struck my shin in mid-cast. I turned to run, but it snapped a pinch of skin on the back of my calf. Panicked, I dropped my rod, saw the goose moving in again and, not knowing what else to do, gripped the bird by its neck, stretching my arm out to keep it at bay. The goose thrashed its wings, honked, shook, fluttered, and made a horrible hiss. The commotion brought about a second goose that toddled in and drove its beak into my Achilles. I buckled over, desperately holding my grip on the first goose to keep it from joining the assault. The free goose came at me again. I managed to dodge the attack by rolling to my right, still clinging to the original goose. I struggled for breath as the second assailant charged again, backing me up against a tree. With nothing to defend myself, the only option was the unthinkable. I swung the first goose. It clubbed the other, knocking him off his feet in a cloud of dust. But the clubbed bird shook it off and steadied itself. Its long neck stretched and arched and weaved like a cobra, searching for an opening to strike. I let go a second swing. This hit square, sending it tumbling back into the river. I released the original goose, snatched up my rod, and fled back to Karla's.

20. Karla drove me all over Calgary,

popping in to several nightclubs she described as *wild*: Cowboys, Coyotes, Morgans, the Ship and Anchor, the Back Alley, the French Maid, the Cecil. We found happy hours and beer tubs and stumbling fights and broken glass and loud bands with large bull fiddles, but we never found Sara Mulligan.

I spent the next three days attempting to fish the Bow, the evenings searching for Sara, the nights laying down on Karla's love seat, being lugged off, and the following mornings waking up in her king bed. Each part of each day equally unsuccessful. Ducks and geese were everywhere on the Bow. Any move I made down from the river path toward the water, they'd swarm. I walked the river for a solid mile, but they followed. Or I simply ran into more. I spotted a couple of men fly-fishing. No waterfowl bothered them. In fact, no birds of any feather seemed to want anything to do with the fly-fishermen. At least the pesky ducks and geese had good taste.

Back at the condo, Karla was every bit as unyielding as the ducks. Constantly nagging me to sign the student loan forms, reading out lists of classes considered painless, rifling off names of instructors and professors rumoured to be merciful.

Each night of searching for Sara in a city of a million people was as unsuccessful as you'd expect looking for somebody in a city of a million people would be. My fourth night at Karla's, we took the night off from Sara-hunting and instead Karla treated me to something I'd never had before: Greek food. The Greek restaurant served everything from roasted eggplant to broiled dandelion to skewered lamb to marinated swordfish. What it didn't have was beef dip. I was starting to suspect Calgary – which misleadingly nicknames itself Cowtown – simply didn't have beef dips. Karla ordered me a dish that turned out to be rabbit. The joint figured out how to roast a rabbit in fourteen herbs but couldn't throw together a beef dip.

After dinner, we strolled around a district Karla called

Kensington. Karla pointed out her favourite coffee shop, her favourite parking spot, the store she'd purchased her pink doily underwear from, her lawyer's office, her other lawyer's office, and a Jugo Juice.

"Ever had a thermo-boost smoothie?" she asked.

I said I hadn't.

"Great! Here comes another experience!" She looped her hand around my arm.

Looking back at the moment, I'm reminded of my timing. We didn't step into any of the other twenty-odd Jugo Juice locations across Calgary. We stopped into the one in Kensington. We didn't stop ten minutes earlier or ten minutes after, we stopped in at that exact moment. And we did so because of my timing.

We entered just as a small, thin man in a black hoodie forced the Jugo Juice clerk out from behind the counter, waving a five-foot metal level like a sword. The hooded man backed the clerk up against a tray of iced carrots just as I noticed the hooded man with the level wasn't a man at all. It was a *she,* and *she* said, "Bacon?"

I watched the she, who I thought had been a he, tug off her hoodie. "Sara?" I said.

"Bacon, what are you – *don't move!*" She thrust the level up against the Jugo Juice man's neck. "Bacon, you lying bastard! Why did you abandon me at the Pure Country?"

"Sara, what are you doing with that level?"

"That's Sara?" Karla said, squinting. "Is she a carpenter?"

"Can I get anyone a smoothie?" the Jugo Juice clerk asked.

"*I told you to shut the fuck up.*" Sara cocked the level ready for a baseball swing.

"Sara, wait!" I said. "What are you doing?"

Sara eyed me for a moment. "I just need a little money." She lowered the level. "And I really felt like a juice. Have you had one of these?"

"Why don't I buy us each a Watermelon Wiggle?" Karla offered.

"Who the fuck's that?" Sara barked.

"Oh, I'm sorry," I said. "Sara Mulligan this is Karla. Karla, Sara."

"I'm Jeff," the Jugo Juice man said.

"Shut up," Sara barked at the man. "Bacon, I don't give a shit what her *name* is. I meant how do you know her?"

"He's been sleeping with me," Karla said cheerily. "Just until he could find you, though."

I'd forgotten how quickly Sara could move. Before I could turn my wide, baffled eyes away from Karla, Sara lunged across the room, thrusting the level like a battering ram. My kidney nearly pushed through my spinal column, and I collapsed against the big window of the Jugo Juice.

"I told you never to lie to me!" Sara panted.

I felt a blow hit my arm. "You lied and then you come to Calgary with her?" Another blow, this time across my other arm. "You fucking liar!" A fourth blow hit my thigh. It was like the geese had returned, only a thousand times worse. Then I saw only darkness, the likes of which I hadn't seen since my father took us camping up the old Lee Lake road. I don't remember what happened next.

Karla would later tell me that it took both her and Jeff the Jugo Juice man, plus another customer who'd wandered in, to pull Sara off. When they finally managed, Sara fled.

It took over fifteen minutes to fully get my breath back. By that time, Jeff the Jugo Juice man had called for help and now a paramedic was holding my head in his lap, another poked at me, and three police officers with folded arms stood over me.

Karla gave a statement to a fourth officer while Jeff whipped me up a thermo-boost smoothie. Complimentary, he said.

"Did she say anything else?" the cop asked Karla.

"Just that she was going to find him," Karla said, motioning toward me. "And that she'd be shoving the level so far up he wouldn't shit right for a year."

"Anything else?"

"Um ... not really – oh, wait. Yes, she said 'motherfucker' and 'cocksucker.'" Karla shrugged. "I guess that was pretty much it."

"ok, thank you," the officer said.

A sergeant asked me all about Sara Mulligan and if I knew where she lived. I said I didn't.

"Don't worry, son." He bent to put a hand on my shoulder.

"We're looking all over the city for her."

"You just got to chop 'er down," I wheezed. "She likes her places *wild*."

21. The doctor diagnosed me with

fierce bruising and some broken skin, but nothing that wouldn't heal. After they released me, Karla drove me back to her place, which she insisted on calling *my* place. She threw one of my arms over her shoulder and eased me into her bed. She gingerly lifted my T-shirt over my head, tugged off my jeans, and draped a blanket over me. "Just relax," she said. But I couldn't. My kidney had an I-shaped bruise as dark as beef dip (though I couldn't be sure; after my time in Calgary, I'd pretty much forgotten what beef dip looked like).

"This will help," Karla said, setting a beer in my hand. She'd poured herself a glass of Hendrick's, even gave it a cucumber garnish. She pushed her face up next to my bruise and took three pictures.

The beer was tasteless. I couldn't even tell if it was cold. It washed over my tongue but it may as well have been poured over the thick-crusted skin of my heel.

The image of Sara charging toward me kept flashing in my mind: the brightly lit Jugo Juice, the tiny potting boxes of well-trimmed wheat grass, Sara's moles flushing so red, her features twisted so tightly, like her whole face was ready to tear apart.

Karla brushed a hand over my forehead, up into my hair, patting down a cowlick. "Let's just hope," she giggled, "Sara has less luck finding you than you did her. That's some angry energy she's throwing off." Karla sighed. "At least you don't have to look for her anymore. You should be relieved."

"I don't feel relieved. In fact, I don't feel all that good about myself at all."

"Oh, Bacon." Karla ran a hand down my cheek. "You're not to blame for her violence. It's inexcusable. But I love that you don't feel good about yourself. It shows just how good a person you are. And you should feel good about that."

I swallowed more beer and pressed the cool, empty bottle against my head.

Karla pushed the student loan forms into my hand, but they slipped from my limp fingers. She corralled them up and pressed them onto my chest with a notable firmness. "Sign this, hon. Then, get some rest."

As I finished the beer, I thought about how I hoped Sara would never find me. I hoped my kidney would find its way back into place. I hoped Karla had more beer in the fridge, tasteless or otherwise. But mostly I hoped the police never found Sara. And that she was safe.

I watched Karla's crinkled lips purse around the straw she pinched between her fingers. Her puckered lips squeezed a smile while sipping her gin. I dropped my glance down to the student loan forms on my chest and watched my limp hand sign.

22. Karla downed her Hendrick's

and explained that she had to get home. Her home. She wouldn't be back until late the next evening. She hoped I'd be OK for the first night alone in what she now kept referring to as "Bacon's place." Sleep didn't come easy in Bacon's place. All night I kept seeing Sara charging me, her twisted face, her angry moles, the glistening metal on that long level. It was morning before I finally drifted off, and I might have slept the whole day through if hunger hadn't woken me that afternoon.

Karla had said she'd left food in the fridge, but I wasn't feeling up to one of her summery or springy or rainy or sunny meals and, since beef dips proved harder to locate then Sara, I simply ignored the hunger and wandered cautiously outside, half expecting Sara's scratchy shriek around each corner. Her eyes had bulged with such rage at the Jugo Juice. But swirled in with the rage of those hard eyes, I also saw something flinching and wavering, a subtle hesitation I'd never seen in Sara's eyes before. I think it was hurt.

I couldn't keep myself oriented when roaming the city with all the skyscrapers shutting out the sky. Every office tower began looking like every other one. I'd have been lost if I'd actually been going somewhere.

I wandered for close to an hour before remembering what Grandma Magic Can used to say about losing your way. So I worked up a mouthful of saliva, spat in my hand, held it up for the wind to sniff. Then I clapped my hands tight. A comet of spittle squeezed out, soaring off in a northwesterly arch. "Spit will show the way," she'd said. After heading northwest for only three blocks, following the spittle's direction, I spotted the river. Apparently the spit didn't figure I was done with the Bow. And Grandma insists the spit doesn't lie. I returned to Karla's building, grabbed my rod, and searched for a fowl-free section of the river.

On a footbridge between the island and the riverbank, an old Asian man was tossing handfuls of breadcrumbs to a frenzy of ducks and geese and other wing-flapping beasts. There must've been fifty of the frenzied birds fighting for handouts in the water. With the waterfowl preoccupied, I hurried upstream and spotted a section of river free of birds. I shuffled down the bank and snapped a cast. The Kamlooper skipped across the water and sank. As I reeled in, the lure rose, and the hiccup splashes told me I'd looped the line around the hook. No fish bit at that crippled motion, of course. A thick patch of cottonwoods and shrubbery crowded the steep bank, making it even more difficult to cast. But I wanted to stay hidden from Sara, from the mallards, the geese, the rollerbladers, the cyclists, the stomp-steppers, A&W clerks, and from everything else that roamed that city. Every now and then I'd glance back over a shoulder, thinking I'd spotted something in my periphery — a movement behind me, the sparkling glint of metal on a level, Sara lunging. But I hadn't.

I fished that same spot without so much as a nibble for I don't know how long. Casting out in one direction then reeling back in, casting out in another and reeling back in. Most fishermen, especially fly-fishermen, refuse to give a spot more than a few minutes. The "ten-cast rule" they call it. Throw out ten casts and, if nothing bites, move along. Maybe I just get lost in the rhythm of casting and reeling, or maybe I can't let go of hope, but I can't seem to leave a familiar spot.

My mother and Grandma Magic Can would return home tomorrow. I'd need to take back the Lancer and inform them I lived in Calgary now. That I had a condo of my own. That I was going to be a student but that I didn't know if it was college or university. Or what I'd be studying.

Upstream at the river's bend, I caught the dusky silhouette of a man, waist-high in the river, fishing. Fly-fishing.

He worked his way downstream toward my line.

I moved myself behind an even thicker cluster of shrubs, clear from his view.

He passed up close, taking gentle steps through the slow-drifting water. When he got up next to the line I was reeling in, he looked up and, despite my hidden position, still spotted me. He nodded hello. "Going to have a tough time landing anything in this river spincasting," he said. I guessed him to be in his fifties. "They won't bite nothing around this stretch this time of year if it ain't a mayfly."

I nodded and waved.

"Green drake still works well this time of year."

I smiled my thanks.

"But, if you *insist* on spincasting," he sighed with a sneer, "least you can do is tie a fly on. Something with olive elk hair. Mimic the dun stage. Clip on a bobber about two feet up." He winked like we'd just shared a deep secret. "The point of fishing, after all, is to catch something."

I crinkled my brow and nodded as though I were interested.

"The hell you got on anyway?"

"Kamlooper." I tried to sound confident; my line reeled in past him. "Orange. Metal."

He plucked the line from the water and held it up, scowling at the dangling lure as though it were tinsel he'd just plucked from a cat's anus. He dumped the Kamlooper back into the water with a thud-like splash, turned, and carried on down the river.

The graceful waving of his long, graphite rod sent out a lengthy stretch of line, weaving an elaborate S in the air.

The evening sun shone between the old trees lining the river, sinking down into the ground it illuminated. The clouds rippled like a washboard in the sky and lit up as bright and pink as Karla's toaster.

I packed up my tackle and headed back down the riverside path to the condo. Passing by the island, I noticed a woman walking its path. Her gait and pink, sleeveless wrap reminded me of Karla. The woman walked hand in hand with a thick, stumpy man. He had reddish-grey hair and wore large burgundy shades that covered most of his face. The woman looked so similar she could almost *be* Karla.

As I watched her turn her face to kiss the man, I realized it *was* Karla. After a lengthy kiss, they strolled off down the path, disappearing from view behind a line of trees. I scurried across the footbridge, chasing them down. A cyclist dinged his bell, veering from me on the pathway. I caught view of them again in time to see them step into a restaurant engulfed in trees and shrubs.

The wood-trimmed building, with its rickety wooden fence, looked more like an old fishing lodge than a restaurant. At the doorway, I stood scanning the tables. A young waiter with too much hair and a bowtie approached me. "Good evening, sir," he said. "May I take your fishing pole?"

"It's a *rod*," I said. "Not a pole."

"Of course it is." He took my rod and set it up against the coat rack. "A *spincasting* rod."

I whirled to face him, but then suddenly Karla stood next to me, holding my elbow. "Bacon! What are you doing here? You should be at home resting."

"Hello, Karla." My eyes held hers and didn't waver. "I saw you."

"OK," she said hesitantly. "And now I see you. Why aren't you resting?"

"No, I mean out there with that ..." I swallowed, almost unable to mouth the words. "Karla, are you with somebody?"

"You mean like right now? For dinner?"

"Yes. I mean no. I mean in general. Are you involved? Karla, are you seeing soemone?"

"*Seeing* someone?" she gasped.

"Yes," I said firmly. "I saw you kiss that man...."

"Oh, Bacon." She let out a heavy laugh, touched a hand to her chest. "I'm thirty-nine years old. I'm a very successful real estate agent. I've got a flat stomach and handfuls of tits. So yes, Bacon, of course I'm seeing someone. I'm married. How would I *not* be married?"

I stared blankly at her for several moments then began adjusting a button on my shirt.

"I wear a bloody ring," she chuckled, thrusting it up under my face as evidence. "What did you think this was?"

"Oh." I gazed down at the two thick bands and the heavy diamond that teetered over, resting against her baby knuckle. "I guess I didn't realize that was a ... *wedding* kind of ring...." I'd never paid much attention to jewellery.

"His name is Laszlo Maximilian Mursky. It'll be eight years this September." She took a deep breath. "He's my someone."

"Your *someone*?" I scowled at the waiter who peeked out from behind the coat rack. "But we ... what about...?"

"Come here." Karla took my hand and led me through the restaurant. "I'll introduce you." We wove through the tables to the far side by the window where the barrel-chested man in the burgundy shades looked up from his menu.

"Laz," Karla said, "this is the guy I've been telling you about – Bacon. Bacon, this is Laszlo."

"You *told* him about me?" I said.

"Bacon!" He stood and snatched up my hand in his chubby fist. "How great to finally meet you."

"She told you about me?"

"Yes, of course. Karly-fry's said such wonderfully wonderful things about you." Laszlo had soft, creamy hands, a light but lengthy grip, and perfect teeth. "Here, Bacon." He pushed out a chair and slapped his fat hand on it. "Join us. Please."

"Um ... I don't know...." My lungs were collapsing, my stomach caving in on itself.

"No, I insist." Every time Laszlo smiled, his eyes disappeared between his swollen cheeks and folded brow. "Seriously. The food here is scrumptious. Insane. ok, come here." He leaned in across the table and motioned us in with rapid flaps of his fat hands. "C'mere, c'mere, c'mere." We bent over the table, down to his level, so close our heads almost banged. His hands made fists with the little finger curled out. "Touch pinkies," he whispered.

"Touch what?" I said.

"Touch pinkies." He shook a curled finger at me.

I turned to Karla. She nodded and grinned her approval.

Karla and I each held a baby finger toward his. Laszlo hooked them with his own and squeezed. "Honestly," he whispered, nodding at each of us. "Swear to God and touch pinkies – the crusted sablefish will change your life. Change it!" Then he sprang back, collapsed into his chair, held his open palms to the sky, and whined, "Herb crusted bc sablefish in a tomato caperberry sauce ... mmm mmm mmm. Heaven and hell, you may as well."

I straightened back up, rubbing my pinky.

"I'll order for everyone!" Laszlo waited for Karla's nod then waved enthusiastically for a waiter. He patted the chair he'd pulled out for me. I sat in it.

Laszlo ordered us hummus and a Fumé Blanc to start. I'd never heard of either, but the waiter brought a dipping appetizer and wine. I had no idea which was the hummus and which was the Fumé Blanc.

As I threw some wine down my throat, I saw, across the room, a goose next to a shrub, peering in the window. Staring at me. Its bill pressed up against the glass, gently tapping. A smug thrust of its chest, a taut sneer on its beak.

"So tell me, Bacon." Laszlo spread his arms out across the table, rapping his fat fingers on the wood. "What did you decide?"

"Decide?"

"Yes, college or university?" His head listed to one side. "Karla said you enrolled in both to be safe. Damn smart move. Damn smart. Which one will it be?"

"I don't know. I never decided."

"Well, no rush." He snatched up his glass, swirling the wine in the light. "Take your time, Bacon. Chew it over. Give it some thought." He stuffed his nose into the glass and inhaled loudly. "Let us know later tonight."

"Tonight?"

"Yes siree, Bacony Boy." He tasted the wine, rubbing his lips over each other. "The bank won't finalize the loan until you choose."

"I'm not even sure what I want to study yet – "

"You could take women's studies," Laszlo offered, almost splashing his wine over me as he pointed with his glass. "That's what I took."

"You don't have to decide that now, Bacon," Karla said, reaching for my shoulder. "You just have to pick which institution. Once you've figured that out, the pressure's off. At that point you don't even have to make any classes if you don't want."

"Why wouldn't I want to make any classes?"

"Or you can," she shrugged. "Whatever. I just mean getting registered is the important part."

Laszlo ordered our dinners. As I'd suspected, he didn't order me a beef dip. They didn't have one. The waiter brought me something called a "morel mushroom and barley risotto," which Karla described as a "perfect summery dish."

I heard a muffled honk from outside and turned to see the goose had moved several panes closer. Its bill tapped up and down the window seam, as though searching for a weakness.

"Oh, and Bacon," Laszlo said, leaning over to me in an overly discreet voice, "I heard about the incident last night at the Jugo Juice. Horrific. Just horrific. I hate violence, Bacon. Despise it. There's no place for violence in modern civilization. You OK? How's the bruising?"

"I'm fine."

"You sure?" He squinted hard.

"Yes," I said. "Having a little trouble getting the image of Sara and that level out of my mind. Otherwise fine."

"I see," he nodded, pondering my comment. The way he rubbed his teeth over each other made me regret mentioning anything. He frowned and turned to Karla. "You know what he needs? A good soak."

"You think I need a bath?" I said.

"Heavens no," he chuckled. "You're not a puppy. I'm talking some good old-fashioned water therapy."

"Like a hot tub?" Karla asked.

"No, no, no, Karly-fry, those are for humping. Which makes me think now we could all crawl into one later if ya like." He threw an elbow into my ribs and winked. "No, I'm talking about some *real* healing. What you need, Bacony Boy ... is a good few runs down a waterslide."

"A *waterslide*?"

"Abso-smurf-ly."

I turned to Karla, checking if this was real. "I don't think I'm up for – "

"Nonsense," he scoffed. "A waterslide's exactly what you need."

"That might be a bit too much excitement for him, Laz," Karla said. "I think he needs rest now."

"Ah, come on, Karly-fry. Pleeease? He needs rest *and* excitement." Laszlo's index finger unravelled from the stem of his wine glass, pointing my way. "Takes both to mend a wound. There's a hotel with a waterslide up in the north end. What do you say?"

Karla considered it for several moments with a restrained smile before finally smirking her approval.

"Finish up!" Laszlo slammed a fist on the table. "We're going sliding." He gobbled up the last of his food, plucked the napkin from my lap, and threw it on my plate. Then he hurried us toward the door. As Karla was paying, I saw the goose again – now inside – ducking around the corner by the bathroom. It honked as it disappeared, but the honk sounded more like a cry than a honk. And the cry sounded just like *piiiigggggs*.

23. The warm, muggy waterslide

reeked of chlorine and roared with the muffled, canned echoes of rushing water, screaming children, and flailing limbs.

Three women stood knee-deep in the shallow end, presumably

waiting for the slides to spit out their squealing children. The women reached the tips of their fingers down to tickle the water, as though that was as close to swimming as they were willing to get. One of them — easily four inches taller than me and twice my width — wore a T-shirt stretched over her bathing suit that read, "Jesus is my homeboy."

Laszlo led us up the concrete stairs to the top platform. "Well," he said, snapping on his goggles and giving me two thumbs up. "Meet you in the pool." He hurled himself head-first onto the slide like he was jumping from an airplane. Sloshing and shrieking around the first bend, he was gone in an instant.

I sat myself down on the concrete platform, carefully placing my feet into the slide, using my fingers to spider myself slowly into the current. The cotton-candy blue swimming trunks Laszlo had lent me filled with water. If Karla hadn't safety-pinned the waist, already four inches too wide, those ridiculous trunks would've washed right off. I eased myself fully onto the slide in a tight, upright sitting position, hands clasped across my lap. The first bend took me slowly as I drifted safely around the corner. But rounding the next bend, deeper into the muggy wafts of chlorine, my speed increased, rushing over each drop.

Veering into a covered corner of the tube, the slide finally flattened out, sending a splash of water in my face. I wiped my eyes clear in time to see something blocking passage just ahead of me.

Laszlo.

Somehow, on that flattened section, he'd managed to brake to a full stop, lifted himself up, and hunched over on his feet. One arm was locked tight against the top of the slide, the other resting on a crouched knee. I couldn't have been more than two seconds from colliding into him, just enough time to recognize his swimming trunks swirling around one ankle, his naked back side thrust up and wagging in my direction, his stupidly grinning face turned back at me — goggles on — and his mouth gaping. "Butt cushion!" he bellowed back at me.

I was headed face-first for Laszlo's ass.

With great desperation I flung my torso back from its sitting position, frantically needing to stretch out as flat as I could get.

But there simply wasn't time. There was barely time to fling back even a little.

I didn't think I could be more terrified. Turns out I could. Because that's when I saw it. Just before impact. Slung well down below his thrust-up rear, like a bulbous butternut squash, swaying like a pendulum, hung the most remarkable scrotum I could've ever imagined.

The last thought I had in the fraction of a second remaining was that there'd be enough clearance for the rush of water to carry me between Laszlo's widely spread, stumpy legs, and that I'd manage to throw myself back just enough to avoid the thrust-out cushion of his back side. But to my great horror, I would not manage, and in fact, *could* not manage, to avoid the slap of that terrible scrotum.

"Oh no!" he cried out after me, his voice echoing down the slide. "You missed the butt cushion.... you got ram-bagged!"

The slide dumped me into the pool where I swallowed three mouthfuls of chlorinated water. Gasping for breath, I flailed for the pool's edge, coughing up water and chlorine and as much of the horror as I could spit out.

"Wooooo hooooo," Laszlo shrieked, splashing his way toward me and slapping a fat hand across my back.

"What is *wrong* with you?" I gasped.

"Honest to goodness, Bacony Boy, touch pinkies and swear to heaven, I was aiming for the butt cushion." Laszlo hiked up his trunks under the water. "I didn't mean for you to get ram-bagged."

"That was disgusting," I cried. "Disgusting!"

"I bet," he agreed. "In any case, I think it worked."

"Worked? What do you mean *worked*?"

"Water therapy, Bacony Boy!" He flipped his goggles up on top of his head. "Water therapy."

"Therapy?" I said. "I'm going to *need* therapy."

"Maybe so, but you're not thinking of Sara, are you?"

"What?"

"Sara," He squeezed his hand around the back of my neck. "You're not thinking of her anymore."

He was right. In that moment I was barely able to think at all.

But one thought eventually came to mind. I was able to at least hold one thought. A thought about something else entirely. Retribution.

At that moment, in that pool, I'd had enough of Karla and Laszlo and condos and ducks and geese and waterslides and everything else that was so exasperatingly strange in Calgary.

Retribution. It was time Calgary ended up on the other end of strange.

Several runs later, enough time to avoid suspicion, I stealthily jumped in the tube first, leaving Laszlo right behind me, eagerly clinging to the slide's mouth.

After the first corner, I sat up, slowing to a drift. When I reached the flattened section with a covered bend, I put the brakes on full and came to a halt. I struggled to my feet, hunched inside the tube, holding myself still, legs bent, feet clamped down. I pressed one arm tightly against the side of the slide, the other resting on a crouched knee. I tugged down my swimming trunks, left them swirling around an ankle. My back side thrust up, wagging. Waiting.

Laszlo, however, didn't appear. Rushing water bubbled over my feet; the grainy fibreglass slide was surprisingly cool on my hand. Still, Laszlo didn't come.

I would later learn that Laszlo had been expecting my retaliation. Anticipating it. He'd guessed right. After I jumped into the slide, Laszlo stepped aside, waved on the next person with a friendly fat hand. Instead of Laszlo's delicately pedicured feet rounding the corner behind me, it was a sore-looking pair of puffy feet that appeared. Connected to two swollen ankles, followed by thick, heavy legs. The next thing I saw was the face of Jesus. For a fraction of a moment, perhaps only a shred of a split second, I considered – maybe only hoped – that it was really him. That Jesus himself had miraculously appeared in the waterslide to rescue me – the only conceivable force that could – from what was about to occur.

But it wasn't Jesus. It was only his face on a t-shirt. And the large lady who claimed him as her "homeboy" heaved around the corner at a terrifying speed.

In that moment, the water seemed to rush faster past me, as though attempting to flee what even it knew was coming. The last image that passed through my mind before the collision—just as those puffy feet barrelled the legs out from under me—was the curious contrast between the tranquil face of Christ and the raw terror on the taught face of the woman I crashed down upon.

In much the way you would a toboggan, I found myself riding atop the woman, speeding down the racing water. I stretched forward from my sitting position to reach Laszlo's baby-blue swim trunks that looked far more ridiculous swinging around my ankles then they did safety-pinned around my waist. But reaching forward drove my weight further down upon the frantic woman beneath me, my bare back side muffling out her cries for help. I gave up on reaching my trunks and resigned myself to riding out—as safely as possible—the duration of the slide. The poor woman who couldn't have had even a sliver of understanding as to what was occurring fought feverishly against the current and momentum to escape from under me. When the slide dumped us into the pool, I splashed for the edge and yanked up my trunks. The frantic woman seemed ensnared in some kind of spin cycle in the frothing water just below the slide. Her head would thrust up out of the water for just enough time to gasp some breath and cry out to Jesus, then she'd roll over herself in the water and her feet would splash to the surface. This repeated itself several times until she washed into the shallow end and eventually gripped a handrail to haul herself out. She screamed out for "holy Jesus" and for "heavenly Christ" and for "the sweet son of God," as though unsure to which name he'd respond. She also called out for "Mother Mary," "God above," "Archangel Michael," "divine Saint Christopher," and "blessed John of Nepomuk." If any of them were at the waterslide that day they didn't come forward.

I fled to the change room, certain the police would soon be called. Laszlo burst in behind me, squealing out a hearty string of squeaky, whiny laughter.

I flung open the locker door, scratched a towel over myself, and hurried to change.

105

We drove back to "my place." Laszlo let us off out front, told us to go up, he'd park his car – a REVA G–Wiz electric car – and then catch up. Upstairs, he explained, I could declare my decision to either be a university or college man. You got yourself two choices, Laszlo said. But I still had no answer. In fact, I had no idea. Lapping thrusts of a headache had been washing over my brain since the waterslide.

Walking past the entrance planters, Karla babbled on about how much I was going to love living here. I gazed at the thick diamond ring on her left hand as she wiggled the key in the lock of the building's front door. While she fumbled with the lock, I turned and headed across the parking lot, slumped into my mother's old rusted Lancer, and turned the engine. I backed out of the stall slowly and then glided out onto the street. As I did, I saw Karla holding the door open with her key, watching me drive past. She didn't wave or call or run after me; she just stood there, as stone-faced and still as the gravelly planters that lined the walk. Her mouth seemed to both smirk and frown at the same time.

I sat hunched forward, staring hard at the road to keep from meeting Karla's eyes any longer.

I drove all the way to the airport.

24. The Calgary airport is a quiet place

at night. The empty carousels sit still and silent, the arrival gates are empty, the few passengers left are all in the process of leaving: waiting on connector flights, boarding red-eyes, flipping through that morning's crumpled, left-behind newspapers. They all look tired, but not an unpleasant tired; their eyes are heavy, mouths closed with just a hint of an upward slant, quietly excited about their departure. I'd seen that look on people waiting for the Greyhound at the Super Stop.

I was every bit as eager to depart. I really just wanted to reel myself in. I couldn't wait to pick up my mother and Grandma Magic Can, for no more reason than I was simply craving the quiet routine of Bellevue. Of our home.

On the second level of the airport, I found a sitting area next to a bronzed statue of a fly-fisherman. I sprawled out across several seats and shut my eyes.

It wasn't long before sleep washed over me and I plunged deep into a dream. I dreamt of fishing in a thigh-high, choppy, sloshing river. A dark, murky water, more than just spring run-off. A sewer line thrust out of a cliff on the opposite bank. Thick, dark clots of sludge oozed out of the line and plopped into the river. Despite the brisk waves, the sludge coagulated into a skin atop the choppy surface, thickening as it slapped up against my thighs. Suddenly my line wrenched down, and not twenty feet away the water thrashed madly. I'd hooked a fish. As I heaved and reeled in, I was certain the line would snap. When I had the fish almost at my feet, I reached for the line and hauled it up from the water. But it wasn't a fish that emerged. The rusted orange Kamlooper at the end of my line had hooked a human body. More specifically, my Kamlooper had hooked the curled baby finger of a body, and the body that baby finger was connected to was the body of Laszlo Maximilian Mursky. "Touch pinkies," he squealed.

I sprang up from the row of seats, gasping, and threw open my eyes. It took me a full minute to catch my breath and realize I was at the airport.

I fled to a bathroom, splashed my face with water, and rubbed my wet fingers through my hair. The soap dispenser, next to a stack of paper cups, released a runny green liquid, not the least bit soapy at all. I unbuttoned my shirt, washed my chest, armpits, shoulders, and stomach, then rubbed the stinging, watery soap over my eyes. I even slipped a cupped handful of the strange green soap into my underwear and scrubbed. I washed all over myself, scrubbing and clawing and raking, hoping to wash away all evidence and memory of Karla and Laszlo and Hendrick's gin and pink appliances and waterslides and psychotic mallards and the Bow River and I guess all of Calgary. I scrubbed until the soap burned my skin red and raw. Then I scrubbed some more. I tried to find my face in the splash-smeared mirror but could only make out a grubby blur.

At 8:35 AM, my mother and Grandma Magic Can waddled through the Arrivals gate; mother dragging her duct-tape-patched, pull-behind suitcase in one hand, the other wrapped around an assortment of small, brightly coloured wooden boy/girl dolls, a pink embroidered bag, three rectangular boxes, and what looked like some kind of ceremonial mask.

"Look, I brought you a box of Choco-Pies," my mother said, tapping her chin on one of the boxes. "Jesus, they make a hell of a Choco-Pie over there. Save a couple for me."

"Bacon," Grandma Magic Can sighed like she was lifting herself off the couch, "this is Mr. Kwon." She thumbed toward a stout, round-faced man in a dark suit behind her. He bowed slightly and took my hand with a shy, polite smile.

"My pleasure to meet you," he said.

"And his daughter." Grandma pointed her elbow to a girl behind the round-faced man. "Meryl Streep." The girl looked about sixteen or so, with coarse, shoulder-length black hair curled out at the ends, and dark eyes that peeked out from between gracefully small lashes.

"Your name is Meryl Streep?" I said.

She cocked her head and held it tilted with her ear nearly touching her shoulder, her hair flung back behind her neck, her mouth opened in a glossy smile. She thrust out a hand toward me. "Thank you," she said.

Somebody cleared a throat.

"Meryl Streep is her English name," the round-faced man explained. "She does not speak good English." He put a hand on the small of her back. "Her Korea name is Young-Mi. But she prefer you speak Meryl Streep."

"I need my weeds," Grandma Magic Can moaned.

"Well, to hell with it," my mother said. "I'm gonna crack open the Choco-Pies."

Grandma leaned over, sniffed my face, and said, "You smell like a bottle of Scope."

"All right, let's get the bloody car and get me home," my mother said through a mouthful of Choco-Pie.

"That doesn't work, you know," Grandma whispered.

"What doesn't?" I said.

"Mouth wash." She made a drinking motion with her hand. "Not enough alcohol to do any good."

"I can't friggin' wait," my mother announced to nearly the whole airport, "to plant my ass on a regular goddamned toilet."

Mr. Kwon heaved the luggage onto a cart, and he and Meryl Streep followed us to the Lancer. He opened the back door and motioned the others into the back seat, rearranged them all, insisting through gestures that Grandma Magic Can sit on the passenger side of the back seat. When the trunk was stuffed full with gifts and luggage, Mr. Kwon pushed suitcases and boxes on everyone's laps. In the rearview mirror I could only see stray strands of Grandma Magic Can's dental-floss hair, my mother's rippled brow, and Meryl Streep's exotic eyes. I climbed into the driver's seat; Mr. Kwon joined me up front.

"Why the hell does he get shotgun?" I heard my mother mumble into her carry-on bag.

"Lord lifting Jesus," Grandma Magic Can moaned. "I need my weeds."

We took the number two to Bellevue. I apologized to Mr. Kwon and Meryl Streep for the thick exhaust fumes filling the car.

"Maybe dangerous," Mr. Kwon said.

"My heart is as drained as melted glaciers," Meryl Streep said overtop of a suitcase.

Mr. Kwon smiled shyly. "Maybe it doesn't sound true," he said, turning to me, "but she really doesn't speak good English." He scratched an itch on the back of his neck. "She only knows English from the subtitles on the Korean dramas. She watches much Korean dramas. Too much Korean dramas."

She'll get along with my mother, I thought.

Mr. Kwon gazed out the window at the nothingness of the number two highway: sprawling prairie all the way to the horizon.

Occasionally he'd tap a finger against the window as if to point at something. Grandma Magic Can and my mother drifted to sleep. Mr. Kwon grunted something in Korean to Meryl Streep. He seemed to groan out the language like he was heaving a sofa up some stairs, one step at a time. He turned back toward the window and said, "You have much land."

I eyed the passing prairie. "It's not ours," I said. "We live in Bellevue." Mr. Kwon turned to me with a puzzled expression.

My mother and grandmother, zonked out in the back, snored in unison. Meryl Streep began making snoring noises too, even though she was wide awake.

"Bacon, what grade are you doing?" Mr. Kwon asked.

"You mean school? What grade am I in?"

He nodded.

"I'm done school," I said. "Graduated in June." I glanced into the mirror to check that my mother and grandmother were still sleeping and continued in a softer voice. "Apparently I'm going to either college or university in the fall." I stopped myself, remembering how I left Laszlo and Karla. "At least I think I still am." I turned the radio down. "I know I have a loan coming ... just as soon as I decide between college or university."

"Which one will you do?" Mr. Kwon asked.

"I don't know yet," I said. "What about you? Were you a college man or a university man?"

Mr. Kwon smiled to himself, like he was remembering something worthwhile. "I was a both man."

"You went to both?" I angled a vent toward my face, relief from the exhaust. "You must be awful smart."

"No, no," he said. "University made me a salary man. Hyundai Industries. I didn't enjoy that. All diligence and long hours. No creativity. Because of that result, I go to the college. I learned to cook as a chef."

"So if you had to go back and pick one," I said, "would you take university or college?"

"Depends."

"On what?"

"On which college and which university." That seemed fair

enough. "I think Korea college and university," he continued, "are different than Canada."

"How so?"

"In Korea, to get to university is more competitive than college. Entrance exams is different in Korea. Very stressful." He folded his arms and stretched back in his seat, letting out a long, echoing snort from somewhere deep in his throat. "In Canada? I'm not sure. But your grandfather said to me that Canada colleges and universities are only a little difference. At one you pay a bit more, at the other you drink a bit more. Maybe that's how you decide."

"You knew my grandfather?"

"Of course," he said with a look like I'd just asked him if we were in a car.

When we reached Claresholm I stopped at the 7-Eleven. Mr. Kwon bought everybody a corndog. Grandma Magic Can refused, even though she normally loves a good corn dog. She even stayed in the car. Meryl Streep gobbled down three before we left.

After my mother finally stopped gushing about the normal toilet in the 7-Eleven, everybody fell asleep and stayed asleep the rest of the way. Except me, of course.

When we finally got to Bellevue, My mother showed Mr. Kwon into the spare room upstairs and led Meryl Streep to my room. "Bacon, you'll have to sleep on the downstairs couch for a while," she said.

"It is my pleasure," Meryl Streep said. "With a love as strong as the universe imploding."

"Sure thing, Meryl." My mother bolted for the bathroom. "Bacon, get me a jug of water and a *Chatelaine*," she hollered. "I want to sit and piss for all eternity right here on this sweet normal toilet seat." She stayed in there for close to an hour.

Just before dinner, Mr. Kwon asked my mother if he could use our shower. He probably feared he wouldn't get another chance at the bathroom. Meryl Streep sorted through my sock drawer. Grandma Magic Can frantically diced up dried weeds on the living room coffee table. I sat on the couch, close beside her, checked over both shoulders before finally asking, "Who *are* these people?"

Grandma peeked overtop of her glasses, carefully rocking the knife over each weed clump. "Our inheritance," she snorted. "Your grandfather *willed* them to us."

"He *willed* them?"

"Yup," she said, twitching slightly. "Meryl Streep's his granddaughter. Mr. Kwon's his son." Grandma crumpled the weed shreds in a small heap on the can.

"Why would Grandpa *will* them to us?"

"Four years ago, Mr. Kwon's wife left him. Divorced him for a guy who ran the neighbourhood *noraebong* – that's some kind of karaoke room, I guess. Kwon moved back in with Grandpa and they tried raising Meryl Streep together. I'm guessing they struggled. Your grandfather's executor says life's gotten tough for Meryl Streep over there. First, because they're not one hundred percent *pure* Korean blood. Second, there's the way she ... but then again, for that kind of thing, I doubt she'll get treated any better here. Guess he wants to open up a Korean restaurant or something." Grandma set the knife down and dropped her shoulders in a show of exhaustion. "Your grandfather's will stated his last wish in life was me bringing those two back to Canada. Help them get set up. For the love of God."

"So Mr. Kwon's my uncle?"

"I suppose."

"Do I call him Uncle Kwon?"

"Call him Uncle Buck for all I care."

Grandma struggled to corral the weed shards with her unsteady hands.

"Well ... it's good of you to grant Grandpa that last wish, I suppose."

"Good of me? Ha!" Grandma's lip lifted up on one side like it had been snagged by a hook. "I would've told that executor to go suck rocks if it wasn't for the forty Gs."

"Forty Gs? What forty Gs?"

"Your bloody Grandpa left us forty grand. But it's *conditional*. Conditional, that is, on us bringing Kwon back to Bellevue and helping him get set up. Boy, your grandfather always knew how to corner us, all right."

"How long are the Kwons staying with us?"

"Until they get their restaurant open, find out nobody's going to eat there, watch the whole darned thing go belly up, and head back to Korea, I hope." Grandma scowled, flicked on her lighter, and ran it over the weeds.

I watched the flame set the weed-crumbles aglow. "We really inherited forty thousand dollars?"

"Conditionally. But we have to put up with Kwon. At least 'til he gets set up. And Bacon, don't you say boo about this. Apparently Kwon knows nothing about the money and if he finds out, the deal's off. We lose every cent of it. That's the other condition. Heck, I'm not even supposed to mention it to you." Grandma made a blowing sound through her nose.

"Wow. Why is it a secret?"

"Oh, who the heavens knows." She took a deep inhale from the magic can and held her breath for a moment. "Then again," she coughed, "who knows why people sit around licking watermelon skins."

I stood watching her breathe in and blow out the garden weeds for a full minute, but no further explanation came. I started to say something more but stopped myself. Instead I grabbed my green and brown second-hand spincasting rod from the car, praying to whatever power existed that the river was still there.

25. Fortunately, I found the river still lazily

flowing past Bellevue. Fly-fishermen still crammed the calm, deep stretches. And I fished my familiar murky stretch alone, as always.

The wind, though, refused to permit my casting. The bullying gusts snatched my line and ran off with it each time I tried. So I consigned the fishing to my fencing-jab cast, thrusting my line into the thick cluster of young alders that lined the far bend of that shallow stretch. I poked the tip of my rod through the mess of branches and leaves, out the other side, hovering it over the river. The surface of the Crow rippled from the feisty wind. I snapped my wrist, sending the rusted old Kamlooper plopping into the water where it vanished in the wrinkled murkiness. The jerking current whisked the lure down several yards, jostling it off the rocky bottom before I reeled it back in. Nothing took the hook, of course. Still, I repeated that fencing-jab cast all afternoon.

I returned to the house just as Grandma Magic Can, bent over the table setting out dinner, announced, "Dinner's ready."

"Shush!" my mother hissed back, playing TV bingo in her slippers. "They're at fifty-eight numbers and no bingo."

Under the B ... seven, the TV caller said.

"No more goddamned Bs," my mother scolded. "We got all our Bs." She spoke half to the TV, half to Meryl Streep, who was playing along, using an ink dauber to blob out the inside of a Canadian Tire flyer.

Still no bingo. Tonight's jackpot is at $4,500, the TV caller reminded.

"Dinner's gonna get cold," Grandma frowned. "Sit down, Bacon." She slapped her hand at the air. "They can eat when they eat."

"Give me an O, for Christ's sake," my mother cried out at the TV. "You call O-67 or I'll tear off your goddamn nut sack!"

Under the B ... nine.

"Jesus!"

And there goes the phones! Looks like several bingos have been called....

"Sonovabitch." My mother threw her dauber across the room. "The bastard called so many Bs he was making up new ones!" Meryl Streep threw her dauber too. "I can't endure," she said, tearing up the Canadian Tire flyer.

Mr. Kwon poured everyone water from the jug, then seated himself. "This cooking looks delicious," he said.

"It's nothing," Grandma grimaced. "Salmon patties. Ain't no deal."

"*Igo mashisseyo*," Mr. Kwon said, chewing thoroughly and snapping each bite.

My mother and Meryl Streep slumped down onto their chairs and took turns plopping patties onto their plates.

"I want to ask questions," Mr. Kwon said shyly. "Is it OK?"

"Knock yourself out." My mother sliced off some salmon patty with the side of her fork.

"Ms. Sobelowski," Mr. Kwon said, "where do you work?"

"A laundromat," my mother replied as she shovelled in a forkful of salmon. "In Blairmore. Be thirteen years this June."

"Do you like your job?"

"No more than I like the blue zig-zagging veins bulging out of my calf. But I tolerate it."

"Mmm," Mr. Kwon nodded. "Your husband – when he lived in Bellevue, what did he do?"

"Just about every tramp in town," my mother laughed. Mr. Kwon looked puzzled.

Grandma frowned and said without looking up, "He drove truck for a living. He was always coming and going."

"Usually *coming*," my mother laughed again. She pushed herself off the chair and grabbed a beer from the fridge. "Anyone else?" She waved the can. Nobody else said yes, so I didn't either. My mother always gets a beer when she says something too crude. That way if Grandma mentions it later my mother can say it was just the beer talking. "Anyway," she dumped herself back in the chair, "about seven years ago he took off with another woman. That was that. We're better off without 'im."

Mr. Kwon nodded, jumped from his seat, plucked the can from my mother's hand, and poured the beer into a glass. "In Korea, sometimes we say, 'love must come before it can go.'"

"I've heard that one," Grandma Magic Can said, her chin lifted.

My mother sat back, startled by Mr. Kwon's move. "Well, I got a saying, too." She gulped some beer. "Love's a load of peanut-packed shit. And marriage is just a means to split the bills." She raised her glass as though to make a toast. "But now I'm as good as married to my mother here, she pays half the mortgage and I get half the headaches I used to."

Mr. Kwon chuckled. "We also say, 'love down is love.'" I saw Grandma Magic Can quietly reach for a pen to write that one down. "It is good that we can rely on family."

Grandma rolled her eyes. My mother was working a fingernail

between her molars. Meryl Streep, sitting beside me, made snapping noises as she chewed. She couldn't understand much of anything being said, yet she still sat cordial and smiling. I imagine it felt a whole lot like my Physics 10 class.

I watched a salmon patty crumble in her open mouth as she chewed wildly, the crumbles bobbling around like bingo balls in a tumbler. She met my stare just as a shard of salmon flung itself out, twirling in the air, diving downward, planting itself on my knee. Meryl Streep's hand, still gripping her fork, moved quickly to brush the salmon shard from my knee. Her tiny hand was awkward in its sweep, then seemed to rest there for a moment. My glance lifted from her hand to her eyes: thin, mysterious, and lonesome, as though peeping through a crack in a fence. Her short, soft, sparse eyelashes lifted like a shy, hesitant wave. Before I could wave back, the hand with the fork left my knee and returned to her plate, and those thin eyes slid their gaze away. I was left staring at the soft caramel skin of her cheek. Strangely, she must've missed the salmon shard; it remained there, resting, balancing on my knee for the rest of dinner.

26. The next morning I did something

I'd never done before. Something I'd not even imagined doing before. I went to the library. I marched up the hill to the old school that's not a school anymore but still has a library upstairs. That library – which used to be full of books for kids but now has books for everybody – is now, in fact, the Bellevue Public Library. The building's insides still smell like a janitor just cleaned up grade-three barf. Maybe the waft of chemical-covered puke never really leaves a school.

I passed by rows of mining history books, fly-fishing books, trail maps, and dog-eared paperbacks by people named Clive Cussler and Nora Roberts, straight back to the small section of travel books. I found one lone book on Korea, flipped to the chapter on language, and began reading.

It turns out the Korean alphabet is called Hangul and it makes just about more sense than anything else I've ever learned from a book.

I guess some Korean king named Sejong up and decided he'd invent an alphabet so simple it could be learned in a day. That way everybody in Korea, even the commoners and peasants, could become literate. King Sejong figured everybody should know what's going on.

He designed each consonant in the shape a mouth makes when it speaks that character. *Nieun* is a character that looks like this: ㄴ. It's pronounced like an English N. You can picture the sideways view of a tongue reaching up and just touching the back of your teeth to make that sound – that's how the character got its shape. Same with the character *giyeok*, ㄱ, pronounced like K or G. Here part of the tongue curves the other way, touching the molar teeth and sticking near the back of the mouth.

The vowel shapes were all based on sky, land, and man. The vowel ㅣ was a man standing, ㅡ was the flat land. It was all so easy. By lunchtime I had memorized all forty alphabet characters. It took me until grade two to learn our own alphabet. By mid-afternoon I had a handful of words. Fish was *seng-son*. Bathroom was *hwajang-shil*. Beer was *mak'ju*. I had to return home to gobble down dinner but ran back to the library while still chewing the last bite.

A few minutes after eight, when the librarian, glaring up at the clock, cleared her throat for the seventh time, I signed out a Korean-English dictionary and read in the parking lot so she could close up.

When the sun slipped down behind the surrounding mountaintops, I started my way home, reading under the light of the streetlights.

As I got within several metres of our house, I spotted an unfamiliar car in the driveway. Even in the darkness I could see the blue-grey paint shine as smooth and even as though it'd had just been painted right there on the driveway. It had a modern shape, streamlined and rounded. The tires looked like they'd never been driven. Even more unexpected was the eerie, flickering candles scattered across the driveway, all around the vehicle. And Mr. Kwon, kneeling beside the car, bent over, bowing in front of what appeared to be a severed pig's head.

By the time I was able to confirm that it was in fact a severed pig's head, I'd reached the driveway and stood staring as stone still as the cracked concrete beneath my feet. I wanted to turn and run but Mr. Kwon lunged at me. "Gausah!" he cried. "Gausah!" He threw an arm around my neck, tugging me toward the car. I threw up my arms trying to bust free from his grip, horrified by the thought of what must've become of my family. I managed to spin from his grasp and darted for the safety of the house. But I stopped just before smashing into my mother and Grandma Magic Can, perched on the front steps – fully alive – pouring themselves glasses of what turned out to be rice wine. Meryl Streep stood behind them, opening and shutting the mailbox lid.

"Gausah!" my mother called.

"Gausah." Grandma Magic Can rolled her eyes.

"Look!" Mr. Kwon waved his open hand at the strange car. "It's Hyundai. Good car!" He opened a door and motioned for me to peek inside. I caught my breath, then cautiously stepped toward the unfamiliar vehicle. The upholstery gleamed with no coffee, root beer, or sweat stains, the dash was free of any rips or tears. The carpet-fibre floor mats had yet to be layered over with rubber mats. Clearly the car was brand new.

"It's ours," my mother said. "Mr. Kwon bought us a goddamned car. Can you imagine?"

"Korean car," Mr. Kwon said proudly.

"Ridiculous," Grandma muttered.

"I'm totally committed to your happiness," Meryl Streep said.

"A goddamned car!" my mother said again, downing her drink.

"Our family needed a new car," Mr. Kwon said.

"We needed nothing of the sort," Grandma snorted.

"Don't get your tits in an uproar," my mother scolded, leaning away from Grandma, looking her up and down. "You're sure the owly one lately. We got us a new car for Christ's sake, lighten up a little."

"Pfft." Grandma bobbed her head dismissively.

I moved back from the Hyundai, stepping carefully overtop of the pig's head.

"We have a perfectly good car in the Lancer," Grandma said to nobody in particular. "What are we supposed to do with *that* now?"

"For all I care we can give the old shit box to that pig down there," my mother laughed. "If it's got a head for driving." She laughed again, waving at Meryl Streep to pour her another glass.

"Maybe," Mr. Kwon said, "we know somebody who could need a car." He turned a firm glance toward me.

"Oh, yeah?" my mother said in a ponderous voice. "Huh. Why the hell not? How about it, Bacon? Want a car of your own?"

The only thing I wanted at that moment was an explanation or two. A sliver of insight as to what was happening to our home. Or maybe just one minute of familiarity. I don't think I answered her but I may have felt myself nod.

"Well then I guess it's yours." My mother finished off another glass. "Keys are on the counter." She eyeballed me expectantly. "Got anything to say to that?"

I looked from her to the car, to the mess in the driveway, then back at her. "Why is there a pig's head on the driveway?"

"Gausah," Grandma Magic Can scoffed, retreating back into the house.

"Gausah!" My mother thrust up her glass, splashing several amber drops onto the sidewalk where they shimmered much like the glow of the Hyundai's headlights reflecting in the glazed-over eyes of the pig's head.

27. Later that night I stopped by my bedroom and gently knocked. The glow of the bedside lamp reached out under the door. I pushed the door open slightly and peered in. Meryl Streep sat quietly in bed, holding one of my socks in her hands like it were a book. She even put a finger on the heel as though marking her place before looking up.

"*Annyong haseyo,*" I whispered.

119

"Ohhhh!" She flung the sock. *"Annyong haseyo!"* Her smile nearly burst right off her face. You'd think nobody had ever said hello to her before.

I scrambled through my notes, searching for another word. But before I could find one she said, *"Gae goo ree yong kal juseyo?"*

I scrambled through my dictionary to check what I thought I'd heard. *Please give me a frog knife.* Admiring the clean, smooth whiteness of her T-shirt, I suddenly realized a girl was in my bed. I'd never brought Sara to my place, and neither Grandma nor my mother ever had any reason to sleep there. *"Eotteohke jinaeseyo?"* I said, hoping it I'd properly said, "How are you?"

"Dok gae goo ree odi it-sum-ni ka?" she said. I fumbled through the dictionary, piecing together her words. Unfortunately, I must have been terrible at hearing Korean because I translated what I'd heard into *where are the poison frogs?*

I excused myself, waved goodnight, and hit the couch. I felt a vague allegiance with Meryl Streep over her isolation. And a peculiar satisfaction that, for the first time in my life, I had a girl in my very own bed. Whatever the circumstances.

28. The next morning, Purolator couriered

a letter to the house. It was addressed to me. I even had to sign for it. It was the first piece of mail I'd ever received, let alone couriered.

"Who the hell are you all of a sudden?" my mother said, her arms folded in her fraying bathrobe, craning her neck to watch the courier van drive away. "Mr. Donald Trump, if you please?"

"What is it, Bacon?" Grandma Magic Can gripped my arm and peered over my shoulder.

"I don't know." I wiggled my way free of their crowding.

"The envelope says KC Enterprizes," my mother pointed. "Who the hell's that?"

"I don't know," I complained, folding the letter and stuffing it into my pocket. "Probably nothing," I said, moving for the door. I had no idea what it was but I certainly wasn't opening it in front of them.

"Whoa, where you going?" my mother barked. "Open it up, let's see what you got!"

"I'm sure it's just junk mail."

"Junk mail?" my mother scoffed as I rushed down the walk. "By courier?"

"Good morning, Bacon." Mr. Kwon popped up from behind the ratted hedge, a pair of trimmers in hand. "Can I give you a drive to where you will go?" Mr. Kwon's wide, eager eyes told me he'd carry me by piggyback if he could just come along.

"No thank you." I hurried passed.

"We can drive with the new Hyundai," he offered, pointing to the car with the hedge clippers.

"No, I'm fine."

"Maybe you can drive with your car," he called out to me as I neared the corner. "The Lancer."

"No thank you," I waved. I hadn't had a chance to digest the news about the Lancer. In fact, I even smiled for a moment hearing it described as mine. Although I'd driven it plenty enough before and knew the car inside and out, there was something new and different now as the rightful owner. Suddenly I couldn't wait to take *my car* out for a spin. But I couldn't just take it down to the library for the inaugural drive. The first spin required a special destination. A meaningful moment.

The anxiety of that letter returned, bulling away my smile.

I leapt up the stairs of the old school, darted into the library, hurried to the far corner, and sat myself down behind a large plant. I tore open the envelope and removed the letter.

Dear Mr. Sobelowski,

We hope this letter finds you happy, well, and smiling. It should, the world's too fun not to smile. But that said, it is with embarrassing regret that we need to inform you your account is in arrears to the amount of $2,505.99. Your prompt attention to this matter – which we know you'll provide – would be super-swell and greatly appreciated.

Please call me at 403-555-9640 to discuss payment options.

Cordially Yours,
Laszlo Maximilian Mursky
κc Enterprizes

Environmentally Friendly, Recycled Paper
(75% recovered material content,
10% post-consumer recovered fibre)

"He's crazy!" I cried out, generating a scowl from the librarian. I didn't owe Laszlo money! I'd never even heard of κc Enterprizes. If anything he should be paying me damages for pain and suffering. I read the letter again, stood up, and sat back down. I jumped up once again, paced around the table, then crumpled up the letter and hurled it into the trash.

It took nearly a full hour of stewing before I could force Laszlo and his incredible letter from my mind, at least enough to focus partially on two more chapters from the Korean travel book.

With a handle on the alphabet, I turned to learning grammar rules and how to group the letters into syllable blocks for writing. I began memorizing words and stringing simple phrases together.

Every morning for a week I returned to the library and studied the entire day. Twice, when the wind blew less ferociously, I fished for a bit in the afternoon. But even then I'd practise speaking the Korean words as I reeled. River was *gang*. Creek was *cheon*. Mountain was *san*. Each night after everyone had gone to bed, I'd sneak over to Meryl Streep's room – which was actually my room, much like my condo in Calgary was actually Karla's – and I'd try out some words or phrases. My pronunciation improved, but my listening and comprehension went nowhere. No matter how hard I studied or how carefully I listened, everything Meryl Streep said sounded like poison frogs. *Poison frogs are in the cereal. Poison frogs have snuck in through cracks in the walls.* When I asked Mr. Kwon about it, he showed more surprise at my learning Korean than at the poison frogs.

"I once said to you that Meryl Streep watches too much Korean dramas. She is obsessed with Korean dramas. In fact, I think maybe she believes that she is *in* a Korean drama. Sometimes poison frogs, other times she has cancer. Almost always she says she is torn in a love triangle. So strange. I can't know exactly, but when her mother left us, Meryl Streep started acting this way."

Mr. Kwon hoped a change of location would help Meryl Streep. Each morning he took her for breakfast and a walk in Blairmore or Coleman or Hillcrest or Pincher Creek. Each evening they sat and chatted for an hour after dinner. He was a busy man, Mr. Kwon. After his breakfasts with Meryl Streep, he'd spend the rest of the day scouting out restaurant locations, research-ing costs and suppliers. In the evening when he got home, he'd water the lawn or clear the slow drain in the tub or patch the hole in the screen door or some other neglected problem the rest of us had stopped noticing. Each night after his chats with Meryl Streep, he'd sprawl out several books across the kitchen table, begin planning and budgeting for everything you could imagine you might need to start a restaurant.

"Canadian restaurateurs think location as the most impor-tant," he told me one night, leaning across the table, tapping on a map of the Crowsnest Pass, shaking his head.

"It's not important?" I asked, resting my chin atop folded arms on the table.

"It *is* important," he said. "But location is only the second most important." He clenched a stack of handwritten recipes and wagged them at me. "A restaurant needs delicious food."

"So delicious food is the most important?"

"No, no." He cocked his head for emphasis. "Delicious food makes you have happy customers."

"Oh," I said. "So happy customers are the most important?" I looked up with confidence.

"No! Happy customers is important but not *most* important."

Mr. Kwon stepped from the table, hands clasped behind him, eyes gazing out the window. "The number one important is the *loyal* customers. When you have the loyal customers, they will come to your location."

I teetered back on two legs of my chair. "OK, how do you get loyal customers?"

"Exactly!" He turned and tapped a fist on the table.

"Exactly *what*?"

"Loyalty!"

"Yes, you said that. But I'm asking *how* you get customers to be loyal?"

"Many ways," he shrugged. "Delicious food, good service, good location ..."

I planted my chair back down with a thud and sighed. "Then *those* things are all the most important."

"No," Mr. Kwon shook his head, "customer loyalty most important."

"Yeah, but – "

"Customer loyalty is not just customers being loyal to restaurant," he said, his chin lifted slightly. "More important is restaurant being loyal to customers."

"How does a restaurant be loyal to customers?" I asked, as he knew I would.

"Many ways." He sat across from me. "Delicious food, good service, good location."

"That's the same thing!"

"Maybe," Mr. Kwon nodded. "But that's not important. The important thing, Bacon, is to be loyal first." He held my gaze with a firm stare. "Be loyal and loyalty will be returned. Eventually." Again his chin lifted as though daring me to defy his words. "Customers are much like family," he smiled, "except customers pay for meals."

"Families aren't always like loyal customers," I said.

"They must be! Your grandfather always told me like this. That loyal family is most important. That I should feel extra lucky and extra loved because we have family in Korea *and* we have family in Canada. When I was a child, he told me all about our Canada family, about your grandmother and your mother. Many times he showed me pictures. He said how our Canada family would always be there for us if we need. Because that's what family does. I couldn't imagine any reason we would ever need, but then sure enough, troubles come."

Mr. Kwon leaned over the sink, gazing out at something in the darkening sky.

"Mr. Kwon, why didn't you and Grandpa ever visit?"

He glanced back over a shoulder. "I'm not sure. Many times I ask like that. Your grandfather always said, 'Maybe next year' or 'Someday soon.' The important thing, he said, is to remember that our Canada family is always there for us. Just like we are for them."

I don't know why Grandpa told Mr. Kwon a story like that. Basically a flat-out lie. But watching Mr. Kwon stand there, hands gripping the counter, leaning over the sink, his proud chin lifted, staring out contentedly at the dusty, wind-blown streets of Bellevue, I suddenly – and desperately – wished I had met my grandfather.

Again that night I dropped in on Meryl Streep. We were now able to exchange small four- to five-word sentences, not in a conversational kind of way, but more simply, declaring things about ourselves. I told her I'd been fishing; she told me she likes green; I told her I'd be going to the library tomorrow; she told me she saw a bus. Then she said something about being betrothed to a crown prince, and I decided that was probably enough for the night.

Each time I left her room she'd smile so hard at me in this incredulous way that it made me feel like I'd just brought her a twenty-five-pound rainbow.

The language barrier actually simplified things, forcing us to speak as basic and direct as possible. No need for reading between the lines or having to interpret meanings. Pure simplicity. Like how Grandma Magic Can says the secret to any Kenny Rogers song is sweet, solid simplicity. It was true. Ah-ah.

Just over a week after that first letter I received from Laszlo, I received a second one. Again by courier. Fortunately, this one arrived when I was home alone.

Dear Mr. Sobelowski,

This letter is a friendly, smiling, good-natured reminder that your account is unfortunately in arrears to the amount of $2,505.99. You no doubt intended prompt attention to this matter and it has inadvertently slipped your mind. Well, that's absolutely no problemo. Fine as wine. But now we'll need to get it right away.

So if you could be a sport and ring me at 403-555-9640 to discuss your plans for payment just as soon as convenient, that would be wonderfully wonderful.

If you've already sent payment, you can magic-marker a big "RB" across this page for "Recycle Bin."

Keep smiling.
Peace,
Laszlo Maximilian Mursky
KC Enterprizes

Environmentally Friendly, Recycled Paper
*(75% recovered material content,
10% post-consumer recovered fibre)*

Several days later I saw the Purolator truck pull up again, and I hurried down the driveway to meet the driver.

Dear Mr. Sobelowski,

Lordy, lordy, you must be awful busy.

It's certainly not my intention to portray an
aggressive tone in any way – nothing ever came
of violence or aggression of any kind. Nor is
it my intention for you to feel disrespected
or uncomfortable. However, that said, we do
require payment of your outstanding account of
$2,505.99.

Won't you please call me at 403-555-9640?

> Cordially, but gently firm,
> Laszlo Maximilian Mursky
> KC Enterprizes

> PS If it would be more convenient, we could
> talk to your mother about your account.
> Please advise.

Environmentally Friendly, Recycled Paper
(75% recovered material content,
10% post-consumer recovered fibre)

Talk to my mother? I ran downstairs and called the number
immediately.

"Happy afternoon," a voice sang.

"Hello? Is this Laszlo?"

"Well, hold on, let me just be certain." A rummaging and
knocking sounded on the other end. "Yup! Just checked the mirror and it is indeed. How can I help you?"

"It's Bacon Sobelowski."

"Bacon! Sonovagun. How the heavens are ya?"

"I'm OK."

"Wonderfully wonderful to hear your voice again. So what's on
your mind, Bacony-Boy?"

127

"You sent me three letters. They said I owe you $2,505.99."

"Oh, that's right. Of course, of course. We can take cash, cheque, VISA, or MasterCard. We can also take American Express, but I'd prefer we didn't if it's all the same to you. For no other reason than they have the *worst* commercials."

"Mr. Mursky, I don't owe you any money."

"You don't?"

"No. I've never borrowed anything from you."

"Oh, no, no, no, you never *borrowed* any. You *spent* it."

"I *spent* it?"

"Yes, that's correct. My apologies, Bacon, my letter was probably a little ambiguous. I should've made it more clear. I just assumed you wouldn't want me to itemize those particular charges in print for you. But let's go over it together. Let me grab your file." I could hear paper shuffling and clips snapping. "Here we are ... um ... invoice #004376. Says here seven nights' rental accommodation at $328.57 a night, five breakfasts at $10 each, six dinners at $26 each, and utilities ... well, I guess utilities were thrown in – that's your cable, water, heat, and electricity. Grand total ... $2,505.99."

"$2,505! Nobody said I was being charged for any of that."

"Well, we're not a homeless shelter, Bacon. Though Lord knows this city could use a few more. I've sent letters to the mayor – "

"$328 a night?"

"Actually that's a blended average. The actual cost was four nights at just $50, and then three nights at $700. I think you'd agree the fiddy bucks a night is reasonable and the seven C-notes ain't much either for what you got on those nights."

"No, I think fifty's crazy and seven hundred is ludicrous! Hotels are less than half that!"

"Well, yes," he chuckled, "but hotel rooms are missing a little *somethin' somethin'*, wouldn't ya say?"

"*Missing* something?"

"Yeah, hee hee. Let's be honest, Bacon. Seriously here – touch pinkies – I'm pushing my pinky through the phone right now. Gimmie your pinky."

"What?"

"Put your pinky to the phone. Come on ... pinky coming, pinky coming. Is your pinky on the phone?"

I put my smallest finger to the phone receiver.

"Is your pinky there?"

"Yes."

"OK, touch pinkies. We're touching pinkies now, Bacon." His voice dropped to a whisper. "You wouldn't be paying a lousy fiddy bucks for a hotel that had Karla in it. Am I right? Huh? Seriously. Darn pooping I'm right. OK, you can put your pinky back."

I tried to spread around whatever moisture was left in my mouth. "Mr. Mursky, are these charges for *Karla*?"

"What's that now?"

"These charges ... they're for *Karla*?"

"The bill you've received is for rental accommodation of Ms. Concolor's Eau Claire condo, plus meals. Utilities are complimentary. Any possible service fee of Ms. Concolor's – if there *was* any – would've been worked into the price."

"What do you mean service –"

"*If* there was any."

"Why is Karla not asking for this?"

"Well, actually, Ms. Concolor *is* asking for this. She's just doing it through me. I'm her business manager. And then husband when we get home. You know I don't get to be the boss in either role. Ha!"

"Are you a *pimp*, Mr. Mursky?" The other end of the phone went very quiet. "Hello? Mr. Mursky?"

"Mr. Sobelowski," Laszlo said grimly. "Did you just call my wife a ... a ... *prostitute*?"

"What? No, I –"

"I'm not sure I know what to do with that."

"Don't do anything. I asked if –"

"You want go around calling me names – fine. Say what you want about me, my hide's rode-hard leather. But if I'm a pimp that means *somebody's* a prostitute. Ms. Concolor housed you, fed you, helped you look for your girlfriend, nursed you when you were injured, and in return for *all* that you go and call her a hooker. Nice."

"I didn't say—"

"What do you think I should tell her tonight when I get home? Oh, hi honey, I talked to Bacon. 'Oh, wonderful Lazzy, how is that nice boy?' He's fine, dear. Called you a dirty harlot."

"I never said—"

"I don't know if I want to continue this conversation, Bacon."

"Wait a minute—"

"Do you make it a habit to call all men's wives whores?"

"Good Lord, no! Listen, I didn't mean to imply—"

"No, that's fine. That's fine. You say what you like. Sticks and stones. Why don't we just get this bill cleared up and be done with it."

"But I don't owe—"

"You don't have to raise your voice, Bacon. Yelling is a form of violence, you know. I have no patience for violence of any kind. Let's just not get into the name calling again, OK?"

"OK. I'm sorry. I didn't mean to—"

"The invoice amount is $2,505.99. How do you want to pay?"

"I don't *want* to pay. I don't have $2,505.99!"

"I know you don't *have* it, Bacon. I'm not stupid. You don't have to go and make me feel all stupid. I just asked *how* you wanted to pay."

"I'm sorry." I wrapped the phone cord around my head, trying to stop the pain. "You're not stupid. But twenty-five hundred dollars just seems a little ... exorbitant."

"You didn't seem to find anything exorbitant about poking your little wick into my wife more than once."

"I had no idea she was married! Nor did she say anything about it costing—"

"It always costs, Bacon. And it's not like we're greedy capitalists hoarding huge profits here. Do you have any idea what we do with the money we bring in? Do you? A full forty percent— *forty percent!* —goes to women's shelters. Victims of violence. I'll never understand why there's still violence in our world, Bacon. Never."

"Look Laszlo, that's very honourable and generous, but it doesn't change the fact I don't owe you—"

"What this all boils down to, Bacon, is you're stealing from women in need. Do you think that's doing the right thing?"

"Now hold on –"

"Oh sure, you're not directly delivering the abuse, but you're perpetuating their victimization."

"That's not fair!"

"Listen, Bacon, let's skip to the toppled fruit cart. Cut the chase scene right out. After you confirm if you'll be attending college or university, just before classes start, the bank will deposit student loan money in your account. Originally we would've waited until that time, but seeing as you ran out on us and we no longer have your presence as collateral, we now require payment immediately. We'll give you five days."

"Five days? I can't –" I heard a click. "Hello? Hello?" Then a dial tone. "Hello?"

I hung up the phone and chewed on my thumb for a half hour.

I didn't have $2,505.99. Was I obliged to pay? What would happen if I didn't pay? I found myself walking upstairs and, even though I was desperately uneasy about it and normally wouldn't even consider such a rash move, in my panicked state I couldn't help myself. I marched right into the living room, right between my mother and the TV. I said, "I need to talk."

"Shhhhh." She flapped a hand at me. "My soap's on."

"I'm serious," I told her. "I have a –"

"Bacon, shush!" she said and I guess thank God she did because who knows how much I would've told her. Maybe the whole story. I know exactly how she would've reacted.

Something in my head was grinding like a worn transmission. I half expected tranny fluid to start spilling out of my ears. I needed to think. To figure things out. So I decided to go fishing.

Outside, Mr. Kwon stood on the lawn, hands clasped behind his back. "*Annyeong*," he said.

A nod was the best I could offer.

"You will go fishing?" He nodded at the rod I was trying to hold behind my back.

I bobbled my head in a half-hearted kind of way that was both a yes and a no.

"Maybe I should come to fishing with you?"

That was the last thing I needed. "I don't know," I said reluctantly. "You don't even have a rod."

He shook his head. "I don't need. I will watch you." Watch me? Fishing is *not* a spectator sport. I'd never had anybody watch me fish before. "Is it OK?" he pressed. "I've never seen Canada fish before."

I fumbled with my tackle box, pretending to check the snaps, moved a little down the drive, but when I looked up he was still waiting for an answer. I sighed and grudgingly nodded.

I took Mr. Kwon to my usual spot, around the bend and past the fly-fishermen. There were three of them out that day.

"Those men have different rods than you," Mr. Kwon said.

I threw him a look of impatience.

When we rounded the corner I clipped on my Kamlooper and flung a cast out into the river. The Kamlooper bounced off a sweeper on the far bank and plopped into the water. Mr. Kwon watched intently. Then he began talking. Mumbling would be more accurate. In Korean. He muttered out sentence after sentence, words I wasn't even able to guess, all while I was trying to fish. "I'm sorry, Mr. Kwon," I finally said. "I don't know what you're saying."

"That's OK," he smiled, "I'm not talking to you."

I looked around, but we were alone. "You're going to scare the fish away," I said as politely as I could.

"Oh no," Mr. Kwon said. "Not at all. That's who I'm talking to."

"You're talking to the *fish*?" I looked into the river, half expecting to see a school of fish hovering intently.

"Of course," Mr. Kwon said.

"Well that's great," I said. Mr. Kwon looked ridiculous standing there next to the river in his black dress pants and shiny polished shoes. All he was missing was a tie.

I tangled up my line on every cast, paying far more attention to his string of grunts and moaning vowels than my casting. It was impossible to fish properly, let alone get any figuring out done. Mr. Kwon kept talking, standing so straight there at the river's edge, staring into the water just like he was teaching a class.

Thirty minutes passed before he stopped talking to the fish. But that was just to the fish — his talking didn't stop. Instead he turned his chatter my way. "What kind of fish will be here?" he asked.

I sighed loudly. "Cutthroat and rainbow. Mostly cutthroat in this stretch."

"*Cut*-throat?"

"Yeah, cutthroat trout. They have a red grin-shaped slice under each gill." I made two lazy slashing motions under my jaw. "Looks like their throat's been cut. Native to this river."

Mr. Kwon nodded importantly. "What you use to catch?"

"This is a Kamlooper spoon." I held up my rod tip to show him the dangling lure. "It's supposed to mimic a little fish. The trout chase the flashing and wiggling. It's instinct."

"You know much about fishing, Bacon," Mr. Kwon said.

"A little," I said. It felt good to know a little about something. I turned back and cast again. "The fish hide behind rocks. The rocks act as a shield from the current." I pointed with the tip of my rod to a large rock jutting out of the water. "They hide there and watch for stuff floating by."

Mr. Kwon stepped closer to the water to inspect, standing directly in front of me. "Why is spoon orange?"

I shrugged. "They seem to like that one best."

He crouched down, flat on his feet, to examine the lure up close.

"You want to cast?" I said. I figured he may as well, he couldn't have been more in the way.

But Mr. Kwon looked at me as if I'd offered him a rattlesnake. "No. I watch. And learn to you."

"From," I said.

"From?" Mr. Kwon said. "From what?"

"Learn *from* me. Not learn *to* me."

"Oh," he said. "Thank you. My English," he said shyly, shaking his head. "Not so good."

I immediately wished I hadn't said anything. "Your English is fine," I told him. "It's almost perfect."

He nodded slightly.

"Did my grandfather teach you?"

Mr. Kwon turned back to the river, as if not wanting to answer but then said, "No. Your grandfather ... he never spoke English in our house. Not allowed. Only Korean."

"He knew Korean?"

"He learned," Mr. Kwon said.

"Why would he ban English?"

Mr. Kwon stood, his back still to me. "My father worried for me, not having the pure Korean blood. Maybe I get teased or disadvantaged in the school. So he tried to hide it. Made me take my mother's name: Kwon. He worried that if I speak good English, people would know." Mr. Kwon pinched his trousers at the knees and sat on a large rock. "I start to learn English seven years ago."

It wouldn't matter what language he spoke, Mr. Kwon sure made you think he knew what was what. His steady eyes and raised chin always looked so proud and confident. If I hadn't twice already, on my way up for late-night soda crackers, seen him sitting alone in the kitchen after he thought everyone had gone to bed, his chin lowered, eyes downcast, lost in the grain of the table – like something in there was going to jump up and maul him – I'd have thought he was the most confident man alive. Both times I'd tiptoed back down the stairs and gone to bed hungry.

I crouched down and grabbed another lure to replace my Kamlooper: a little silver Panther Martin. The smaller lures never cast as far, but the river was narrow enough to compensate.

"Bacon," Mr. Kwon said, scooping up a handful of gravel, "you look serious today."

I gave him a look that offered reluctant agreement. "I just need to figure some things out."

"Why not ask the fish?" Mr. Kwon skipped a pebble across the water.

I squinted into the river. "Do they answer?"

He shook his head hesitantly as if I had asked the peculiar question. "No," he said. "They *listen*."

"Maybe I should ask the universe," I said. "Apparently *it* answers."

"Fish are good listeners."

"I don't know," I said. "I wouldn't feel right catching one after it'd been good enough to hear out my moaning and groaning." Mr. Kwon actually laughed a little at that. "Can I ask you something, Mr. Kwon?"

He nodded.

"Let's say you had a restaurant, but it wasn't really a restaurant, it was actually just your home, and you didn't even have any menus or signs or prices posted." I stood up, watching the Panther Martin spin and sparkle at the end of my line. "And if you invited somebody over for dinner, could you then charge them for that dinner? Send them an invoice?"

"Did I tell them I would charge them?" Mr. Kwon dropped the rest of the pebbles and wiped his hand on his pants.

"No," I said. "Not at all."

"Does my restaurant have the business licence?"

"No, I doubt it would." I kicked the lid closed on my tackle box. "Especially seeing as your business is illegal."

"*Illegal?*" His face clearly showed he was now giving my question grave consideration. "What kind of illegal?"

"I don't know," I shrugged, "let's say you're serving food you're not supposed to sell."

"What kind of food can't I sell?"

"I don't know. It doesn't matter," I said. "Whatever. Isn't there some kind of food that's illegal to sell?"

He nodded thoughtfully, folding his arms. "You mean like tiger or gorilla?"

"Sure, that'd do," I hurled out a cast but the Panther Martin didn't sail out with anywhere near the distance my heavy cast implied. "So the question is: would you charge somebody you invited over for *that* dinner?"

"I would never serve tiger or gorilla," Mr. Kwon said sharply.

"ok well, that's not the point," I said, tugging my line free from a stone or weed it snagged onto. "The point is ... ok, let's say somebody *else* had the restaurant, and you were invited to eat there. Then *they* gave you a bill for that meal. Would you pay it?"

"I would never *eat* tiger or gorilla."

"ok," I dropped a hand off my rod. "Not you. Somebody else.

135

Somebody *else* owned the restaurant that was really just their home, and somebody *else* was invited to eat there. Do you think *that* person should pay for that meal?"

Mr. Kwon put a curled finger to his lifted chin. "If the restaurant does not have the business licence, and they serve illegal foods, then no. No pay," he said. "What can restaurant do? Call the police? It is restaurant that is doing the illegal."

I stopped reeling.

"You're right," I said. "That's right! I'd never even looked at it that way. Of course." Laszlo couldn't do anything. What would he tell the police, that I didn't pay for his wife? This was great news.

"Bacon?" Mr. Kwon was suddenly solemn, stepping closer to me. "Yeah?"

"You haven't been eating gorilla?"

Mr. Kwon and I stayed out fishing all afternoon. I kept casting and reeling back in, tying different lures and spoons, and Mr. Kwon kept talking to the fish. I even showed him my fencing-jab cast, reaching my rod into the thickets and snapping off a few flick casts. Neither of us noticed when dinnertime came and passed.

29. One afternoon, Grandma Magic Can

caught me in the living room rummaging through her Kenny Rogers CDs. I had liner notes unfolded and spread out across the carpet. "Do you think it matters that Kenny Rogers didn't write the song?" I asked.

"What are you talking about?" she said, peering down at my mess.

"I mean do you think there's someone for everyone?"

"Oh, *that*." Grandma eased herself onto the couch. Either her or the couch made a groaning sound. "I'm sure when Kenny sings it, it's true."

"But in general, I mean?"

"I hope not," she mumbled, sorting through the magazines on the coffee table. "Look Bacon, Kenny's a bloody beautiful man. But not everything he sings about actually happened. Sometimes you have to just dream shit up. And believe it. It makes for a better song. Nobody wants to listen to some song about the excruciatingly dull hands real life deals you."

I leaned an elbow on the coffee table. "When did you know Grandpa wasn't your someone?"

Grandma's eyes shut for a moment; it was longer than a blink. "Maybe when he messed around over in Korea." She licked a finger and snapped over a page of her *People* magazine. "Or maybe when he came home with someone else's baby. Or when he asked me if *we* could raise it." She shut her eyes again. "The asshole didn't know anything. Dumb as a ham steak."

"But Mr. Kwon seems like he'd have been a nice son to have around."

Grandma turned toward the kitchen and didn't answer.

"Did you know that *Kwon* is Mr. Kwon's mother's maiden name?" I said. "Grandpa made him use it." Grandma Magic Can ran a finger along the words in the *People* article, her lips moving as she did. "And Grandpa never let Mr. Kwon learn English when he was growing up. He protected him from teasing and discrimination for having a non-Korean father —"

"Bacon, please!" Grandma said, her voice unusually firm. "I'm reading." Even though I stopped talking, she chucked the magazine onto the coffee table; it slid across and fell to the carpet. Grandma touched her fingers to her forehead. We both sat quietly for a while before she stood and stepped out of the room.

30. In what had become a routine,

I ended the night hovering in the bedroom doorway practising Korean words with Meryl Streep. I delivered my usual slaughtered attempt at how are you. "*Eotteohke jinaeseyo?*" But this time my words were met with silence. Instead of responding with a rapid phrase I couldn't understand or giggling at my pronunciation, Meryl Streep simply stared. Then she shuffled over and patted the mattress beside her.

That was unusual. I pointed at myself, then to the mattress, asking if that's what she wanted. She patted the mattress again. So I sat.

"*Eotteohke jinaeseyo*?" I said again. This time she replied.

"*Sarang habnida*," she sang. I immediately thumbed through my dictionary, but she plucked the book from my hands and set it on the headboard behind her. "*Sarang habnida*," she said again. Then she threw her arms around me and pulled me close. The soft touch of her cheek pressed against mine made my back straighten. "*Kamsa hamnida*, Bacon. *Kamsa hamnida*."

I turned up my hands to show I didn't understand and reached for the dictionary, but Meryl Streep pulled me back by the arm with a gentle grip, and kept that gentle grip resting right there on my arm even after I sat back. "We must never forget what we've shared," she said.

"OK," I replied.

Her graceful eyes and their wispy lashes looked so delicate, like I could scatter them away with a whisper. "Such tragedy that our love is forbidden," she added. I wasn't clear what she meant by *our* love. Did she mean my search for my someone? Had she found a someone herself? Was she referring to *us* together? That would be strange because I didn't feel love for her – not in that way. I'd need to tell her.

The awkwardness of sitting there next to her on my bed, fumbling for a way to ask her to clarify her comments, caused a gripping in my lungs. But Meryl Streep took my face in her hands, softly cupping my cheeks. Neither of us seemed to know what to do next; we just sat there staring at each other, my face in her hands. Maybe she really did mean *our* love. But now, as her soft breath brushed my face, I no longer wanted anything clarified. Instead I remembered what Karla had said about being a man. That I couldn't sit waiting for a woman to grab me by the throat each time. And so I felt myself leaning over to Meryl Streep, pressing my lips against hers. She flinched like a spooked trout. She even raised a hand to her startled mouth. When she settled, she whispered something in Korean. I reached for the dictionary, but she pushed her lips back onto mine, and we were soon both still again, our closed lips pressed together tightly. I held my lips against hers, but her rigid mouth wouldn't open. As ungraceful as it seemed, all I could do was poke tiny pecks on her trembling lips like some kind of industrious woodpecker.

"In the next life," she whispered, "let us never meet again."

Why would we never meet again? What was the next life? Perhaps out of habit, I found myself reaching for the Korean-English dictionary, as though it might contain an explanation. But Meryl Streep reattached her closed mouth to mine and we continued to hold our closed mouths together until, to my surprise, I felt my hand slipping onto her back, under her shirt, gliding over her soft, thin skin, lifting up near her neck, dragging her T-shirt up. The whirling wind rattled the thin glass of the small basement window. I tugged at her bra — a bra so white and simple compared to Karla's doily garments — hoping a snap or clamp would give and sort itself out. Both Karla and Sara had always removed their own. Meryl Streep's bra remained firm, so I reached both hands around behind her, feeling about for some kind of clasp, a button or Velcro. Again she spoke to me in Korean. Again I reached for the dictionary, a difficult stretch while keeping my closed mouth to hers. She snatched the dictionary and flung it across the room. Then she removed the bra herself. We both worked to tug her T-shirt up over her head, letting her bra slide down her back, revealing tiny, soft breasts with small, sausage-slice nipples no bigger than my own.

I traced my finger over her skin, as smooth as polished walnut. Could Meryl Streep be my someone?

"If only you had your eyesight," she whispered.

"Eyesight?" I said, almost letting go of her breast. "I see fine."

She ran her fingertips over my eyelids. "Such tragedy that you shall never see my face."

"No, I can see perfectly well," I said. "Your face, your eyes, your neck. I can see everything." I put my other hand on her other breast as evidence.

"I shall always be haunted by what could've been." She turned her face to the ceiling, forced a tear out of an eye, and let out a long, loud sigh.

That's when a splash of light filled the room and a startling roar came from the doorway. *"Anneeyo!"* Mr. Kwon stood gaping at us. *"Anneeyo! Anneeyo!"*

I suppose I shouldn't have been surprised. Sure, Mr. Kwon had never come downstairs to speak to Meryl Streep before, but maybe it was just one of those nights he needed to tell her he loved her once more, or maybe he wanted to change the time of their breakfast the next morning. Whatever his reasons, there was no doubt it was my timing that had called for his presence.

"Chweesung-hamneeda," Meryl Streep cried out, moisture flooding her eyes.

"Anneeyo!" Mr. Kwon howled again. He pulled a blanket from the bed, wrapped it around Meryl Streep, hugging her tightly. I tumbled from the bed and collapsed on the floor. *"Wae!"* he cried out at me.

"What's all the—Jesus, Bacon!" my mother said, appearing at the doorway, pinching her housecoat tight. It was amazing how her thin frame could fill a room. "Holy shit ... she's your *cousin*, for Christ's sake!" Each word crackled on the verge of laughter.

"What's going on," Grandma Magic Can said, waddling into the room, rubbing the sleep from her eyes.

"Bacon's poking his goddamned cousin," my mother coughed. "Not to mention she's also ... *oh, Jesus Christ!*" My mother blew out the kind of sudden laugh she gives watching clips of skiing accidents on TV. She turned to Grandma. "Behold your grandson, the perv."

Mr. Kwon still clung tight to his daughter, brushing her hair with his palm.

"Chweesung-hamneeda," Meryl Streep wept. *"Chweesung-hamneeda."*

"Bacon!" Mr. Kwon demanded. "Why do you do like this?"

I didn't know what to say. I had no answer. I wanted to ask myself the same question. I felt like I didn't have an answer for any question in the world. I looked up at my mother standing there staring at me like she'd found me sitting in a puddle of my own pee. "I'll tell you why," she said, and for the briefest moment—perhaps out of desperation—I thought she might actually have the answer I needed. "It's because he's got a *problem* with his pecker. He's become his goddamned father."

"Hold on —" Grandma Magic Can started, but my mother wasn't finished. She leaned back against the door like she couldn't be bothered to stand.

"I knew he wouldn't turn out any different," my mother groaned. "It's that age," she sighed. "There's no stopping it."

"Lydia, please," Grandma said, trying to hush her.

"His father had the same problem," my mother continued, handing Meryl Streep the T-shirt I'd removed. "But even his father —" She stopped to snicker like she'd thought of something nearly unimaginable. "Even *he* wouldn't have tried doinking his cousin."

That was when I ran out. I busted straight through my mother and Grandma, fled upstairs, and bolted out of the house. I kept running and didn't stop until I'd reached the Bellevue Inn Tavern.

31. I finished my first beer in just

over a minute — tipped the empty glass forward signalling for another — and finished that one in under a minute. I also ordered a rye and coke, tried a rye and ginger, asked for a rye and water, and ended with a rye and vodka.

At that point I decided I best be going before my problemed pecker impelled me to ask the waitress home, or move in on the old Barrow sisters competing for dust at the shuffleboard table, or before I simply dropped my pants and stuffed myself into the pickled-egg jar.

I bought a six-pack of off-sales and stumbled out into the warm, gusting July night air. I staggered through the back roads, keeping clear of the dim streetlights, even though they threw down barely more than a headlamp's worth of light. A cat, perched on the hood of an old abandoned Impala, perked its head up as I passed down the alley behind the Moose Mountain Grill, guzzling off-sale beer as fast as I could swallow. I slinked down around the Crowsnest Angler, all quiet and dark inside except for a tiny dot of red light flashing sporadically. A message indicator on the phone, maybe, or a resting security alarm. The town was silent other than the constant murmur of the highway.

I eventually found myself at the Wayside Chapel – the littlest church. I hunched down, stepped inside, and squeezed into one of the seats. I finished two more beers inside, glaring at the podium as though waiting for somebody to speak, to explain themselves, to explain me. Nobody did.

I've no clue how much time passed while I sat – I'm sure I slept for a stint. At some point I woke, hauled myself up, and shuffled back out the door, pinballing off the doorframe. Outside the dark shapes around me came alive: the mountains swayed, the chapel leaned, the trees smeared. I glanced around for a single object to hold my focus. The dark, silhouetted crow's nest, towering over me on its twenty-foot pole, seemed to step forward. The crude sculpture lurched from side to side but, squinting through one eye, I was able to hold it mostly steady. Even in the darkness the large white eyes of the mother crow stared down at me. Watching. Waiting. I pushed my hand through one of the plastic rings of my six-pack and began climbing the pole it sat on, the two full cans bouncing against my arm as I wormed my way up. I gripped onto the lip of the nest, heaved myself up and in, sprawled out on my back, and nearly rolled out the other side.

The giant nest wasn't hollowed out like I must've expected. Instead it was filled in and inverted so my mid-section shot up higher than my head or feet, giving me the sensation of drifting. The awkward, unsteady nest was no place for a sober person, let alone one in my fog. Yet, at the same time, the big crow was a shield from the wind; it kept me warm, gazing down with those large, white eyes, her head tilted in concern, her mouth gaping knowingly – knowing all the things we're all supposed to know about, all the things I didn't.

My heavy eyes narrowed, reminding me of Meryl Streep and her thin, exotic eyes, the alluring, oily smell of her skin, the terrible mistake we made. I thought of Karla and her ale-coloured nipples, of Sara and her long, soft legs. Even with the sharp sting of shame still fresh in my chest, I couldn't stop thinking of them.

Any of them. That only added to the shame. I scratched at my stomach, ran my hands down along my jeans. I couldn't hold one thought steady. Each arousal from the past eight months flashed through my head like a depraved and frantic slideshow. I tugged down my zipper as, above me, dark mountain shapes closed in on all sides. A charcoal cloud-cover blotted out the stars, my eyes reached up at the giant crow, her long black beak gaping, her black and beautiful face almost smiling. I had so many questions for her. My head grew heavier, the crow's white eyes watching, protecting. I felt my cold hand on my penis trying to hold on and, as the sage old crow blurred from sight, I wanted to reach for her, to call out, but my head rolled back on its weak and wobbly neck. Again, I would fail to finish. Her wise, nourishing beak disappeared through the mesh of my closing eyelashes. At that moment I wondered about so many things, so many things the old crow would know. That I didn't. I hungered for understanding. I hungered and wondered so hard I nearly knocked myself out. I lifted my chin with whatever consciousness remained and, like the begging nestling beside me, I too stretched open my mouth, hoping to be fed.

32. What I recall next was waking to a

blaring squeal. My skull shook and rattled like the track beneath a shrieking train. I couldn't pull open my eyes to see where the noise was coming from. Every part of my body ached. I had a knot in my neck, my throat was raw, my legs and arms were numb, my back throbbed. The squeal returned, like a siren or passing freighter. Every limb iced over, my whole body shivered from the unrelenting blasts of wind. Only my eyes felt warmth, the slow-rising sun just beginning to touch them, to soften the sleep that glued them closed.

The noise came again.

Hoooooooooooooooonnnnnk. It was a car horn, not far off in the distance. And then another.

Hooooooooooooooooonnnnnk. By the fading sound I could tell they were passing cars. I finally managed to pry open one eye to the sight of the giant crow gazing down at me. It took close to a minute to remember where I was.

Hooooooooooooooooonnnnnk.

I lifted my head, peeking out at the highway. Each passing car honked, some passengers even waved. I felt the crumpled weight of my jeans dangling around one leg that hung numb over the lip of the nest. The other leg sprawled off the opposite side, naked except for a sock and a runner. Each arm shot out straight, draped over the edges of the nest. A six-pack ring with two full beers dangled from my wrist, battered about by the wind. The inverted hump of the nest forced an arch in my seething back, lifting my body into a painful pyramid. Mount Bacon. Marked at its peak by a flaccid flag: a tired penis, fallen dead like a shot gopher.

Everything from the night before came back to me: Meryl Streep, Mr. Kwon, my mother's snickering, the tavern, and my understanding of how very little I understood of this world.

I remember when my father used to reel in a fish; he'd let it slap and skip itself across the rocks on the river's edge. When the fish wore out, my father would wrap his large hand around it but, before cranking down on it with a fist-sized stone, he'd wait a few seconds, just until the fish had kicked its tailfin one or two last times. "There," he'd say, winking at me. "Now it's got no more kick left." That's how I felt lying there in the giant crow's nest. I had no more kick left.

I knew what was next. Like everything else that stumbled into Bellevue, Mr. Kwon and Meryl Streep would soon be on their way out. But they'd be leaving not because Bellevue was old and dull or deprived of culture, or because they needed some place wild – they'd be leaving because of me. Mr. Kwon wouldn't start a restaurant here, Meryl Streep wouldn't get the new start she so badly needed, and Grandma Magic Can wouldn't get the forty Gs. And as I pictured my father's hand gripped around that stone, heaving down upon the head of the trout with no kick left, I decided I too had had my fill.

Attempting to sit up, I rolled off the nest, nearly smashing open my head as I crumbled to the ground. I managed to land most of my weight on my side, but still lay there for several minutes before pulling up my jeans and limping home. The Hyundai was gone. Mr. Kwon probably left during the night, unable to sleep one more minute under our roof. I crept inside the house and found Grandma Magic Can asleep at the kitchen table, a half cup of tea still in her loose grip. I snuck around each corner until I was sure nobody else was home. Nobody was. But I found Meryl Streep's clothes still filling my closet and dresser drawers. She hadn't packed yet. They must've decided to stay the night at least. True to their routine, Mr. Kwon had most likely taken Meryl Streep out for breakfast as he did every morning. Get a meal in before the long drive. Before they did their leaving. But that, of course, meant they'd be back soon. I quickly stuffed my daypack full of clothes, scribbled a note, and left it by Grandma's hand: *I've moved out. Left Bellevue.*

I grabbed the keys to the Lancer, walked out the front door — which, it dawned on me at that moment, had a fifty-fifty chance of being the same fucking door my father had — and drove away.

33. Maybe there wasn't someone for

everyone. Maybe the whole idea was crap. Maybe Kenny Rogers just threw a lousy song together to make some money and maybe there's a reason nobody but Grandma Magic Can and my mother listen to him anymore.

I'd failed three relationships in five weeks, still hadn't found my someone, and was no closer to figuring out what love was all about. Maybe I never would. Maybe nobody ever does. Or maybe it just doesn't happen to people who have a "problem," as my mother had said of me. The only thing I needed right then was to get away. I was done looking for my someone. I was through watching *other* people leave. And even more important than leaving Bellevue was leaving Bellevue before Mr. Kwon left. My turn to do the leaving.

Calgary had felt as jarring as cracking through the ice-crusted skin on a winter river. Everything there was different. And that was just one city. There were whole other provinces out there, whole other countries. The US border was only an hour away. A whole month still remained before I'd need to swap out the tackle in my backpack for textbooks. Until then, waiting for me was a big world of crappy towns and crappy cities full of crappy people listening to crappy singers tell us how they think the world is. Surely there was somewhere less crappy than Bellevue. I'd found the perfect inaugural drive in *my* Lancer: leaving. The moment was monumental.

I pulled the Lancer up to the highway intersection and stopped. In the rearview mirror I could see the tiny Wayside Chapel and the giant crow's nest. That big crow had watched so many people leave – so many people bail on Bellevue – and she'd watched it all right at this same intersection. She'd be watching Mr. Kwon and Meryl Streep bailing soon enough. But first she'd watch me. One secret she'd surely learned, a secret I now knew too, was the people those leavers left behind – people like me, the ones that did the staying – got left behind for no greater reason than because they didn't do the leaving first. This time was my turn. A rusted old Lancer, a daypack stuffed with clothes, eighty dollars in cash, two beers on a six-pack ring, and a green and brown spincasting rod with the thumb-button trigger. It was all I had.

Idling at that intersection, what was once an intimidating rest of the world suddenly looked naked to me. Like I'd snuggled up under the sheets sneaking a look-see at what had been underneath all along. Now I was ready to tear away those sheets, gawk away at any stretch, gully, or curve of the whole darn world I desired. I even stepped out in front of the Lancer to consider my options. A left-hand turn would take me east, past corn fields tall enough to hide cars, deep into bald prairie, all the way to Manitoba, maybe to some secret lake nobody knew about. And if I kept going, who knows, maybe even to whatever was east of that. A right-hand turn would send me into British Columbia with mountains even bigger than the ones around Bellevue, totem poles, rivers stuffed with salmon, and union jobs where my

mother said you can work laundry in a hospital and rake in
as much as a doctor. Which way to go? Only the spit would know.
I worked up a wad of saliva, spilled it into my hand, and held my
palm out for the wind to sniff. My direction ... my future ... all at
the mercy of the spit. A crow glided overhead, scolding me. Probably irritated at being left behind. My hands clapped shut, a tail
of spit squeezed out, shooting through the air, arched in a south-
ern direction. The saliva strain splashed onto the asphalt, and I
could almost hear the tide of my future begin to lap. South.

South would take me to the border. The United States and,
if I kept going, maybe even Mexico. I'd seen movies of people
escaping to Mexico, fleeing the law or other troubles. More often
than not, they were never heard from again. That's a place you
leave for to stay left. Excitement rippled over my skin.

I peered down the number three highway, east. Not far down
I knew of a turn-off that forked south. In the distance I could
see the hills flatten, the trees scatter into patches, and the jut-
tings of rock submerge under the grass. I slipped back into the
idling Lancer, adjusted the seat, clicked in my seatbelt, and
flicked on the signal light, flashing left. "Bring it on," I said to
the eastern horizon. I gripped the wheel tight, waited for a truck
to pass, eased out on the clutch, hit the gas, and headed into
my future. As I turned onto the highway I threw one last glance
over at the giant crow's nest, her large, white eyes still watching.
Then a great thud filled my ears. A shattering screech. My body
thrust forward, the seatbelt snapped me back. The back end of
the Lancer lifted, the engine screeched and moaned. Everything
stopped. I opened my eyes to a caved-in windshield, shattered
into a crooked web of cracks and splinters. It had a strange,
brown blur to it that I couldn't see through. I stumbled outside,
my steps crackling on the glass and plastic and pieces of car
strewn across the highway. Part of the side panel hung from the
frame, a tire had blown from the impact, and there, sprawled up
against the windshield, its weight crushing down on the hood,
was a large, brown, enormously antlered male moose. Its massive
head and rack dangled off the side, and steam and smoke spewed
from under the animal.

147

A cluster of cars flashed by, swerving on either side. *Hoooooooonnnnnk! Hooooooooonnnnnnnk!* I jumped, gripped an antler point, and threw myself up against the car to keep from being hit. When a break in traffic finally appeared, I crawled back into the Lancer and turned the ignition. The engine wouldn't take. I tried several more times. Nothing. After another cluster of cars passed, I staggered back out, still dazed from the impact. I remember glancing back at the winding road into Bellevue, checking for Mr. Kwon's car before I stammered over to the hood of the Lancer, hunched down, gripped my hands onto the neck of the moose, and began pushing with everything I had. I could still leave first. But the moose wouldn't budge. I pushed and heaved, my runners scratching the pavement for traction. It took everything out of me just to lift the massive head upright; I was never going to shove it off the car. I slipped and fell, and the Lancer began to roll. It rolled and rolled, slowly at first, then with increasing speed, rolling right down the highway – backward. Westward.

Hooooooooonnnnnk!
Hooooooooonnnnnk!

I chased down the rolling Lancer, jumped in, and gripped the wheel. The rusted old car built up more momentum down the incline. A Shell station sat around the bend at the bottom of the hill. I aimed for that. The giant crow watched it all, her white eyes sad now, her beak still gaping but silent, maybe too sad to speak.

The Lancer cruised down into the parking lot of the Shell station while I repeatedly glanced over my shoulder for any sign of the Hyundai leaving before me.

Simone, the mechanic – the one everybody in town calls Mony Mony – stood propped up against the pump watching me.

The Lancer glided safely into a parking stall. I got out, hunched over with a hand on my knee, caught my breath, wiped the sweat from my brow with my shoulder, and asked Mony Mony what he thought.

He circled the car, took off his hat, and scratched his oily hair. "Well," he moaned in a nasal tone – he had a chronic sinus infection that left his nostrils so badly clogged and crusted up with such a great mess it was often difficult to look him straight in the face – "I think she's done."

"The car," I said, "or the moose?"

He looked back at the steaming heap. "Both."

I turned toward the highway, staring eastward. A wind that was something more than air left my lungs.

"You suppose I could have it?" Mony Mony said.

My knees nearly buckled and I had to step forward to steady myself. I tossed Mony Mony the keys. He caught them against his overalled chest and moaned. "Naw, I mean the moose."

Just then, with a deep gurgling groan and a raspy gasp, the moose's legs began kicking and jerking until it wiggled itself off the hood and righted itself up on its hooves. We watched it stumble and drop to a knee. It collected itself and limped across the highway, down the bank, and into the river valley out of sight.

Mony Mony rubbed his chin with the back of his wrist. "I'll still take the car if you ain't wanting it."

I didn't want it. Any of it. I grabbed my green and brown spincasting rod with the thumb-button trigger from the back seat, threw the two beers into my daypack, tossed the pack over a shoulder, and began walking. Bellevue could throw whatever it wanted at me, I'd do no staying that day. I wouldn't be left behind again. Not on that day. I hurried down the highway at a fast jog that turned into a full sprint. Fleeing Bellevue. Headed south.

34. I'd made it about seven kilometres

outside of town but still hadn't found a ride. Exhausted, I dropped my thumb and slid down against a guardrail on the side of the highway. The whir of passing traffic and the wail of cutting wind sent me drifting off to sleep. To the passing cars I must've looked like road kill. I slept like it. In fact, I slept right through lunch and continued sleeping right past dinner before a cloud of dust and gravel woke me, all kicked up by a large RV with Ontario licence plates, pulling over just in front of me.

A tiny, smiling, grey-haired man limped out of the side door. His short body was almost entirely torso, like a wiener dog standing on hind legs. He tugged up his belt, almost as if hoping hiked-up trousers might give the illusion of legs. "You OK?" he said with a soft, timid voice.

I waved that I was.

"You hitchhiking?"

I nodded.

"That thing there a spincasting rod?" He pointed to the gear behind me. I looked at the rod, almost surprised to see it. I nodded reluctantly. "Well, galldarn, Vronnie," he called inside. "Have a boo here. Somebody still spincasts." He pushed his face right up to my rod. His hands he kept at his sides, as though afraid to touch it. "I figured I was darn near the last," he laughed.

I couldn't pry my eyes from his legs. They were clothed in a pair of hiking shorts that fit him like pants, covering him almost down to his ankles. "Yesiree," he continued. "Everyone else fly-fishes these days, don't they? Not me. Give me a bobber, a worm, and six cold ones, and you may as well just impale my wrinkled bum right on the pearly gates." He rubbed his hands together with excitement. "See, I like to rest my eyes in the sun, lay back and maybe have a snooze, you know? Tie one of them little bells on the rod that rings and wakes you when a fish bites. Can't do *that* fly-fishing, eh?" He grinned warmly. Welcomingly. But I sighed to myself, thinking that if he was a supporting argument for spincasting, the fly-fishermen had already won.

"Come on in, son." He waved me into the RV as he scampered back into the driver's seat. A quick survey of the inside revealed nobody else in the motorhome. Though I did see a framed eight-by-ten photograph of a stone-faced, square-headed woman, perched upon the passenger seat. "We got a spincaster here, Vronnie," the grey-haired man said to the picture. I watched him whisper something else to the photo as I took a seat at a table further back.

The short-legged man started the engine. I stretched my neck to see how those tiny legs would possibly reach the pedals. "You headed out to do some fishing?"

"I'm definitely headed out," I said. "And fishing's all I'm going to do."

"Oh, wait! How rude of me." He spun the framed photograph and angled it to face me. "This is the wife, Veronica." He even extended a finger out toward the picture, I guess in case I mistook her for the radio or cup holder. "And I'm Alfred."

"I'm Bacon Sobelowski."

The photograph didn't say anything.

Alfred pulled the big motorhome back onto the highway, thrusting his chin up to see over the wheel. "*Bacon*, you say? That's an interesting name. Bacon the spincaster." He stretched up, almost falling out of the chair, his feet slipping off the gas, just to adjust the rearview mirror so he could smile back at me. "So, where'd you say you were headed?"

"South." I ran my hands across the table. "Anywhere south."

"Well, that's where *we're* headed." Alfred shuffled excitedly in his seat. "We're going to Waterton Lakes National Park. We can get you that far. After that I'm afraid you're on your own. We're camping there for a couple weeks. Right, Vronnie?"

The photograph didn't answer.

"We just did our usual BC run and now we're making our way back. Like I say, you're welcome to join us that far."

"That'd be fine." I tried to smile. Waterton was a small mountain park stuffed into the most southwest corner of Alberta. I recalled seeing it on a map once. Just one road going in and that road ended right there. A dead end. The park was only an hour away so it wasn't going to be a new country or even a new province, but I'd never been before and it was as good a starting point as any. At least it wasn't Bellevue. Or Calgary.

"Vronnie and me, we're from Etobicoke, you see. We've been camping out west every summer for the past forty-three years. That's how long we been married. Forty-three years. Every one of them a galldarn blessing, right, Vronnie?" He threw out a thumbs-up at the photograph.

"How many of those has she been a photograph?" I asked. Alfred's face went as solemn as if the stomach flu had just kicked in. I immediately wanted to stuff the question back in my mouth.

151

"She's been gone now eight years," he said.

"I'm sorry." I shook my head partly for Veronica and partly at myself. Neither Alfred nor I said anything for a spell. I wished we could've stayed like that all the way to Waterton, but it seemed somehow disrespectful not to ask how she passed.

"*Pass*?" Alfred wheeled around in his seat, sending the motorhome veering into the next lane. "She isn't *dead*. Cheese and rice!" He yanked the wheel, swerving us back into the proper lane. "She moved to New Brunswick to live with her mother."

"She's not? Oh, I'm sorry, I thought – "

"No, no, no. She just up and left one morning. I found a sticky note on the waffle iron. Haven't heard from her since."

The oncoming traffic gave Alfred's swerving motorhome a wide berth. I wondered if Veronica had left because of his driving. "But you still keep her picture?" I said stupidly.

Alfred turned and looked me over. "She's my wife." I met his gaze, trying to will his eyes back to the road. "This here's the one picture where she's smiling." I peered at the stone-faced woman in the photo, at that mouth that could've been drawn with a straight-edge, and wondered what her frown might have looked like.

"You ever been in love, Bacon the spincaster?" Alfred finally returned his eyes to the road; it was the first question he didn't ask while watching me, waiting for an answer. "Well, there you go," he said, adjusting the seatbelt strap around his waist. "If you had, you'd have answered right off. And then you'd understand that photograph sitting there."

I looked at Veronica's hard, flat mouth, her preoccupied lowered glance. She had a startled tautness to her face, like she'd just been served the wrong meal at a restaurant.

"I tried finding my someone," I said. "But I have a problem controlling my pecker."

35. Dusk settled in as Alfred's big RV

passed by patches of white birch sitting just a few metres off the highway, rows of barbed wire clinging to weathered and rotting fence posts, and dusty ranch road turnoffs marked by sun-bleached cow skulls or wood slab signs seared with ranch brands.

When we arrived at the tiny resort village of Waterton, it was too dark to see anything more than the red glow of a Coca-Cola machine in front of an old lodge, a series of No Vacancy signs lining the otherwise dark road, and the dim blue light of a phone booth out front of a garage.

Alfred asked where I'd be staying for the night. I told him I didn't know. He said he and Vronnie kept a dome tent and sleeping bag in the RV for the grandkids. Said I was welcome to borrow it all for as long as I needed. Alfred and the picture of Veronica dropped me off at the town site campground; I thanked them both, found a tent pad in loop B, and set up camp for the night.

I should've borrowed a flashlight. Cloud-cover had blocked out any possible glimmering aid from the moon. With nothing to look at but blackness, I crawled into the tent and finished the two beers I'd packed. As warm and flat as they tasted, I wished I'd packed two dozen more. Listening to the breeze brush the nylon walls in the unbroken darkness of that tent, my thoughts couldn't help but turn back to Meryl Streep and what had happened. What I'd done. I wished I had an answer for Mr. Kwon when he asked why. My mother was certain she knew *why*. I had a "problem," she'd said. She'd emphasized "problem" in a way I'd heard it spoken on the Maury Povich show when Maury was talking about some lady who couldn't stop stuffing coins into slot machines. She'd stuff coins into those machines sometimes for ten hours a day until she had no money left for groceries. Eventually she stuffed every coin and every dollar she'd ever saved into those slot machines. The whole time her two boys waited at home. I guess if she could've, if it had got her another spin, she probably would've stuffed those boys in, too.

I'd also heard "problem" spoken that same way by Oprah Winfrey. She was talking about a man who couldn't stop eating. It got to the point where he'd eat four whole chickens in one day. He was nine hundred and twenty pounds. They had to cut a hole in the side of his house just to get him out.

I wondered if I'd end up on Maury Povich or Oprah or Regis or Larry King. Maybe I needed to see someone, a specialist, an expert, someone who understood peckers better than I did. I lifted the sleeping bag and peered down inside. Unable to see anything in the darkness, I listened nervously, as though fearing what my problemed pecker might be up to.

36. I zipped open the tent the next morning, forced to squint from the bright sun glistening off the gentle laps of a river I'd had no idea was running so close in front of me. The river emptied swiftly into a large lake I also hadn't expected. I cowered back in the tent, shocked. Steep mountains thrust up along the perimeter of the campground, miles and miles of limestone peaks stretched down the lake, poking out behind each other.

I hadn't been many places but still I could hardly imagine a more dramatic setting for a town. The snuggling mountains, so steep and immediate, hovered right over the tiny village. With just that one road in, the town was cornered. Like the prairie had collided into a wall.

That morning I strolled up and down pretty much every street the little village had to offer. The seclusion and silence made me feel like I was playing hooky from the world. Waterton was only about an hour from Bellevue, but the abruptness of the mountains felt like I'd reached the end the world.

The previous night I'd expected to spend the morning searching for a Greyhound station, a shuttle bus, or something that would carry me to my next stop, but that morning, staring up at the crowding mountains, I felt hidden. Hidden made me feel a little better. Any thoughts of a quick exit sank into the deep lake that ran alongside the tiny town.

With my stomach groaning, angry at me for having slept through all my meals the day before, I popped into a lodge hoping for breakfast. Behind the front desk, a twitching budgie paced anxiously on its perch, berating me with a series of angry squawks. Nobody else appeared behind the desk, so on the off chance the bird knew and could say so, I asked about a restaurant. The budgie shrieked wildly and set into some kind of spasm before I heard a voice call from the small adjacent lounge. A barrel-chested man in a cowboy hat sitting on a stool against the bar called out again, "Any experience working maintenance?"

"Me?" I pushed open the saloon-style swinging doors. "Maintenance? No, not really."

The barrel-chested man reached across the bar for a coffee pot to fill up his cup. "None at all?"

"No."

"Never helped your daddy change oil? Build a fence?"

"No."

He scratched at his goatee. "Really?"

I nodded.

"Can you cook?"

"Not so much."

"Ever served food?"

"No."

"Bartend?"

"No."

"Good," he nodded, sipping from his steaming mug of coffee. "We need a dishwasher. You can start in an hour."

"Start?"

The budgie squawked.

"Yeah, apron's hanging next to the sink," he said. "Kitchen's that way."

"I just came in looking for breakfast...."

"Breakfast is included. Go ask the cooks for some eggs. You can eat in the back room. Then get to work."

The budgie shrieked and fluttered, small feathers scattered in the air. The barrel-chested man scooped the angry little bird up with his finger, carried him over to a cage by the window, and closed him inside. This seemed to bring the bird either resignation or tranquility.

I hadn't even considered working since the Super Stop. Then

again, I only had about eighty dollars left on me, and I'd sure as beans bark need some money to keep going.

Dishwashing at the lodge only paid minimum wage plus tip-outs from the servers, but it did include staff meals and my own room in an old, seven-bedroom staff cabin just off the lake. The cold cabin smelled of old books and wet leaves. Half a charred barstool rested in the soot of an old fireplace, a duct-taped sheet of plastic covered a missing window pane, and the living room sofa was short three legs and a cushion. The bathroom had a yellowed sink with a mismatched faucet handle for cold water, and a pair of pliers pinched around the nub where the hot water handle must've once perched. A half roll of toilet paper sat on the tank instead of the cracked roller half hanging from the wall.

I spent the next few days fishing each morning and washing dishes each night. Nothing else. Exactly what I needed to do. I didn't know anybody in the town, other than Alfred, the picture of Veronica, and the barrel-chested owner of the lodge, whose name was Jim. But I was in no hurry to meet anyone else. I didn't even meet all my roommates for over a week. The first room-mate I met was Poke from Halifax. He ran the maintenance shop where they housed long racks of tools, rolls of carpet, spare odds and ends of lumber, and hundreds of half-used cans of every kind of paint you could imagine. Poke spent most nights at the local bar, the Thirsty Bear Saloon, purchasing Alabama Slammers and Long Island Iced Teas for girls, never getting home until the following morning. When he did get home, he usually carried with him a small kitchen appliance: a toaster, a blender, a garlic crusher, a kitchen scale. At first I worried he secretly burgled cabins, but later he explained that the appliances were just souvenirs, much like the tourists collected snow globes and teaspoons from the places they stayed. By the end of summer we accumulated five toasters, three blenders, four coffee makers, a juicer, two waffle irons, and a whole assortment of other small kitchenware.

Poke showed me a hook by the door where he hung his keys. "The blue Firefly out front is mine," he said. "Borrow it any time you want. If you ever want to do more than borrow it, I'm selling it for five hundred dollars." He was the friendliest of any of my roommates, and I decided if I earned five hundred dollars dishwashing, I would indeed buy his Firefly. I'd need a car to get wherever I ended up: university or college or otherwise.

Shortly after, I met my next roommate: Kyle Cruikshank out of Prince Albert. He worked in maintenance. We passed in the doorway one particularly warm afternoon as I left for my evening shift. He'd just returned from his day one. Cruikshank threw up his hand in a stopping motion, wagged a finger in front of me, and said, "It's Phil Collins out there."

"I beg your pardon?"

He tugged on my fleece. "No Jacket Required." Then he asked me what I'd been doing with my days since I'd arrived. I told him fishing. "Oh, yeah?" He eyed me up and down. "We fish, too. Me, Gibson, and Peritz." Two other roommates I'd yet to meet. "What time you usually head out?"

"Eight or so."

"Acceptable. The three of us have next Tuesday off. I'll let you fish with us." Before I could say one way or the other, Kyle Cruikshank made a clucking sound with his tongue, gave me a thumbs-up, and walked away. "Tuesday at eight," he said, and disappeared into his bedroom. I'd never even imagined a scenario where someone would invite me fishing. Just a few days in Waterton's embrace and already I'd made more potential friends than all my years in Bellevue. A vague warmth washed over me, a warmth I'd only otherwise felt at the start of a fishing day, the brief moment just before the first snap of a cast. I think it was buoyancy.

37. It turns out dishwashing, like so many things, was all about timing. I found it impossible to clear out the bus pans before they spilled over with more dirty dishes. I could never re-stack the steaming hot, freshly cleaned glasses before the shelves emptied. And every time we ran out of clean dessert plates, you could bet a server would fly over to the dessert counter to dish up chocolate brownies for a table of six and

end up spitting out cuss words of frustration even my mother wouldn't speak.

The servers nicknamed me Stoner, on account of my sleepy eyes. They towered dirty dishes in swaying stacks that teetered right over if I didn't hurry out from behind the dishpit to catch them. When I pointed this out to the servers, it seemed to actually encourage higher stacking.

The cooks stuck to themselves and concocted their own name for me. They called me Dishpig. They said that was what dishwashers were and it wouldn't be right calling me anything else. They never talked much, other than to splash pots and cookware into my bus pans and grunt, "Clean 'em, Dishpig."

Despite the challenges, whenever the dining room manager reminded the servers to tip me out, I made surprisingly good money for just dishwashing. Every few days I bought a new T-shirt, and once I bought a pair of shorts (I mostly didn't want to be wearing the same dirty clothes everyday). The rest of the money I stashed away in an emptied deodorant stick in my room. When the deodorant stick was stuffed with five hundred dollars, I'd buy Poke's Firefly.

In Waterton life felt less complicated again. Simpler. I worked. I fished. I slept. What I didn't do was look for my someone. I kept to myself, and I didn't listen to one lousy Kenny Rogers song.

A calm began to settle over me, a quiet comfort I hadn't felt since before Sara.

On one of my afternoons alone, while lazily sloshing my way up a quiet run of water called Cameron Creek, I watched the soft sand squeeze through my toes and smother my bare feet. With its slow drift, clear water, and lack of fly-fishermen, Cameron Creek soon became my second favourite fishing spot, second only to the Crow.

I snapped out a cast and the rod whipped forward, my thumb catching the release trigger just in time. The spoon sailed through the air in a gradual incline then dove down, cutting into the water with a smooth plop. The creek averaged a depth of only about two or three feet, so I reeled in quick to keep the Kamlooper up off the bottom, clear from hooking any rocks or weeds, while also holding the rod tip down to avoid skipping the lure across the surface. Nothing took. I cast again, this time jerking the line occasionally to mimic the anxious darting of a minnow. After several more casts, I took a break to lie down in the August sun.

Resting my head in my hands, peering over the bank, I spied a small brook trout swimming through my reflection. Well veiled against the river's bottom, I wouldn't have even spotted him if he hadn't darted to the surface to inspect a passing fireweed petal. Easily holding his ground against the slow current, he sat ready and waiting, watching what the creek served up that day.

The little brookie snapped at everything that passed. *Chomp! Spit! Whoops, just part of a leaf. Gulp! Spit! No, no, just some bark.* The small fish couldn't have been more than seven inches long, and I guessed from his unparticular eating habits, he probably wouldn't get the chance to grow much bigger. Not if any other fishing lines stalked that creek.

For a moment I considered snapping on a tiny Panther Martin, tossing it out a few feet upstream, cutting it in across the current just in front of him. He wouldn't stand a chance. If I so much as jiggled a shiny beer cap his way he'd dart straight for it. I left my rod on the grass.

I once read that it took a million years for gills to evolve so that brook trout could exist and breathe under water. Probably took another million to come up with those short, wormy markings on their dark, olive backs so that when the sun shines through the rippled water and casts shadows down on the dark river bottom – just as long as that brookie's keeping still – the only thing fish-eating birds and fishermen like me will see is river. But even more amazing to me was that, after fifty million years of perfecting themselves, brook trout still couldn't tell food from shiny, twisted crap. That's the secret to fishing. The advantage anglers have over the fish is that the fish thinks it's looking for food. It doesn't even realize it's actually – out of pure dumb instinct – looking only for allure.

38. I was scouring an onion soup bowl,

crusted with charred cheese and burnt onions, when the laundry girl whispered at me for the first time. I peeked out from behind a stack of bus pans. She was leaning out a large window that opened from the laundry room where the servers chucked through stained tablecloths and soiled cloth napkins to be washed, dried, and folded. Her huge eyes, spaced widely apart, stretched so round and open that she looked in perpetual shock, like she was forever being told the filthiest joke imaginable. She attempted to hide at least one large eye behind long, brown, unevenly chopped sideswept bangs, but any shake of her head or breeze through her hair quickly revealed both alarmingly wide eyes and their black pupils. Her mouth was remarkable in its size, too. Her lips long and fat. Obese even. Just as plump and full in the corners as they were in the middle. The huge eyes and mouth left little room for much else on her face. Her nose was small, her chin undersized, and her ears would've been almost invisible if not for a small plastic hearing aid coiled behind her right ear.

"Hey," she hissed from the laundry window. "Hey, what's that?" She pointed toward the dirty dish a busser had just dumped off.

"What's *what*?" I said.

"That plate." She flicked up her undersized chin, her hands folding the corners of a towel. "What's on it?"

I lifted the plate. "Looks like it was pie." About four forkfuls had been removed, the rest lay toppled on its crusted back.

"Strawberry rhubarb, isn't it?" She clutched the towel to her chest.

"I'm not sure," I shrugged. "The filling's red – "

"Strawberry rhubarb," she confirmed sadly. "They never finish the strawberry rhubarb. They almost never order it to begin with, but when they do, they either send it back or leave it unfinished. Four bites taken, tops."

"Looks about right," I agreed, holding the plate at eye level.

"Everybody orders the *Saskatoon* berry," she snarled, clearly bothered by this. "The *Saskatoon* berry always gets eaten."

I supposed that's why five of those pies crammed the dessert fridge to just the one strawberry rhubarb.

"Bring it here," she demanded.

"What?"

"The pie." She pointed to the half-eaten piece. "Give me the poor thing." She began shifting on the spot, pacing from one side of the opening to the other. "*Quick!*"

I carried the plate with the half-piece of strawberry rhubarb to the window. A hand shot out, snatching the baking like a trout at a stonefly. She pushed the entire half slice between her fat lips and licked her palm clean with a long sweep of her tongue. She waved a pie-stained hand of thanks, rubbed that hand off on her sweater, and continued folding linen. The strawberry-rhubarb smears blended almost naturally with the red speckles of her brown sweater.

"Clean this, Dishpig." One of the cooks clanged a strainer into the sink.

Not ten minutes later I heard the laundry girl whisper again. "Pssst," she said. "*Hey,* what's that?"

"What's *what?*" I said impatiently, jet-spraying coagulated hollandaise from a saucepan.

"Come *on*," she whined, shaking aside a wisp of hair from her wide eyes, beginning to pace. "That stuff." She pointed to a plate.

I tipped up the dish. "Cheesecake."

"Peach?"

"Smells like it," I said.

"They always finish the blueberry or the strawberry or the chocolate. And of course the *Saskatoon berry.* Never the peach. Bring it here."

I got within two steps of the laundry room when she lunged out of the window, snatching the cheesecake with her fist, almost flipping herself through the opening. She gobbled down the dessert before she'd even steadied herself, much of it smudging across her cheek.

I worried the poor girl hadn't eaten in her life.

Later that shift, the busser dumped off a stack of dishes. One plate had a steak with barely a corner sliced off. "Hey," I called. The laundry girl was stuffing an armload of tablecloths into the industrial washer. "Hey!" I called again. She didn't respond, I assumed because of the hearing aid. So I carried the plate to the window and waved it through the opening.

"There's most of a steak here," I said. "Barely even touched."

She brushed away a sweep of hair, knocking a crumble of cheesecake from her cheek. "*So?*"

"Well ... I thought you might still be hungry –"

"Are you nuts?" she sneered, shoving a second load into the washer and slapping the door shut. "Everybody eats *steak*. Steak doesn't need any more eating. Just like Saskatoon berry pie and Saskatoon berry cheesecake and Saskatoon berry soufflé don't need any extra eating. It's the disregarded coleslaws and key lime pies of this world that need eating." She snapped a towel in the air, pinching a corner in each hand and letting it fall out flat on the folding table. "Dump the steak in the ice cream pail." She nodded at a bucket next to the freezer. "I'll see if the campground owner's Lab wants it."

I swept the steak off the plate with a knife. It landed in the pail with a thud. The steak must've spooked the laundry girl because she didn't pop her head out to ask for any of the half-slices of pie or partially picked brownies that got dumped in the dishpit the rest of that night. Which I found a little disappointing. I didn't mind delivering her the desserts. Up close, the laundry girl had a slight smell of algae and river foam, which in its subtlety I found strangely inoffensive. Almost agreeable.

39. ●"Bacon the spincaster!" Alfred

said, grilling a burger on the barbecue off the side of his RV.

"Hello, Alfred." I held out the sleeping bag and tent he'd lent me. "The sleeping bag's washed. I took it to the laundromat this morning after fishing."

"Goodness gracious, son, you didn't have to do that." He gaped at me like I'd hand-quilted the thing. "You hear that, Vronnie? The boy went and had the sleeping bag laundered." Veronica sat propped up on the picnic table next to a speckled-blue dinner plate and an open bag of Cheetos. The barbecue hissed as Alfred plopped on another burger.

"I got a job," I told him. "I'm a dishwasher. They even gave me a place to stay."

"Holy mackerel, that's great! Dishwashing, eh? Most important job in the kitchen, you know." He squinted hard and serious. I nodded like it was common knowledge. Alfred tossed the sleeping bag and tent in the RV. "I guess you're sticking around then."

"I guess I am," I said. "It's simple here. I like that."

"May as well stay," Alfred smiled. "You can't go anywhere but back the way you came. We're standing at a dead end." He motioned toward the steep thrust of mountain behind us. "Your folks must be pleased," Alfred said. "About the job."

"I haven't told them."

He let the screen door slam. "Why the heck not?"

I shrugged. "I don't know where my father is, and my mother ..." I shrugged again.

"For God's sake, get the cell phone, Vronnie," he said, grabbing it himself. "Sweetness mercy, son. You have to call your mom. That's just common courtesy. Here, use our phone." He snapped it open and shoved it in my hand, closing his small hand with a firmness you couldn't argue against.

I stepped around the front of the motorhome and dialed.

"Hello?" Grandma Magic Can's voice sounded tired.

"Grandma?" I put a hand over my free ear. "It's Bacon."

"Bacon! Where are you? Are you OK? The call display says this is a 416 number."

"I'm in Waterton."

"I know 416 ... that's Ontario. You're in Ontario?"

"I'm in Waterton, Grandma."

"What the hell are you doing in Ontario?"

"No, Grandma, I'm not –"

"Good lord, Bacon. Have you got enough money? Are you safe?"

"I'm ok."

"How did you get out there?"

"I'm not in — I'm working, Grandma. I'm a dishwasher. I live in a cabin with six other guys."

"You got a job?"

"Yeah. I'm a dishwasher. I get free staff meals."

"Thank heavens you're safe. How long are you staying out there?"

"I don't know." Alfred squeezed a splotch of barbecue sauce on the burgers, pretending he wasn't listening.

"I'm going to save a little money and I guess I'm going to school. At least I think I'm still going."

"School? Bacon, what's going on? What school?"

"I don't know yet. I haven't figured out if I'm a college man or a university man. Or what to study."

"Bacon, did you have the grades for school? And where are you getting the money for all this? And why did you run off the other night? That bloody Kwon's been out driving around looking for you since you left."

"He what? You mean he's still there?" I was shocked to have beat him leaving by nearly a full week. "Why hasn't he left for Korea yet?"

"Why would he leave for Korea? Though Lord love him if he did. I don't think we'll be ridding ourselves of him anytime soon."

"I don't understand ... and you said he was looking for me. Why is he looking for me?"

"To find you, of course." She made a puffing sound. "None of us knew where the toot you went! Damn fool's been running all over town asking about you. We don't need the whole bloody Pass knowing our business. He and Meryl Streep spent the last few days split between looking for you and looking for a location for that cockamamie restaurant."

I'd have been just as likely to believe my mother had given up bingo than Mr. Kwon and Meryl Streep were still in Bellevue. "Did they find a spot?"

"No. Doubt it matters. One spot's as bad as the next."

"I hope he finds a good one."

"What's that?"

"Nothing." I dug out a half-buried stone from the ground with my shoe, peered down at the damp little crater it left, then nudged it back in.

"Bacon, you got another letter couriered from KC Enterprizes."

The thought of Laszlo tightened my gut. "Just throw it out. It's junk." Just the image of his fat face threatened to pollute the sweet, clear, simple mountain air I'd found.

"Bacon, how long will you be gone?"

"I don't know, Grandma. I have to go to work now. I'll call you in a few days." I closed the cell phone, imagining Mr. Kwon in his dress pants and ironed shirt, driving around dusty Bellevue asking people if they'd seen me.

Alfred scrubbed away at the grill with a steel brush. "You make sure you call home more often," he said, rubbing his hands off on his shirt. "Don't leave family forgotten." He took the phone from me and replaced it with a plate. "Here. I made you a burger."

40. Pretty much every evening

I worked, the laundry girl worked, too. And pretty much every evening I worked, I delivered her half-eaten meals from the dishpit. But she was a difficult person to predict. One night I brought her a partially picked-over strawberry rhubarb pie. She continued folding laundry like I was nothing more than the smell of algae around her. "I don't *feel* like pie," she finally said. And sure enough, the only thing she'd eat that night was cheesecake. The next night she craved only partly spooned-up sundaes. Sometimes she'd snub the entire dessert world and decide to munch only on half-eaten salad. But not Caesar salad—Caesar salads didn't need any more eating. And certainly not Greek salad, everybody ordered Greek salad. All I know is she decided what to eat and it was too bad for me if that wasn't something I brought her.

Her name was Woodrat Lynn-Marie Seever. She'd often lift ants off the syrup bottles and carry them outside to release them in the grass, calling it her "troubled ant relocation program." People step on ants, she said, kids fry them with magnifying glasses. On her way back inside I saw her swat down a butterfly that had fluttered in her path. Some nights she'd nap on the linen piles instead of folding them, if that's how she felt. Some nights she'd wash, dry, and fold her loads with such focused vigour, her face would sweat. She lived not in a cabin, but in a tent at the campground. Some servers suggested that's what was responsible for her unique algae smell.

"Woodrat?" I said one evening, after delivering her two-thirds of an order of potato skins. She was only eating leftover appetizers that night. "Now that's a strange name. Is it short for anything?"

"Yes, it is," she said, scooping up three fingers' worth of stray bacon bits.

"What's it short for?"

"Katherine."

"*Katherine*? Woodrat is short for Katherine?"

"Un-huh." She popped the last half-wedge of potato skin into her large mouth, then handed me the empty plate.

"How is Woodrat short for Katherine?"

"It's got fewer letters."

I watched her scratch an armpit, pinching at something clumpy under her shirt.

"More dishes, Stoner!" A server plunked down a stack of dishes, teetering on the edge of the dishpit. I darted over to steady the plates before they toppled.

"They torment you because you're new. Just learning your job. Because you're quiet and timid." Woodrat sunk into an unfocused gaze on the wall above me, like she was remembering something. "You'd think they'd do the opposite."

The servers were also supposed to clear the plates for me. At least that's how the manager explained it. But they never did.

"You've been here what, three weeks?" Woodrat said. "How come I never see you at the saloon?"

"I don't know," I shrugged, scraping salmon skin from a plate. "I never see you at the saloon either."

"That's because you're not there."

"Oh, right."

"You don't hang out with many people, do you?"

I shrugged. "Do you?"

"Just one." Her arm was bent up under her shirt, rummaging and shifting like she was sorting through a junk drawer for change. "I don't need *many*. There's no point in hanging out with people who are already hanging out. They don't need hanging out with." The *one* was her friend Chris. Almost every night Chris met Woodrat at the end of our shifts and they'd walk each other over to the Thirsty Bear Saloon. Chris bartended at another restaurant. She was quiet, never said boo to anyone, kept her sharp-edged chin and brick-like grimace to herself. She carried an expression of frustration that never changed, like she was stuck endlessly trying to twist open a jelly jar that just wouldn't pop. Chris was the target of many unflattering comments I'd overheard from the servers. Woodrat said the servers were cruel and Chris was sometimes funnier than you'd expect.

"You work evenings," Woodrat said. "So what do you do all day?"

"I go fishing."

"Fishing?" Her lips spread into a wide smile. "What a perfectly good way to spend a day."

"You fish?"

"Of course I fish." She flipped the hair from an eye with a flick of her head. "I'm from the Yukon. I've caught lake trout fat as a beer fridge and jackfish long enough to surf on."

I imagined her crouched under a wave, her thick, red arms stretched out, riding atop a giant pike. "Do you fly-fish or spin-cast?"

"I do both," Woodrat said. "I do neither. Depends on the day. I'll catch a fish with a meatball tied to a wad of yarn if that's what I feel like using. Mostly I just use a twig."

"A twig?"

"A twig."

"You can't fish with a twig."

"But I already have." The innocent confusion in her eyes suggested she wasn't putting me on.

"I spincast," I said.

"Potato-of-the-day," she shrugged. "Whatever greases your reel."

It was relieving that she didn't smirk or frown at my mention of spincasting. I guess it doesn't rank too far below the twig in the accepted hierarchy of fishing instruments.

"So that's why I never see you down at the saloon. Because you spend your days fishing and your evenings working."

"I guess," I said. "That and I need to save money instead of spend it." And save I'd been doing. The emptied deodorant stick, hidden inside a slit of my pillow, was stuffed full with even more than the five hundred dollars I'd hoped to squirrel away. Now I could look at covering school costs, too. As soon as I figured out if I was a university or college man.

Woodrat sprayed stain remover on a tablecloth. "What are you saving for?"

"I'm going to buy my roommate's Firefly," I said proudly. "And drive it to school."

"And study what?"

I shoved a tray of glasses into the washer and tugged down the door. "I don't know yet."

"Potato-of-the-day," she shrugged.

"Potato *what*?"

"I've been saving, too." Woodrat chucked the spray bottle down and leaned in through the window, resting her elbows on the windowsill. "For adventure. I leave right after the September long. I'm going to the Bahamas to do something nobody's ever done. *Ever*."

"Ever?" I held a scrub brush to my chest. I didn't know there was anything left that nobody had done. "What are you going to do?"

"I'm going to do some good in this world."

"Nobody's ever done good before?"

"No, lots of people have done good. Lots are doing good. But I'm going to do the good nobody else is doing. That nobody's ever done." A proud look came over her face. Her fat lips parted slightly, as if mouthing something silently. "I'll be the first. You'll see. A pioneer. It all starts in the Bahamas."

"So, nobody's helping the people in the Bahamas?"

She considered me for a moment. "I don't know," she said. "I'm not sure many Bahamians need help. But I'm not going there for them." She glanced to both sides and lowered her voice. "I'm going for the dogs."

"The dogs?"

"Shhhh!" she hushed, continuing in a whisper. "Eleven thousand stray dogs roaming the streets of Nassau." She gripped her hands on the windowsill as if it were a podium. "Eleven thousand hungry, neglected dogs suffering from abuse, burns, broken limbs, all limping around with open wounds and who knows what else."

"Nobody's helping the dogs," I said triumphantly.

"No, no, no, no. There's lots of people helping dogs." She glanced over her shoulder, checking the dryer. "Humane Societies, PETA, local groups. Some people feed the dogs, some get the dogs spayed or neutered, some fix broken limbs."

"Well, then what are *you* going to do?" I hunched over the dishpit, stretching to hear her.

"What nobody else is doing. What nobody else *will* do. Help the unhelped dogs."

One of the cooks frisbeed a saucepan from the kitchen into the water-filled bus pan. "Wash it, Dishpig." Water soaked my apron and splashed onto the floor around my feet. I plucked the pan out and set it in a rack.

Woodrat glared toward the kitchen. "I wash their whites, you know."

"Their *whites*?"

"Yeah, their cooking clothes."

"Oh," I said. "Yeah, I guess you would."

"I'll put urushiol in his pants."

"OK," I said, wondering if I should be putting urushiol in my pants. "But the dogs ... what are you going to do for the dogs?"

She motioned me over to the window with her finger. "If I tell you," she whispered, "you can't tell anybody else. Nobody."

I agreed.

"Promise me."

"I promise."

"You're supposed to use my name when you promise." She jabbed a finger at me. "That makes it contractual. Promise me and then say my name."

"OK, OK. I promise ..." I paused for a moment. "Do you prefer Katherine or Woodrat?"

"Woodrat, of course," she scowled. "Or I wouldn't have shortened it."

"Right. Sorry, I just never heard that name before."

"What about your name? I only know you as Stoner or Dishpig. What's your real name?"

"Bacon!" Jim the barrel-chested owner stomped into the kitchen. "Phone!"

"Phone?"

"Yeah, the phone. The noisy thing that rings. That little device we use to take reservations. It ain't taking any reservations right now because somebody's on it for you."

I followed his heavy steps over to the front desk. He held the phone out at me like it was a rock he'd found tossed through his front window.

The little budgie behind the front desk screeched in a reprimanding tone.

"Hello?" I said. The other end was silent. "Hello?" It was an uncomfortable silence, the kind where you just know somebody's there. You could almost swear you *felt* them. Or hear the string of spit stretching between their parted teeth, right next to your ear. "Who is this?" I demanded.

Finally, a cold, flat voice answered. The familiar croaking made me stiffen like a frightened cat. "Hello, Bacon," the voice said.

My mouth went dry. "*Sara*? How ... how did you find me?"

"Called your Grandma. Even introduced myself. She said you were in Ontario. But I knew that couldn't be. You don't like to go too far from home. Or is it that you just don't like to go with me? Seems Granny jotted down a number you'd called her from. A 416 number. So I called it." A rush of heat passed through my body. "Had a nice chat with Alfred. You're in Waterton, Bacon. I sweet-talked old Alfie good. But he was still a little shy about telling me where you worked. We negotiated a little, but he wasn't caving. So I threatened to crawl through the phone and eat his fucking face off. That's how I found you, Bacon."

Jim the barrel-chested man threw an exaggerated glare at the watch on one of his folded arms.

"What do you want, Sara?"

"Oh, listen to you. Bacon's gone all business. Growed right up, eh?" She chuckled in a way that sounded like it was oozing through a snarl. "I need you to come get me. Take me to Vancouver."

"Vancouver?"

"Yeah, I hear it's *wild*."

"Sara, I can't take you to Vancouver. I have a job —"

"Listen you little cocksucker, I have a court date tomorrow because of you. You'd best come get me the hell out of here before they start looking for me again."

"Sara, I don't even have a car anymore. And you can't skip out on a court date —"

"I'll skip out of whatever the hell I decide to skip out of. Borrow a car. Rent one. Buy one. Steal one. I don't give a shit. You just be here tomorrow. Pick me up at noon at the Smitty's in Westbrook Mall. You got that?"

"Sara, I'm not —"

"Smitty's at noon. You stood me up once, Bacon." Her voice dropped to a caged whisper, and I could just see her words seething through clenched teeth. "You don't want to do it again." I heard her end click dead and felt the phone drop away from my ear.

41. I needed beer.

I hurried the last tray through the washer with shaking hands, dumped the plates on the shelf, pushed a mop over some of the dishpit floor, hung my apron, and bolted for the saloon. I didn't even wait for my tip outs. My first ever steps into the Thirsty Bear were slow and cautious. I peeked around the doorway and scanned the large room as though half expecting Sara to be lurking somewhere inside. I retreated to a table in a dark corner to the side of the bar, as far from anyone else as possible. When the waitress approached I asked what was on tap. She didn't know.

Neither did the bartender. For my benefit he pulled forward the unlabelled handle, letting a stream of golden liquid spill freely onto the floor to prove something was there. I ordered whatever that was. Then ordered another.

Beer pooled on my tabletop, splashing down from the mug in my trembling hand. The third beer eventually steadied my grip.

Halfway through my fourth beer, a freckle-faced girl with blue eyelids and a Simpson's overbite slinked up to my table. I saw her all at once and jumped in my seat. She had on a white tank-top with spaghetti straps, and low hanging jeans. A small push of belly arched out over her belt line. "Your name's Bacon, right?"

I confirmed that my name was Bacon, but not before scanning the bar nervously, wondering why she was asking.

"Is that your real name or a nickname?"

She had a slick, downward sloping nose that forced my eyes right down to her tight fitting top. I had to keep adjusting my glance so as not to be rude. "Bacon is my real name," I said, squinting down inside the narrow neck of my beer bottle.

"Great." A row of protruding top teeth flashed within her smile. "I'd heard that was your real name. That's wonderful news." Her breath carried a strange wisp of tennis ball scent. I couldn't imagine what odd diet or curious toothpaste or peculiar chewing gum stood behind such breath, but each time her mouth opened I could almost hear the cracking tin lid rip from a fresh can of tennis balls. "Would you like to neck?" she said.

I looked up from my beer. "I'm sorry. Did you say ... *neck*?"

"Yes, that's right." More tennis ball breath escaped from her overbite. "We can neck either here or out back by the garbage bins. Wherever you prefer."

I felt like I'd been hit with a forehand volley. No words reached my mouth. All I could do was stare. There wasn't a square speck of skin on the girl that wasn't painted with freckles. Even the soft puff of her belly. The shakes returned to my hand, and a grow-ing warmth in my groin reminded me of the problem my mother cursed me for possessing.

My grip on Waterton's simplicity was slipping. I sat fumbling with the label on my beer, when Kyle Cruikshank appeared at the table, squaring his shoulders at the tank-top girl. He wore a desert-patterned camouflage ball cap and a Dri Mesh long sleeved shirt with "Trophy Fisherman" embroidered over a twisting trout on the left breast.

"I got maybe two songs left," Kyle Cruikshank said to the tank-top girl, "then I have to Michael *Bolt*on out of here. We're fishing the narrows early tomorrow." He stopped himself and turned only slightly in my direction, adjusting his black polarized sunglasses, and added, "My roommate and I will both need our sleep."

I'd forgotten about our fishing arrangement. Or perhaps it just seemed so implausible that I'd be joining *the boys* for a day of fishing that I'd simply denied it. But it was real. Maybe it would become a weekly outing. A set day we'd commit to. A custom. A ritual between men. Years from now we'd still converge annually, leaving our families for late September trips to northern Saskatchewan or the Queen Charlotte Islands. For a moment, Waterton seemed right again.

The tank-top girl threw an arm over Kyle Cruikshank's shoulder. "Are you asking me to dance, Kyle?" As she whirled to face him, I saw a slow, soft, bobbing swing to her tank-top that tugged at the spaghetti straps, and squeezed my throat closed. The grip on my bottle nearly broke it.

"We can dance if you want to," Kyle Cruikshank said.

"You know how much I love dancing. But Kyle, I'm concerned your asking has less to do with dancing and more to do with keeping me from sitting here at this table with Bacon. You're a possessive little fellow."

Kyle Cruikshank pressed his mouth shut, then said again, "We can leave your friends behind."

The tank-top girl made a pursed smile. "ok, Kyle. We'll dance." She took his hand, patted it, and turned back toward me. "But I still need to neck with Bacon." She twirled a freckled finger at me. "So hold tight, Bacon. I'll be right back."

Kyle Cruikshank led them away and, while he did, he tugged down the brim of his camouflage cap.

That night, Waterton, my haven of simplicity, had been

invaded. On multiple fronts. After finishing the last swig of my beer, I hurried back to my cabin. I took the dark, lakeside path, keeping an eye out for everything.

42. The next morning I scuttled down-

stairs to wait for Kyle Cruikshank, Gibson, and Peritz a full hour before we were even supposed to meet.

I scrubbed the outer-casing of my closed-face reel with a knuckle brush, cleaned and greased the gears, and spooled on new line. Then I pulled off that line and spooled on more. I cleaned each grommet on the rod with a Q-tip, and carefully washed the rusted hooks of my old Kamlooper spoon. As I did, the front door crept open and Poke tiptoed in, a food proces-sor tucked under an arm. He set the appliance on the counter, covered a yawn with the back of his hand, threw me a lazy good-night wave and shut himself away into his bedroom. I could hear him snoring within seconds. I found it odd how he always insisted on sleeping as soon as he rolled in from his all-nighters. He'd be up within twenty minutes anyway, strolling off to work in his paint splattered coveralls to spend his day painting fences or ceiling stipple or countertops or concrete basement floors. Then again, there was a reasonable chance those twenty minutes were all he was getting for sleep.

All at once, I heard three bedroom doors slam closed, two on the top floor, one on the main. Then heavy marching down the stairs. Cruikshank, Gibson, and Peritz turned the corner and stepped into the living room in unison, as if choreographed.

The three of them stood in a line before me, each clad in shiny black neoprene waders, black polarized sunglasses, black three-quarter-finger spandex gloves. Hardwood teardrop fishing nets draped over each of their backs. Their left fists clutched pairs of full-foot-design fins, their right hands gripped tightly around long, thick, black, cloth-covered rod tubes. Tucked under each of their left arms, stretching from the floor to their armpits, turned on their sides, were black vinyl float tube belly boats. Not since Sara Mulligan sat on top of me, whoofing and snarling had I seen anything so menacing.

"Cool belly boats," was all I could say.

"They're Fish Cat 4s," Kyle Cruikshank said, pushing his sunglasses up his nose.

"Deluxe," Gibson added.

I stood scratching an itch on the back of an ankle with the toe of my tennis shoe – the pair I didn't mind getting wet. In the silence that followed I tried to keep my green and brown spincasting rod with thumb-button trigger hidden behind my back.

"What is that?" Peritz said, craning his neck to see.

"Is that a...?" Gibson's face twisted like he'd just caught wind of a fart. "That's a ..." He couldn't bring himself to say the word. The three of them exchanged glances. For a moment they all stood staring me down. The only sound in the cabin was muffled snoring coming from Poke's room.

"Listen, Bacon," Kyle Cruikshank finally said, looking from me to the other two and back at me. "There're some docks just out back here." He nodded at the window facing the lake. "Maybe you can try your spincasting off those. We're going a little further out in the lake. Fly-fishing. I think you'd best go David Lee Roth. You know? Go solo." The three of them rolled their Fish Cat 4s out the cabin door and down into the lake. As I watched them slipping into their belly boats, kicking up their fins, gracefully splashing themselves further out into the lake, I found myself thinking of those trout my father gripped on the rocks along the river's edge, those ones too small for frying, my father's big hands shoving the small, thin fish back into the water, clumsily smearing away the thin layer of slime that protects the fish from infection.

I snatched Poke's keys and dumped myself into the Firefly, headed not to the narrows where Kyle Cruikshank, Gibson, and Peritz wielded their nine-foot thunder rods, and not to the shallow bays of the upper lake where I'd likely run into other fly-fishermen, and certainly not to Calgary to pick up Sara and drive her to

Vancouver. My destination was the one spot simplicity might still exist: the trickling creek I'd been so fortunate to have always enjoyed to myself. Cameron Creek. But just before I squealed the Firefly out of the driveway, the passenger door hurled open, a slight waft of algae brushed across my face, and Woodrat Lynn-Marie Seever heaved herself in. "I snatched some leftovers from last night's shift." She wagged a brown bag clenched in her fist. "In case we get hungry." She must have read the startled look on my face because then she added, "You *are* going fishing, right?"

"Where did you come from?" I glanced out the windshield like she'd fallen from the sky.

"I was at Chris' last night." She pointed to another cabin across the street. "I saw you pulling out, so I ran over. You spend too much time alone." She pulled out a flattened half-slice of strawberry rhubarb pie and stuffed most of it into her mouth. "Guess I'm hungry now. Want some?" She held out the crumpled remains of pie crust in her hand.

I shook my head partly at the pie, partly at Woodrat, and partly at the idea I spent too much time alone. I *wanted* to be alone. As grateful as I was to see Woodrat not packing a nine-foot fly rod, or sorting through a box of hand-tied flies, or wearing a mushroom-coloured fishing vest, or rolling a vinyl belly boat, I still wanted to fish alone. Actually, I didn't see any kind of rod with Woodrat. Or any tackle, for that matter. All she'd brought was pie. "Look," I explained, "I'm sorry but I want to fish alone today."

"No you don't. You were planning on fishing with your idiot roommates. Seeing as I watched them roll off without you, that means you've got room for me. Besides, I want to teach you how to fish."

"Teach me? Teach *me*?" I yanked up the parking break. "What makes you think I need teaching?"

"We all need teaching. There's always room for learning."

"And *you're* going to teach *me*?"

"That's right. I'm going to teach you how to fish. What I show you, you can take or leave. But I've certainly got something to show you."

"Why?"

"Because your roommates are assholes and I want you to know more about fishing than them." She shoved the parking break down. "Now drive."

Maybe it was the confident line across her wide mouth, or the unblinking glare behind the brown hair that draped over her huge round eyes, or the small squish of pie clinging to a strand of that hair. Maybe it was the strawberry rhubarb stains on her outstretched hand that still offered the crushed pastry. Maybe I just wanted to know what she was going to do for the Bahamian dogs that nobody else had done. Maybe I wanted to see what she thought she could teach me. Or maybe I really did want some company. Whatever the reason, I didn't argue. I drove.

As we wound up Cameron Road, Woodrat lurched in her seat, rubbing her arms against her ribs, grunting and pinching at her chest. Finally I had to ask, "Are you all right?"

"Mmm." She shook her hair. "It's this bra. *Way* too tight. It's killing me."

"Why are you wearing it then?"

"It's not the sixties, Bacon." She ground her back hard against her seat. "Women wear bras."

I felt my face flush warm at the thought of a whole generation of women not wearing bras. "No, I meant why don't you wear one that *fits*."

"This is the one I grabbed," she shrugged, bending an arm behind her back, adjusting the bra's strap. "How am I supposed to know what's going to be in someone's dryer? Potato-of-the-day."

"Potato-of-the-*what*? You keep saying that. Wait—what do you mean someone's *dryer*?"

"I grab other women's bras from the dryers at the laundromat."

"You *take* bras? Why?"

"What's the alternative?"

"To *buy* bras," I said. "Bras that fit."

"Exactly," she nodded as though some point had been made for her. "Potato-of-the-day."

"What does that mean?"

"Potato-of-the-day? It means potato-of-the-day. Just means

whatever. I hear the servers calling it out in the kitchen all the time. A cook will ask, 'What side for table twelve?' and the server says, 'Potato-of-the-day.' I love that. They don't say stuffed potato or baked potato or roasted potato wedges or whatever the hell the potato actually is that day. They just say potato-of-the-day. Even the menu out front says, 'Comes with potato-of-the-day.' The customers don't even know what the hell it'll be. Only some-one who just doesn't care would order that. It could turn out to be fries! If some guy is the type of guy to order potato-of-the-day, well, you could bring out a raw fucking potato still clinging to big fat clumps of garden dirt, drop it on his plate, and say fuck you, and he'd just shrug and say, 'Whatever man. Potato-of-the-day.' That's living. I love that phrase."

"But wouldn't people in the restaurant just ask what that night's potato-of-the-day was before ordering?"

Woodrat faced me, blinked. "Maybe," she said. "Never thought of that. Who cares? Potato-of-the-day. Speaking of the servers ..." Her chin further receded as her mouth turned taught and seri-ous. "Are they tipping you out?"

"Yeah," I said, gearing the Firefly down for a tight turn. "Some nights."

She nodded slowly and knowingly. "You make sure they do it every night. If they don't, you tell me." I didn't know why she cared one way or the other about my tips.

We parked the Firefly at a picnic pull-off and wandered upstream to find some pools. The creek plunged down into a shallow gorge where the grey rock of the steep walls glared in the morning sun.

"Let's fish," Woodrat called out like she was announcing the start of a horse race.

I readied my green and brown second-hand spincasting rod with the closed-face reel and thumb-button trigger, but Woodrat simply stuffed her hands into the back of her jeans.

I fired a cast upstream. Not the ideal direction to spincast; the lure loses much of its action riding back with the current. Woodrat watched. We moved our way up the creek, I'd throw out casts and occasionally she'd scurry ahead, scouting out the water, watching.

I had no idea if she could fish but she was a natural trout spotter. She'd creep up quietly to a bend in the creek, crouch slightly, peer up around the corner, and whisper the locations of the trout she saw up ahead in the clear water. And she'd do it without spooking any of them.

"Know any secrets?" she said.

"Secrets?"

"Yeah, fishing secrets."

"Not really," I shrugged. "A guy back home says you're supposed to talk to the fish." I laughed, remembering Mr. Kwon in his dress pants and shiny black shoes standing in the muddy bank.

"I think that's a good idea," Woodrat said. "What are we fishing for again?"

"Cutthroats."

"And if we catch one we're supposed to just throw it back?"

"Yeah. There's zero possession for cutthroat on this creek."

"Zero possession," she chuckled. "That's a good phrase. Maybe that explains lots of things. So really," she turned a lip out pensively, "we don't even need a rod."

"What? Of course we do. It's not fishing without a rod."

"Nah." She yanked the rod from my hands and tossed it aside. "I've found all the fish today. And I didn't have a rod. Spotted them from a good distance, too." She dropped herself down, sitting cross-legged next to the creek, holding her knees like she was about to pray. "If we're not going to keep any, we may as well just watch them."

"No, no, no," I said, retrieving my rod. "There're only two ways to fish for trout: spincasting and fly-fishing. And both ways need a rod."

"That's stupid. There's always another way."

"No. No, there isn't. Not in trout fishing. There are basic rules. You need a rod to *go* fishing, you need to cast that rod to *be* fishing, and you need to *land* the fish to say you caught it. Those are the rules."

"Who says? Don't be silly, I've got six fish today, you've got none. Who's doing more *fishing?*"

179

"No, neither of us *got* any fish. You just *spotted* some – "

"Look!" Her arm flung out, pointing to the water. "There's another one. That's seven. I'm good at fishing."

"You don't understand – "

"I understand perfectly. It's you who's constricting himself to goofy rules and *two* ways. I'm fishing *my* way. The Woodrat way." She sprang to her feet and tromped further ahead. "And here's another way," she called back, crouching down at the edge of the bank, feet flat, knees thrust out in opposite directions. She hovered a long twig out over the water, stretching so far I half expected her to fall. She wagged the twig's tip in slow circles, just a fly's wing from the surface, slowly around and around, occasionally dabbing the budded point on the water with the slightest touch – not enough to even form a ripple. She continued the slow sedative circles, like handwriting across the water's reflection.

"What are you doing?" I said.

She lifted a finger to her mouth to shush me. The circles continued, slow and entrancing, around and around. The three little buds of the twig's end passed just over the water. Then a fish appeared. About an eight-inch cutthroat, drifting to the surface, transfixed on the slow-circling twig. Woodrat wagged the twig into tighter, tinier, and even slower circles. The fish rose slow but deliberate, even breaking the surface, bobbing the tip of its head out from the water. It hovered there almost motionless, watching the circling tip. Woodrat dipped the twig just below the surface, reached just under the trout's crimson gills, and tickled its chin. She turned toward me, her plump lips smiling. "There's always another way," she whispered. She withdrew the stick and the fish drifted slowly back down to the creek bottom, swimming leisurely away.

I'd never seen anything like it.

Just seconds after, I already began wondering if I really saw what I thought I saw. I stood mute, unable to think of anything to say.

Woodrat set down the twig and touched the yellow flower of a strawberry weed beside her. I knew the strong-stemmed, hairy-branched weed from helping Grandma Magic Can pick them from the hill out back. It was one of her favourites. I remember she said it was also called "cinquefoil." Grandma could well have been out back picking cinquefoil right then at that same time Woodrat and I were peering down silently at the one between us. She would've claimed I stole her magic can and sucked up too much stinkweed if I told her what I'd just watched Woodrat do with that twig.

Woodrat looked up at me, her hand shielding her eyes from the glaring sun. "It's not just the Bahamas, you know," she said. "After I help the dogs there I'm going to do the same thing in India. Then Thailand. Turkey. Central America."

I nodded, still stunned by what I'd seen.

"Philippines. Laos."

"That's a lot of travelling," I said absently. "When would you come home again?"

"I don't know," she said, reflecting for a moment. "I think maybe wherever I am will become home." Woodrat used her thumb to dig a little moat around the strawberry weed. "Sometimes you have to leave home to find home."

"Won't you miss your family?" I asked. "Being gone so long."

She touched a hand to her hair, flipping forward some strands to cover her hearing aid, then shrugged. "There was zero possession in that creek," she said, pulling up the strawberry weed by the stem. She shook off a clump of soil that clung to the pale roots.

The high sun was catching the tiny crests of the creek, like sparkling streams of tinsel on a fan.

"What do you eat?" Woodrat asked, flinging the weed into the creek.

"What do you mean?"

"Did you have breakfast? Did you bring a lunch? What will you eat today?"

I pulled from my pocket a bag of sunflower seeds. "I brought these," I said. "And we get a staff meal before work."

"We get hamburgers and fries."

"Usually," I nodded. "Sometimes it's mozza sticks."

"Crap and crap." She snatched the bag of sunflower seeds from my hand. "And crap."

181

"They're just sunflower seeds," I said.

"Read the label." She shook the bag. "Cholesterol free! The factory's got so much cholesterol, they throw it in for free. You need a home-cooked meal."

"I don't think I'm ready to go home just yet."

"No, I don't mean *home* home, as in wherever you're from—"

"Bellevue."

"OK, Bellevue—potato-of-the-day. You need to cook something once in a while. Your cabin's got a kitchen, doesn't it?"

"I guess, yeah."

"You've never cooked for yourself, have you?"

I shook my head. "My mother did most of the cooking. Never looked much fun to me."

"Fun?" She pushed a handful of hair from her face. It swung right back down. "I'll bet that cabin's kitchen has never been used," she frowned. "Tell you what. To christen your kitchen, Chris and I will come over and cook us all dinner. In exchange, you have to start making one home-cooked meal a day in that kitchen for the rest of the summer. It's good you learn now for when you're at school. You can't live off mozza sticks and sunflower seeds. Fair deal? Not that anyone ever keeps deals, but deal?"

I didn't know why she cared what I ate or didn't eat. I'd never really given my diet much thought. But we agreed and even shook on it. "But you also have to tell me about the dogs," I said, not letting go of her hand.

She smiled a fat-lipped smile. "Agreed."

43. "Bacon, thank God!" Grandma
said. "It's about time you called. How's Ontario?"

"Grandma," I said, leaning against the glass of the phone booth. "I'm not in Ontario."

"You're not? Good heavens you're not. This is a 403 number— you're in Alberta now!"

"I'm in Waterton, Grandma."

"You're in Waterton? What happened to your job?"

"I still have it … I'm a dishwasher in Waterton."

"Did you get transferred?"

"No, I was never in … nevermind. How're you doing, Grandma?"

"Me? My bones are tired. You need to phone me, Bacon."

"I am phoning."

"I know you're phoning. I don't mean right *now*, I mean you should phone more often. I'd prefer once daily. Even twice if you can. Especially if you're going to be traipsing all over the country."

"OK, but I wasn't –"

"How's your job?"

"Fine. Dishwashing's all about timing."

"Is that right? I guess that old Kwon would know, too. He's been doing the dishes every night since the washer broke last week. Says he's just doing his part. Right. Doing his part mixing up the whole bloody kitchen. I can't find a thing anymore; who the hell knows where he puts anything."

"He's still there?"

"Of course. The fool's still fumbling all over the Pass each morning looking for the perfect spot for that bloody restaurant I doubt we'll ever see. Though better he's off wasting his time driving around than screwing things up around here. Yesterday he messed up our fence with some God-awful brown paint."

"He painted the fence?"

"If that's what you want to call it."

"Isn't that good?"

"It's ugly! And a waste of time. I was planning to tear the damn thing down soon anyway. Put up a new one." As I remembered it, Grandma had always talked about wanting to *paint* the fence, not tear it down.

"Is Mr. Kwon doing OK?" I asked.

"How would I know?" I heard a puff of dismissive air snort from her mouth. "He did say to say hello, though."

"He what?"

"He said hello."

"I didn't hear him –"

"No, he's not *here*. He just said to say hello the next time I talked to you."

"Why did he say that?"

"Why? I don't know, Bacon. Why does he do anything? Why the hell is he even here? I guess he just wanted to say hi. No biggie. He asks about you."

"What does he ask about?"

"Everything. What you're doing, how's your job. He was pleased as punch when you got a job."

"Tell him I was asking about him, too."

"What on earth for?" I could almost hear her frowning. "I'd pass you over to your mother, but she's at bingo."

"How come you didn't go?"

"That bloody Kwon and Meryl Streep went with her. Nothing's sacred anymore. He said we could make it an 'outing.' Can you imagine? Everything's upside-down around here, Bacon. You should come home."

"Maybe soon, Grandma," I said, but I didn't even sound convincing to me. I envisioned Mr. Kwon at the bingo hall, his dark suit against a sea of Northern Reflections sweaters, greying T-shirts, and frumpy golf shirts. A tray of bingo nachos and those extra large Cokes. Meryl Streep blotting her own forehead with my mother's dauber.

"Grandma," I said, "have you ever heard of anyone fishing with a twig?"

"A what?"

"A twig."

"Fishing for a twig?"

"No, fishing *with* a twig."

Grandma went silent, likely considering the idea. "Never," she said. "But I'll tell you what I have heard: don't cover the sky with the palm of your hand."

"What does that mean?"

"Actually, I don't know what that one means, but what the hell does fishing with a twig mean?"

"Nevermind."

"Oh, Bacon, did your nice friend Sara get a hold of you?"

The mention of her name turned my mouth dry. "We talked," I said.

"Oh, good. She sounds lovely. You've been popular around here, Bacon. That charming man from KC Enterprizes who'd been sending you couriered mail showed up at the door this morning."

"He what?" One of my knees buckled; I had to brace myself against the glass of the phone booth. "What?"

"Wonderful man. Very pleasant. I told him you weren't home and we didn't know when you'd be coming back."

"Oh, thank God...."

"So I gave him that same number I gave your friend Sara."

"You what?!"

"Why, is something wrong? Bacon, what's the matter?"

"Nothing. Nothing's wrong." I pushed the phone so hard into my forehead I thought it might bust through and stab me in the brain. "I have to go now, Grandma."

"What's going on, Bacon?"

"Nothing, I just have to go." I darted across the street, back to my cabin, flew up the stairs and into my room.

I was too late.

The place had been ransacked.

I knew instantly. The floor was clear of clutter and tracks in the shag suggested the carpet had possibly even been vacuumed. My strewn clothes were now folded and stacked neatly in the drawers of my dresser. The bed was made, sheets tucked tight and crisp. The pillows appeared fluffed and set perfectly centred at the head of the bed. The hidden deodorant stick removed. Gone. It had been stuffed with nearly eight hundred dollars.

44. ● Trudging into the lodge, I

passed by a gust of laughter exploding from the lounge. My feet planted firm and still in the lobby, listening to two familiar laughs. The sharp, abrupt heaving *har hars* I attributed to Jim the barrel-chested owner. The other whiny laugh that squealed like a dropped accordion was unmistakable. My feet shuffled me toward the laughter. I poked open one of the saloon-style swing doors and peeked into the lounge.

"Bacony Boy!" Laszlo Maximilian Mursky raised a mug of draft. "There ya are!" The swinging doors creaked and swung to a stop, fanning the air behind me.

"That's the dude you're looking for?" Jim snorted.

"Yes, indeedy doo," Laszlo said. "I hope you'll excuse me while I grab old Bacony Boy." Laszlo hopped off the stool and dug for his wallet while making a scribbling motion to the bartender.

"Don't bother." Jim threw up a lazy hand. "It's on me. You made me laugh, Mr. Mursky, and I don't laugh easy. I'm buying your beer." Laszlo objected, Jim insisted, and they repeated that routine several times before Laszlo relented. I stood staring stupidly, mouth slightly open, unable to speak a word even if I'd had one. I watched the two of them shake hands, slap each other's shoulders, and continued watching while Laszlo guided me out the front door.

"It's my weight, isn't it?" Laszlo said, stuffing his hands into his pockets as he led us through the parking lot. My lip twitched, trying to answer, but no words materialized on my parched tongue. Laszlo stopped, turned his back to me, and stared down at his Birkenstocks. "That's why you ignore me." His head nodded so hard it vibrated. "You're not interested in communicating with pudgy people, are you?"

"That's ridiculous," I finally managed. "Look, Mr. Mursky, I want my money back—"

"It's a pudgy thing." Laszlo's head shook.

"Give me my money back."

"Understandable," he said. "Many people judge pudgy folks."

"Good Lord, you're not even that big—"

"*Big?* I never used the word *big.*" He whirled to face me. "I said *pudgy.* You said big. You think I'm *big?* Why don't you just say fat-ass or lard-face or seven-chins? Get it all out, Bacon!"

"I didn't say anything like that!" Laszlo turned from me again. When I stepped around to meet his eyes, he shuffled around, keeping his back to me. "I said you *weren't* big—"

"Nevermind. You've ignored my letters, refused to return my calls, and continued to ignore your debt. Then to top it all off, you're back to hurling names at me again. You made me get in my car, drive three and a half hours, all the way to the deepest, darkest God forsaken corner of the province to track you down. Well, now here I am. Problems people create for themselves don't just blow away in the wind, you know. These kinds of things always catch up to you."

"Look, Mr. Mursky, give me my money back. I have to work soon. Do you know what time it is?"

"I haven't the slightest. I don't wear watches or jewellery. I don't believe in it. It's excess and consumerism."

I squinted at the lodge's front window. The lobby clock read 4:51. "I have nine minutes. You took my money from my room."

"No, I took *Karla's* money from your room." He spun back around, handing me the emptied deodorant stick. "And I cleaned up a bit while I searched for it. Honest to goodness, touch pinkies, your room was a pigsty. Good thing I keep a bottle of concentrated orange cleaner in the car — completely organic. Made entirely from plant-based ingredients. It's wonderful."

"That money was to buy a car and pay for school."

"You have student loans to pay for school. And that money quite simply couldn't have been for a car because it was already spent and spoken for. And not to further piddle on your procession, Bacony Boy, but you still owe more. I found just under eight hundred dollars in that deodorant stick. You owed twenty-five hundred, five dollars, and ninety-nine cents. That leaves some seventeen hundred bucks or so."

"This is insane," I said.

"I talked to your boss Jimmy-Boy in there," Laszlo said. "Hell of a man. Hell of a man. Jimmy says he'll let you double shift the next few days to make the cash. I guess this little pimple of a town dies right down after the September long. That's only five days away. And then you'll have to get your buns — little dinner rolls — up to school. You got yourself five days to make seventeen hundred."

I thought back to the casual nature Mr. Kwon's shrug when he said, "No pay." I wished Mr. Kwon were here right now. I could

just see him kneeling on the dark asphalt of the parking lot, sur-
rounded by candles and bowing toward a severed pig's head.
Laszlo would've had one look and fled back to Calgary before you
could say *gausah*. Mr. Kwon had been so certain. And he was
right. What could Laszlo do?

"No pay," I said as brave and casually as I could.

"No pay?" Laszlo repeated. "What is *no pay*?"

"I'm not paying you. What you're doing is illegal. Besides, what
can you do? Call the police?"

"Of course I'll call the police." He fumbled out a cell phone
from his pocket. "What *you* did was illegal, Bacon. What *you*
did."

"What do you mean?" I lifted myself up on my toes to see if he
was really dialing. He was. "How was what *I* did illegal?"

"You're the *John*. The solicitor. You're the guy they'll look for.
They'll print your name in the paper, too. Hold on – it's ringing."

"Wait!" I reached out and shut his phone. "I'm the John? I
didn't even – "

Laszlo tugged the phone away from me. "Oh, so suddenly you
now have a little more interest in talking payment? That's fine.
Look, if you can't bring your stubborn, greedy little self to make
peace over paying us back, make a cheque for the balance out to
a women's shelter. Or Mothers Against Drunk Diving. We'll just
end up sending the money there anyway. But, Bacony Boy, I'll tell
you this: I will not sit by and watch you get away with filching
my wife's services."

"Laszlo, I'm not going to – "

"Hup, hup, hup!" His hand stretched up nearer to my mouth
and his face turned away from me. "I'll be back in five days. You
get earning."

"Lasz – "

"Hup!"

"La – "

"Hup, hup!" Laszlo threw a fat finger up to my lips. Then he
turned his back to face the lake. "Five days," he said, nodding his
pleasure at the view. He strolled over to his REVA G-Wiz electric
car and drove away.

45.

I not only toiled through a double-shift, as Laszlo suggested, I actually endured a triple-shift. Dishwashing shifts were six hours each. I worked for eighteen hours. I scrubbed and scoured every dish, glass, pot, plate, pan, fork, knife, and spoon the morning, lunch, and dinner rushes could throw at me. When the restaurant was quiet, I pitched in to help the housekeepers. They paid me ten dollars for each toilet I scraped. I scraped twelve. From dust one can build a mountain, Grandma used to say. But not a rat cent of the money I was slaving for would feel Laszlo's fat-fingered grip. I'd spend my slaving on Poke's Firefly. What I should have done when I had the money before. The second I earned the five hundredth dollar, I'd bust away on that beautiful blue ride and disappear before Laszlo returned. The money he'd taken, I accepted as bad timing.

My only break in the exhausting day entailed sprinting back to the cabin to cook a meal in my own kitchen—keeping up my end of the deal with Woodrat. I made Manwich. I even hollowed out a big crusty bun until it was all bowl-shaped and poured the Manwich inside like they do with the chili at the lodge.

Waterton now felt the furthest place from quiet and simple. In fact, I now saw how, underneath its layer of tranquility, Waterton was pulsating, raving, and unhinged. The whole town was on vacation, and not just the tourists—the staff, too. They'd all come from somewhere else. Just for a summer. Everyone was temporary. The Thirsty Bear Saloon came to life each night, cramming with restaurant staff who'd sprinted over after their late shift just in time to order eleven drinks for last call, joining the housekeepers and front desk staff who'd been there since six. Each night after the saloon closed, a crowd would spill into the street with armfuls of off-sales and unfinished highballs or jugs of beer snuck out under jackets. The crowd would swarm aimlessly up the street until a stumbling someone was liquored up in the excitement enough to step forth and volunteer his or her cabin. The swarm would change direction accordingly. Poke stumbled home with a new appliance just about every morning, and just about every night you could find a body passed out in our cabin's living room, on the kitchen floor, in the shower stall, or out front embedded in a hedge. Waterton had a bingo game, but not like the bingo my mother and Grandma Magic Can played. One evening in the lodge staff room, while I chewed on a mozza stick, I overheard three waitresses talking about daubing a number on a bingo card for each person they "snogged" that summer. Under the N, Nathan, under the G, Gary. The whole game was a race, they said. First one to get four corners or a line won the pot. I guess they threw in a bunch of money on it, too. It all made me think Sara was wasting her time in Calgary or trying to reach Vancouver – this tiny resort village was wilder than any city she could flee to.

[**Fourth-last day of the season**]

46. Again I triple-shifted. Again, my

only break in the exhausting day was sprinting back to the cabin to cook a meal. I'd planned on Beefaroni, but when I reached the cabin, it was filled with the smell of simmering olive oil and the warmth of a baking oven. The old round dining table that had been mostly used to stack empties was now cleared, the tabletop even wiped clean. Woodrat gripped two plates with tea towels, carrying them out from the kitchen. "This is my end of the deal," she said.

Three place settings were laid out – presumably the third was for Chris – but Chris was nowhere in sight. She'd originally agreed to come, Woodrat explained, with just a hint of irritation in her voice. But she hadn't actually seen Chris in a full day.

Woodrat set out a box of red wine – no glasses. She said red wine was better drunk from a box, straight from the spigot, without the disruptive brokering of a glass. Even though I had to return to work, we each took a turn lifting the box over our heads and carefully trickling a stream of wine into our open mouths.

On my plate was what appeared to be a large slice of ham steak and a mass of strange, green, poofy matter. "What is this green stuff?" I poked at it with my fork.

"Try it."

I corralled a small puff of the green material and lifted the half-forkful to my mouth. "It tastes like eggs."

"It should." Woodrat smiled proudly. "It's food-coloured scram, Bacon I am."

"I don't get it."

She leaned back in the chair, grinning. "Why, Bacon Sobelowski, your lack of creativity startles me. Maybe I should have served this on a boat, or had us eat it with a goat ..."

I looked down at my plate, pushed around some of the green fluff, then looked back up. "You made green eggs and ham?"

Woodrat nodded. "Better than sunflower seeds or staff meal fries and gravy."

"In what way?" I said.

"Cute," she said. "The point is you're eating a home-cooked meal and it's fun."

Woodrat ate her green eggs and ham slowly, and I guessed from her frequent glances at the door that she was buying time for Chris to arrive. Chris never did. Chris could've up and left Waterton, been plucked right off the planet, and if it wasn't for Woodrat, I don't think anyone would've known the difference. Woodrat was the only person I'd ever seen talk to Chris. The only person Chris *allowed* to talk to her.

Woodrat fixed her gaze out the window. "You ever had a hemorrhoid?" she asked.

I turned and peered out the same window, checking if one was outside. "No," I said. "I haven't. I've heard my mother complain about them."

"They're painful," she said, her eyes still fixed out the window. "It's a bulb of swollen veins and tissue on your anus."

The green eggs shuffled a little in my stomach at each of the words "anus," "veins," and "tissue." My queasiness with medical terminology hadn't wavered. "Do you have one?" I asked, blushing at my own question.

"An anus? Yes," she said, turning her gaze to me. "A hemorrhoid, no. But did you know dogs get them, too?"

"Dogs get hemorr—" I couldn't finish the word, "—those things?"

"Especially stray dogs. Dogs that sit a lot or eat a diet too filled with garbage."

"I get it now," I nodded. "You're going to help dogs with hemorr ... those things."

"Nobody else does," she confirmed. "Nobody pays those dogs any attention. They're alienated. Ignored."

"What can you do?" I said. "To help with ... those things?"

"I've created a kit." Woodrat slid to the edge of her seat, like she'd just then fully returned from her gazing. "A K-9 hemorrhoid kit. Tea tree oil, steroid ointment, Proctofoam, and suppositories." Clearly Woodrat had researched the subject well. She told me all about how she planned to apply the treatments and every time she spoke the word "fissure" or "vessels" or "suppository" I felt the green scrambled eggs rumble and bounce in my gut like popping corn.

"Why are there so many stray dogs?" I asked.

"That's life, Bacon." She ran her fingers along her forearm. "Some things just get thrown back."

The nausea I felt competed with a rush of admiration at Woodrat's drive and direction. She was so sure of herself. Of what she'd be doing, where she was going. She knew exactly what she was supposed to do.

The door threw open. Woodrat looked up hopefully, but it wasn't Chris who walked in. It was Kyle Cruikshank. He was holding the hand of the tank-top girl. They kicked off their shoes and stopped to hover over the table. "Hi, you two," the tank-top girl gleamed. The soft freckles drizzled across her cleavage were reddened by the sun. It was impossible not to stare. "What a scrumptious-looking meal!" she said. "Bacon, I must've missed you the other night. I couldn't find you. But we still need to meet up, OK?" A fork fell from my hand.

Kyle Cruikshank tapped his black polarized sunglasses down the bridge of his nose and peered at our meals. "Thought so," he nodded. "So sure, in fact, you could say I had Gwen Stefani's old band." He pushed his sunglasses back up his nose. I saw my elongated face in their dark reflection as he turned to me. "Just knew it wouldn't be *fish*." Kyle made that clucking noise with his tongue, nodded at Woodrat, then disappeared into his main-floor bedroom.

The tank-top girl rolled her eyes, touched Woodrat's shoulder, and said, "Nevermind him. You two enjoy your ..." she bent closer to our plates, "... your ... food." She, too, disappeared into the bedroom.

Woodrat excused herself, stood from the table, and carried the box of wine over to the door. She bent over Kyle Cruikshank's black mesh Techamphibian sport shoes, pinched the spigot, and filled each shoe with dry red wine.

When she sat again, she held the wine box over her thrown-back head and let the red stream trickle into her mouth. At that moment, I suddenly became aware of a strange ginger-ale feeling that had been carbonating up from my stomach into my lungs since I watched her tickle the chin of that cutthroat trout on Cameron Creek. The bubbling soothed over the uneasiness the tank-top girl had left me with and replaced it with a no less tolerable anxiousness. Kenny Rogers would've written a song about those kinds of feelings. I don't know what words he'd have chosen but the only word that took shape in my mind was "problem." Problem because that ginger-ale feeling hadn't really begun its bubbling from my stomach. The source of the bubbles' inception was, as my mother would easily have guessed, my groin. And if my mother were there beside me she would've somehow heard the carbonated fizz bubbling inside me, raked her fingers rapidly over her hair, and reminded me, for the ten thousandth time and with great exasperation, what to stay away from.

"I need to get back to work," I said, fighting the rise of my bubbling problem. Immediately I realized how rude that sounded with Woodrat still eating.

Her huge eyes looked startled, but then again they always looked startled. "OK," she said. "You go. I'll clean up."

"No, no. Leave it. I'll do it later."

"It's no problem," she said.

"What problem?" I said.

"What?"

"You said *problem*."

"I said *no* problem."

"I don't have a problem," I said.

"What the hell are you talking about?"

"Do you want to spend the night?"

Woodrat jumped like something had pinched her seat. She stopped chewing and pushed a chunk of ham around the inside her closed mouth with her tongue, as though searching for a comfortable pocket to store it.

The words had formed on their own in my throat, had thrown themselves out of my mouth without permission. I bit down on the inside of my cheek, seeing myself sitting on Oprah's couch or perched on a stool on Maury's stage. I wanted to punch myself in the problem.

Woodrat's gaze slowly turned from shock to such a sad kindness I worried she might apply tea tree oil on me. "I think," she said, "maybe that question requires an answer a little more complicated than we need to get into right now. How about we just meet at the Thirsty Bear after work?"

I nodded, mortified at my brash offer, unclear if I should actually be feeling so mortified, confused why the brash offer was more complicated than we needed to get into, and desperately fighting a gnawing crave to make the offer again. So I simply nodded. Mostly I just wanted to crawl into a heap of poofy green eggs and cover myself with a sheet of ham.

After work, Woodrat and I met at the Thirsty Bear. Neither of us spoke much, the distracting awkwardness of that afternoon sitting between us as ignorable as a hovering wasp. She did say she still hadn't heard from Chris. She also said I should try asking someone to dance. Then she left. We'd been there less than half an hour. Woodrat was not one for late nights, always leaving the saloon long before closing. She said she liked her sleep.

Watching her leave, my thoughts drifted to the rapidly approaching season's end. Only three more nights remained until the summer staff left. All week I'd overheard people coordinating rides back to shared cities, organizing pick up times with family members over the phone, and I'd watched the staff-room corkboard crowd with posted requests for rides to the Calgary airport. There'd be quite an exodus parading past the park gates Sunday morning. A long line of leavers, with no giant crow to watch us all leave.

I left the Thirsty Bear and put myself to bed even though I wasn't the least bit tired. I lay awake, gazing into the bedroom's darkness, imagining a long line of cars filing out of the park gates. Through the back windshield of the last car I could see the back of Woodrat's head, not once turning around as that car carried her off. It was impossible not to imagine what those full lips would feel like to kiss. Like pushing your mouth into a glorious mound of soft, satin throw pillows. Or nuzzling between the cushiony cleavage of swelling breasts. ·

I flipped and rolled and shuffled in the bed, trying to shake myself to sleep. My eyes finally shut just as the red dashes of the clock radio reorganized themselves with great digital speed to form 1:32. At that same moment, a strange, muffled whimper rose up from under the carpet in my room, from below the floorboards. It had come right through the first floor ceiling, from the bedroom immediately below mine. Kyle Cruikshank's bedroom. The whimper sounded again. Then again. I listened closer. Soon I was able to make out the source of the increasingly loud whimpers: they were the rhythmic whines of the tank-top girl. After some time, her whimpers turned into grunts, which turned into a high-pitched wheeze that squeezed through the floorboards below me, shoved through the carpet, and hovered in the air above my bed, brushing past my ears like the whining of a mosquito. The knocking of Kyle Cruikshank's bed frame against drywall soon joined the wailing of the tank-top girl. I folded the pillow over my face, smothering my ears and wrapping my head like a taco. I should have felt happy for a roommate who may have found his someone, but I didn't. Instead I lay there alone, feeling the way the lodge's front budgie must, its cage cruelly placed next to a window, where it can see the big, blue, wide sky.

[Third-last day of the season]

47. After nearly a full hour's worth of sleep I

lugged myself out of bed, teetered downstairs, and poured myself a bowl of cereal: my home-cooked meal of the day. The door abruptly burst open and Poke barrelled in, bringing with him a rush of cool, early morning air. He clung awkwardly to a large microwave slipping from his grip. Three stumble-steps into the cabin and the microwave dropped, clanging to the floor. Poke threw himself back against the door, slamming it shut. He snapped closed the deadbolt, pulled down all the blinds, and hissed, "Do *not* open this door!" Then he fled to his room, hauling the microwave with him. His bedroom door lock clicked behind him. Seconds later, the front door shook, a fist hammering hard against it. Kicks thudded the heavy wood lower down on the door. I sat silent for several minutes, my mouth clamped down around a spoon, holding myself still, waiting for the pounding to stop. When the banging and rattling ended and I heard the sound of stomped gravel disappearing down our drive, I withdrew the spoon from my mouth and finished the rest of my Count Chocula. I'd need the fuel of a solid breakfast to survive another exhausting triple-shift at work.

That evening, when Woodrat arrived at work, her huge eyes looked like she'd just walked out of a dust storm; they were as red and swollen as cold sores.

When I asked if anything was wrong, she shook her head. "I'm fine," she said in a voice that wasn't hers, and clearly wasn't fine.

"Do you want to take our break down by the lake?" I suggested, hoping that was the right thing to suggest.

Woodrat nodded. I had a feeling that if I'd suggested we walk right down to the bottom of the lake, she'd nod at that, too.

We shared a bench looking out over the big lake that laid so calm and still you'd almost swear you could walk right out across its glassy surface, supported by nothing but your own reflection. The big mountain across from us was throwing down the blushing reds of its sun-sparked warming rock and the hazy blues and plums of the deep limestone folds. The calm-mirroring lake was throwing it all right back so clearly it was hard to tell which was real.

"Did you find your friend Chris?" I said.

Woodrat nodded, but not at first, it took a moment, and when she did, the nod was so slight it could've been mistaken for a hiccup. "She left."

"She left?" I said. "But the season's not over 'til Monday. Why did she leave?"

Woodrat shrugged.

I watched one particular cloud's reflection on the lake and wondered if fish could see the underside of reflections.

"She was going to join me in the Bahamas," Woodrat said. "To help with the dogs."

I counted nine small clouds in the sky.

"Nobody keeps their word, you know?"

I nodded as though I knew.

"I think maybe I've been declared a protected species," she mumbled. "I keep getting thrown back."

Her big eyes somehow looked smaller that day, like they'd shrunken or her face had almost grown into them.

"Why don't people keep their word?" she whispered.

"I don't know," I said. "I try to. I've kept our deal about making one home-cooked meal a day. I had Count Chocula this morning."

Woodrat was about to continue but she paused. Her face started but gave up on a couple of different expressions, before settling on a slight grin. For just a moment.

She sat with her knees pulled up to her chest, her arms wrapped around her legs, her feet set on the bench. She scrunched herself up right close, even tilted her head onto my shoulder.

I wished we could've sat like that all evening. And though I knew it wasn't appropriate for the moment, my problem was enjoying it, too.

Staring out over the big lake, it struck me that, when you're away from home, some place temporary, the days move just a little differently. They feel more like weeks. And the weeks feel like months. And now there were only two more days in Waterton.

"What are we?" I asked.

"What do you mean?"

"You and I. We go fishing together, eat our staff meals together, sit on benches. Does that make us something?"

She slid her head off my shoulder and straightened herself on the bench. "We have... *obstacles* ... Bacon. The least of which is the fact we have two days left to know each other."

"Yeah."

"Do we *need* to be something?"

"I don't know," I said. "I guess you just seem disgruntled with people right now and I don't want to be grouped in with that. I'd like to maybe be something else to you."

She nodded like I'd just told her some little-known, fascinating fact.

I started thinking about if there really was someone for everyone. And if there was, what if Woodrat was actually my someone? But she was going off to the Bahamas and I was going off to school and we'd never see each other again. We'd never know. "What if it turns out Kenny Rogers isn't full of shit?" I said.

Woodrat showed only a hint of confusion but didn't take her glazed eyes off the lake. "I suppose that's possible," she said.

I nodded.

"You know, Bacon." She faced me. "You're right. You could turn out to be the first person I've ever met who is as good as his word. So yeah, you are something else to me. And I'd like to be something to you. Even if that something is only for two more days." She rubbed a knuckle under her eye. "We just have to figure out what that is. What to call it. I think it should be a partnership. All things considered, with our particular 'obstacles' and constraints, with us being limited to two days, and I suppose with us never seeing each other again, our partnership would be clearly limited. Limited in time and liability. I say we call ourselves a 'limited liability partnership.'"

"I like that," I said. "What does it mean?" The problemed part of me hoped it meant she could stay over now, but I didn't ask.

"I'm not sure," she said. "Maybe it simply means that for these next two days, we just keep doing what we've been doing and agree we won't throw each other back. We'll keep our word about everything we say. If we can't keep our word for two days then I guess we're no better than the rest. Bacon Sobelowski, do you take me to be your two-day limited liability partner?"

"I do."

"Well, then I do, too."

And with that, I guess Woodrat and I were limited liability partners. It took all my sober strength to keep from kissing her right there on that bench.

Woodrat pulled my arm around her, sank down on the bench, resting her head back on my shoulder, and shut her eyes. I took slow, deep breaths, breathing in her sweet algae smell. We sat like that right there on that bench for the rest of our break, without a further word between us. Limited liability partners.

After work Woodrat and I hit the Thirsty Bear, but she went home just as early as she always did. I still didn't know if a limited liability partnership meant she could stay over, but if it did, she wasn't doing so on that night. After three triple-shifts and another coming the next day, I needed my sleep. So I left the Thirsty Bear and headed back to my cabin. On my way, I stopped to call home.

"Bacon!" Grandma coughed into the phone. "I wish you were here. I'm watching an infomercial about the Exercise Rock. You can do all the same weight training and muscle-building exercises as in a gym, but all you need is the Exercise Rock. It looks and feels just like a real rock, but it comes in three different colours. I like the red."

"Cool," I said, standing in the phone booth at the garage across the road from my cabin.

"Do you want to come up for dinner tomorrow?"

"Not tomorrow, Grandma. I'm dishwashing."

"When can you?"

"I don't know yet." The summer had darted past me like a trout that nibbled a hook and fled. I still hadn't decided if I'd stop at home before heading up to school or not, or what kind of school I'd be heading to. "I'll let you know."

"I've got some news," her voice droned, clearly implying it was the bad kind.

"What is it?"

"Kwon found a location."

"He did?" I tugged at the phone cord, almost pulling the receiver out of my hand. "So then they'll be ... *staying*?"

"God help us, yes. He bought a lot right on the bloody highway, for God's sake. Smack dab between here and Blairmore. Can you imagine? Too bad it's not further over Blairmore's way, where it is now we're still in smelling range. He figures a Korean restaurant will be a tourist attraction for the busloads of Asians that roll through."

"That's smart."

"Smart? It's stupid. We don't get busloads of Asians. And if we did, they wouldn't stop. If Asians wanted Asian food, why the hell would they fly all the way over here?" I stood silently in the phone booth, still in shock that somebody in Bellevue was staying. And not just somebody, but Mr. Kwon. I guess I'd still expected he'd pack up his things and haul Meryl Streep back home because of me. "Anyway," Grandma said, "now we're stuck with him for at least as long as it takes for that idiotic restaurant to go under. The worst part is he's gone and asked your mother to waitress. She said yes! She'll be quitting the laundromat as soon as the restaurant's built. The only secure income this house had."

"She said yes?"

"Yup. Now she bounds around the kitchen risking our health by experimenting with goofy Korean recipes for dinner. Haven't seen her this chipper since Princess Di died. Heck, she doesn't even sleep in on Saturdays anymore. Like she thinks she's all worldly now because she'll be waitressing in a Korean restaurant.

Then Kwon was fool enough to ask me to hostess. Pfft. Fat chance."

It was strange how much Grandma had changed since the Kwons had arrived. It was like her and my mother had swapped souls.

"Anyway," Grandma said, "I was just about to flame one up and hit the fart sack before you called. Bacon, you should come home for a dinner."

"I'll try Grandma," I said. "Goodnight."

That night, as I fought for sleep in my bed, again I heard the tank-top girl's muffled whimpers rise up from Cruikshank's bedroom. This time her rhythmic whines were met by raspy groans discharging from Gibson's room across the hall.

The whimpers and groans from each bedroom seemed to clash in the air just above me, brawling to be heard over each other. My problem stretched like it was reaching to peek out from my underwear, peer over the waistband at all the excitement. I spun onto my stomach to smother it.

That night I slept like a log — meaning I spent the night wincing and turning as though a thousand ants were gnawing at my timber.

⌈ Second-last day of the season ⌉

48.

I slogged through a third straight triple-shift, my sluggish limbs and drifting mind sleep deprived, my stomach empty and cantankerous, the pale skin of my hands raw and reeking of rubber gloves but, by the end of it all, I'd accumulated $485 in tips and toilet bounty. I now only needed to work the morning shift on the last day of the season to make it five hundred and then bolt. As soon as I owned the Firefly, I'd offer Woodrat a ride to the airport. It seemed the least a limited liability partner could do.

This time I kept the money stuffed in socks—the socks I wore. So long as I kept the bills unrolled, laid out flat beneath my feet, they didn't scratch or chafe my skin too much. By that end of the third triple-shift, the bills had, to say the least, lost their crispness.

If it hadn't been the second-last night I'd ever see Woodrat in my life, I would've simply collapsed into sleep under the sink of the dishpit. Before I could even remove my apron, I'd be dreaming of Sara Mulligan's long, butterscotch legs or Karla's heavy, slumping breasts or Meryl Streep's tiny, egg-shaped nipples or the tank-top girl's tank-top or Woodrat's plump, moist lips. But it was the second-last night I'd ever see Woodrat, and it's startling the energy a depleted body can unexpectedly unearth when that body is propelled by a problemed pecker that knows a window is closing. My tired mind was too done in to reason or fight or wallow in guilt. Besides, Woodrat and I had agreed to meet, and limited liability partners must keep their word. So I hauled myself down to the Thirsty Bear, led by my problemed pecker, hoping the clouded, cool night air would diminish Woodrat's attachment to her nylon tent.

"You've been working hard lately," Woodrat said, pinching up wine with a straw, lifting it and releasing a dribbling stream into her gaping mouth. The saloon didn't have boxes of wine and wouldn't permit her to drink from the bottle.

"Extra money for school," I said. I hardly wanted to explain Laszlo to her. "Sure cooling off out there." I motioned her to turn toward the window.

"Those servers been tipping you out?" She wiped a hand across her mouth.

"Yeah, quite well," I said, still facing the window. "I think a storm's coming."

"All the servers?"

"Yes."

"You sure?"

"Yes, of course."

"Good. Some of those sons of bitches can be tighter than fishing line hooked on a forty-pound lake trout."

"It's definitely going to rain," I said.

"So what did you decide? College or university?"

I shook my head.

"School starts in three days, Bacon," she straightened. "You waiting for someone to decide for you?" I had no idea what I'd been waiting for. "Bacon, do you even want to go to school?"

"Of course. I mean, I should. Everybody goes to school. And I don't want to get left behind." I tapped a finger on the window glass. "Going to be a cold rain, too. Real cold."

"Not *everybody's* going," she laughed. "I'm not. And just because other people are doesn't mean you have to. Take a year off. Go next year. Take two years off. Three, if you want. Or don't go at all. It's whatever you want, Bacon. Potato-of-the-day."

"I don't know what kind of man I am. College or university."

"What if you're neither?"

"You don't think I should go to school?"

"You should do what you want." She stirred her wine with the straw. "There's not one way or the other. There's always a third way. *Your* way. Call it the *Bacon way*."

"The Bacon way?"

"Absolutely."

"Which way is the Bacon way?"

"It's your way. That's exactly the point. It's what you decide. I can't tell you."

"But you think I shouldn't go to school."

"No, I didn't say that. I think you should do what you want. The Bacon way. I just think if you really wanted school right away you would've picked some classes by now." Maybe she was right. Everything seemed so simple and sure to Woodrat. Potato-of-the-day.

I returned my gaze to the window. "Might even snow," I said.

"It's not going to *snow*," she laughed. "What the hell's with you and the weather all the sudden?"

"Me?" I said. "Nothing. Just looks cold out."

"Doesn't look too bad to me. Besides, we both have shelter."

"Tents can leak," I said.

"Mine doesn't."

"It could tear."

"Bacon, I need to get to bed," Woodrat announced. "*My* bed."

"But it's our second-last night...."

"I know and I need to rest up for tomorrow. It's late and I have to get up early. I switched shifts so I could work the morning instead."

And just like that, even though it was our second-last night together, my limited liability partner headed home to bed. I hated how much she loved her sleep. Actually, I found it endearing, but it infuriated my problemed pecker.

As Woodrat joined a line of people stepping outside into the rain, I watched as the others lifted their jackets over their heads. Woodrat walked straight and unbothered. Dampness seeped in through the thin wooden structure of the saloon. I turned to see the moon blurring through the staggering streams of rain on the dark window beside me and cursed my problem for chasing her away.

"I finally have you alone," the tank-top girl said, snagging the stool next to me. She didn't just sit close, she seized personal space as though it were her only source of nourishment. As she leaned her elbows onto the table, my eyes drew to the exposed stretch of freckled skin below her arm, an extended crook of soft skin unclaimed by armpit or breast, revealed through the window of an arm loop on her black tank-top. The further back I leaned in my chair, the more of that stretch revealed and the more I found myself wondering if the tank-top girl might have been a recent victim of Woodrat's thefts. It seemed she didn't have a bra to wear.

"My three friends over there and I are going to enjoy a soak in the hotel's outdoor hot tub tonight." She clasped her hands together like she was praying. Her three friends were known as the 'bingo girls.' They huddled together over the same table in Thirsty Bear each night, plotting strategy on napkins, pointing around the room with sideways glances, their bodies jiggling from failed attempts at holding in giggles. "Are you able to join us?"

"I don't have a swimsuit," I mumbled.

A smile like a stretching snake twisted across her freckled face. "What on earth would you want with one?"

I could see the tank-top girl easing her soft skin into the hot tub, dressed in nothing but a collage of popcorn freckles, steam lifting over her patterned skin, the puff of belly disappearing under the warm rumbling water as her body submerged, only her hair remaining visible, swirling on top of the bubbled surface. Sitting in the water just behind where the tank-top girl submerged was a wetted Woodrat, steam-soaked hair clinging to her face. Her round eyes watching me.

"Look Bacon," the tank-top girl said — the one at my table, not the one in the hot tub — "you're the only boy in the whole town whose name starts with B. Amazingly, this town has no Bills or Brents or Brads or Bens. Just a Bacon." She glanced back at her three friends, all of who, as if on cue, raised their drinks. "At least one of us girls needs to get a B tonight. We've got a game to conclude and obviously we can't end the summer without a B."

I saw all four of them in the hot tub now, crowding out Woodrat, forcing her from the water.

"You two OK?" a familiar voice barked. I snapped out of my gaze to see a waitress standing next to me, her black money apron and round cork tray at my eye level. "Nothing for me," I said. In the blur of the bar-room air it seemed, for just that moment, the waitress' head wasn't her own. Instead, at that moment, she had the head of a goose, its long, snaking neck, its glossy beak. "You sure?" the goose-faced waitress said in a voice that wasn't hers either. Nor was it the voice of a goose. The familiar voice was my mother's. "How about a mystery draft?" my mother's voice said, the waitress tipping her long goose neck toward the bar where Maury Povich was now the bartender. Maury tipped forward the draft handle, letting the beer flow down onto his shoes and waved a large friendly hand our way. "*Piiiigs*," the goose-faced waitress hissed.

My chair tipped over as I jumped to my feet. I excused myself, apologized to the tank-top girl, the waitress, and the chair. I said something about needing to get to sleep, hurried out of the saloon, and raced out into the drizzle, keeping a darting eye out for Laszlo or Sara or fly-fishermen or any other geese. I ran to the campground to pass by Woodrat's tent. I guess I hoped to catch her awake, maybe find the glow of a flashlight illuminating the tent walls. Her tent was dark. I even walked up to her front vestibule, listening for a sigh or movement. I waited for a moment, imagining Woodrat lying awake, wondering if I'd be walking by, and maybe she'd zip open the front flap to check for me. She didn't.

Before reaching my cabin, I spotted Laszlo's REVA parked out front. He could have been in my room waiting for me. Or down at the lodge, slugging back beers with Jim the barrel-chested owner. Now, I couldn't go to work or home. I needed to leave. But not without Woodrat. I'd have to hide out until she finished her shift.

I snuck along the side hedge and crawled into a tight cluster of shrubs out back of the cabin. The thickly leaved, overhanging branches of an old cottonwood kept the cluster of shrubs dry.

I could see the silhouetted shadow of two embracing figures on one of the upstairs window shades. My mind tried to fight the images it so likes to imagine at such times. But the those images appeared anyway and, as they did, and even though I didn't have any memories of how Woodrat's lips tasted, or the weight of her breasts, or the shape her nipples, I imagined it all just the same.

Even from the bushes and through the drizzling rain I could again hear rhythmic whines from Cruikshank's bedroom. And those whines were again joined by a whimpering moan from Gibson's room. Sharp grunts could also be heard heaving out of another room upstairs, paired with the shuffling and creaking of an old metal bed frame. Soon, all six other bedrooms in the cabin – every bedroom but mine – revved and thumped like the old Lancer. The entire cabin seemed to shake in the night, dancing and celebrating the season's end – the drumming of wooden headboards providing percussion.

My problemed pecker reached up for the hand resting just below my stomach, like a kitten nudging for attention. I pulled my hand away, stuffed it under my back, furious that my mother may have been right about there being too much of my father in me.

That night I slept like a baby – meaning I woke sporadically with a yearning to cry.

49.

What woke me from the cluster of bushes was not the hairy leaves and coarse stems scratching my cheek. Nor was it the frantic mob of mosquitoes stabbing their syringes into my hands and neck and face. What woke me was a distant cackle, increasing in volume and drawing closer. My tired, itching eyes felt as blotchy red as a pizza-pocket stain, which was the exact stain that, had I wanted to confirm the comparison, sat conveniently smeared across my white long-sleeved shirt. The remains of my previous night's home-cooked meal. I rubbed open my sore, pizza-pocket stained eyes, and turned them back toward the bend of the street behind me. A man staggered hurriedly down the middle of the pavement, lugging some large object on a two-wheeled dolly. As the man neared, I was able to make out the flustered, exhausted, and sweating face of Poke. As he drew into focus, it became evident he wasn't wearing clothes, with the exception of one sock covering his left foot. The object he awkwardly zig-zagged up the road was a standard-sized refrigerator-freezer. The fridge veered and swayed and wobbled as Poke scrambled to right it while maintaining the forward momentum, the cord snaking like a tail behind him. His hearty cackle overtook him as he struggled to keep a running pace. Frequently he glanced over a shoulder, clearly concerned about something behind him. He heaved the dolly with a great, wobbling thrust up the curbed drive, using the momentum to propel the fridge toward our cabin.

Laszlo's REVA was now gone; perhaps he'd seen Poke and became worried for the inventory of his own kitchen. So I crawled out from the shrubs and sprinted to the cabin door just as Poke wheeled up the refrigerator. I pointed to the Firefly and held out a handful of limp, sweat-sodden bills. "Four hundred and seventy," I said. I'd spent fifteen at the saloon. "Close enough?" Poke plucked the bills from my hand, almost losing the refrigerator as he did, but not once breaking stride.

It was all the money I had.

"Deal includes a fridge if you want it," he said as the appliance careened violently off each side of the door frame and into the cabin.

Of all the things I might have imagined wanting at that moment, a fridge would seem amongst the last. Even, as it was, a thirty-cubic-foot, side-by-side, double-door, luxury fridge with water and ice dispenser. But Poke's offer sparked an immediate thought in my mind, and though, as my mother had often reminded me, I've never been one for ideas, the thought Poke's offer had sparked was indeed an idea. A good idea.

"I'll take that fridge," I said.

Poke nodded firmly, signifying a transaction was complete, then kicked the door closed behind him. I heard the deadbolt snap into place like a hammering gavel.

I had plans for that fridge.

The sun hauled itself up, peeking over the surrounding mountains and down at the little town. The sky was a contrasting mix of morning glare and dulled, thickening cloud cover. The streets were silent and still. I crept down the drive to the Firefly, glancing all around for Laszlo. I wondered how Grandma Magic Can, my mother, Mr. Kwon, and Meryl Streep were spending their long weekend. Did they play TV bingo? Set up the fan on top of the VCR? Curse the heat? Barbecue baseball-shaped burgers stuffed full with onion shards? I wondered what Mr. Kwon thought of burger balls. Was he still living with us or had he found a place of his own? Had he started constructing his restaurant?

I was now the proud owner of a blue Firefly. And a fridge. But I decided at that moment I was no longer the owner of a job. There was no longer a reason to work. Laszlo would likely be waiting for me at the lodge. And I needed time. Eventually he'd come back to the cabin. So I had to work fast. I ran down to Poke's maintenance shop for assistance.

When I was done with my idea for the fridge – the whole

process took about an hour – I hauled the large luxury appliance out under the carport. Now it just required time.

Until then, I needed to lay low. To hide from Laszlo. At least until the fridge was ready. I grabbed my green and brown second-hand spincasting rod and climbed into my Firefly. Down the lake, the sky crackled and screamed as the dark cloud cover tumbled and thickened. Waterton had a storm coming.

50. I raced up Cameron road to one

of the uppermost stretches of Cameron Creek, a section I'd yet to fish. I parked on the shoulder, snuggled the Firefly up tight against a guardrail, and shuffled myself down a steep embankment to the creek. I trudged upstream, working against the flow, climbing around the small waterfalls and slippery rocks. After a full month of days spent fishing this creek, different canyons and pools, gradually working my way a little further upstream each day, I wondered if I was finally nearing the creek's source: Cameron Lake itself. The land around this new section of the creek flattened out into a mess of fallen logs, berry patches, shrubs, trees, and beaver dams. The surrounding ground was soft and boggy and, in most places, it was easier to travel by balancing atop the criss-crossed logs.

As the creek snaked through the thick foliage and forest debris, more and more pools opened up, and each little fish darting from my splashing steps was less little than the last.

The dark blanket of cloud pulled right overtop of the Cameron Creek valley and the first stabs of rain jabbed my skin. The thick forest blocked out most of what little light the heavy grey clouds hadn't already.

As I rounded the next bend, I heard the gurgling of water spilling over the cluster of sticks and branches and mud of an abandoned beaver dam not far ahead. For the trout fisherman, beaver dams drum up the kind of heart thumping you'd otherwise only get in a bingo hall one daub away from a blackout and an announced bonanza of twenty-five thousand dollars.

I stood scanning the creek ahead and at first couldn't see the spill of water, only hear it. The current appeared to run swiftly and evenly past the dam. Then I spotted it. While most of the creek's flow ran past the mess of sticks clogged along its right bank, a separate stream broke from the flow, pouring over and down a foot or so into a deep scoop in the soft soil. A pool formed, almost entirely hidden behind a thick cloak of willows and scrub. When a pool opens up off a creek with a streaming feed of water throwing in nutrients and washing in insects, you can be as sure as Kenny Rogers' beard is grey, there'll be something lurking in that pool. Something large.

I guessed the pool at about six feet long by six feet wide. Impossible to know for sure because it sat safely guarded on all sides by the thickest of thickets and fullest of shrubs. The pool had been nearly completely grown over by the huge leafy branches of surrounding trees, forming a ceiling over the spot.

I scanned for any break or entry, but the pool was wedged in tight. As if Mother Nature herself had sculpted together one tiny pocket of the planet perfectly designed for nothing else but my very own fencing-jab cast.

What regal trout had earned such a safe and protected throne? Clearly the most prime pool of the entire creek. A flash movement caught my eye in the shadows further up the creek, around the bend opposite me. I squinted upstream and watched a dark figure step out from the darkness like a cat. Reaching high above the dark silhouette, an enormously long rod swayed in the growing storm's gust. Kyle Cruikshank had found my creek.

Even from that distance I could see his eyes darting. Stalking. Analyzing. Taking in how the creek moved. Where the current flowed. Where the bottom dropped. Cruikshank's brain rendered and layered and mapped out the creek. When he abruptly froze, I knew he'd spotted it. The garble of logs and branches and twigs and mud where water spilled over and disappeared behind a thick wall of foliage. His eyes roamed the perimeter, widening with the hunger of a stalking animal. Those eyes followed the creek downstream, to the bend opposite him, then lifted up to meet my own eyes. Thunder cracked. A shot of lightning lit up the chisels of Cruikshank's face.

I charged upstream, sloshing through the water as quickly but as gently as I could, trying to keep from frightening away whatever sweet-prized beast lay hidden in that pool. More importantly – scrambling to reach it first. Cruikshank calmly assessed the clearing around him, lifted his rod, and began working it into a rhythmic sway. His free hand threw the coil of line dancing into his rod and out into the freedom of the sky above.

He had no chance of clearing that wall of brush, regardless of the length of his rod. I closed in on the dam, wafts of boggy mud and pooled water filling my nostrils, sopping, heavy mud filling my shoes.

I glanced back in time to spot the faintest upward slant in Cruikshank's mouth just as he launched a cast that sent his line hurling forward, unravelling like a frog's tongue down the creek. The fly coasted to a soft touch atop the water, six feet up from the dam. Now he let it drift. In that instant I knew the plan he'd concocted. He was letting the current do his work. Carrying his fly downstream, over the spill of logs and into the pool.

He cocked his long rod to the side, holding the tip high, attempting to guide the fly into the split of current that flowed off to the right bank and spilled over the logs.

I pumped my knees – splashing be damned – and raced his fly the last ten steps to the log dam. The rain now began drumming across our backs; thousands of tiny ripples littered the creek's surface. Thunder cracked again.

I reached the dam just as Cruikshank's fly caught the right bank flow and trembled toward the spillover. I searched frantically for a break in the foliage wide enough to jab a rod through. Nothing. Cruikshank's fly bobbled over some dips in the water, lifted up on the lip of the dam, where it seemed to pause for a moment, then popped over. As it sailed down, the fly caught a twig, stopped, and hung suspended, swaying, only a few inches over the water below.

Cruikshank could tell from my sudden smile he was snagged. He jiggled the rod, hoping to nudge it free and send it over. It wouldn't go. I ran my hands along the thickets until I found a broken branch that opened up just enough of the thicket to stab through. I reeled in my Kamlooper tight up against the last grommet, lifted my rod like I was pulling a sword free from its sheath, and with my best fencing-jab, thrust the rod into the brush. I could almost hear a metallic glint, like steel piercing bone.

Cruikshank reeled in the loose slack and yanked at his line to pull the fly free. It hopped back up over the logs and into the main stream behind me. He hauled the line frantically back in and immediately worked up a second cast.

I angled my rod downward, carefully through the mesh of branches, my rod tip hovering just above the still water of the hidden pool. Cruikshank, observing my peculiar method, made a face like I'd wiped my mouth with a tablecloth. He fired off a perfectly placed cast, landing softly just above the lip of the dam; the fly sailed swiftly into the flow and bobbled over just as I snapped my wrist, released the thumb-button trigger, and watched the Kamlooper sail into the middle of the pool. The Kamlooper plopped into the water and I reeled. Cruikshank's fly teetered over the lip of the logs and it, too, plunged into the pool. I reeled evenly, fighting the panicked urge to hurry the line unnaturally. Cruikshank's fly bobbled to the centre of the pool. The race was on.

Then I felt it.

At first it was like child tugging on your coat. A dog on a leash suddenly stopping to sniff a fence post. Then the line pulled hard and taut. My rod dipped, bent over, the wildly shaking tip pulling down almost into the water. Another tug, a pull, and then what I could only describe as a violent wrench, yanking at my line from somewhere below. I had latched onto something wild. Something uncontrollable.

The splash I heard next was the sound of pure muscle flexing, the beast thrusting itself up and out of the water. I lurched back, dodging my head to peek through the branches, half expecting to see a bear rising out of the water, roaring into the rain. But it wasn't. It was a beautiful, thick, long, massive rainbow trout – as big a rainbow as could ever exist in a creek so small. It soared up above the water, twisting and turning its giant frame, its glossy black spotting across its olive flesh, a fiery red band stretching from its flaring gills to its thrashing tail. The enormous fish crashed back into the water as my eyes dared to veer from the sight for only a second – just one essential second – long enough to take in the look on Kyle Cruikshank's face. He couldn't see the fish from his vantage, but he most certainly heard the splash. Cruikshank's mouth plunged open, his eyes spread as wide and dull as old spoons. His arms dropped to his sides, and the tip of his great fly rod sagged down into the water, bent on the gravelly creek bottom.

This wasn't to be Kyle Cruikshank's day. It wasn't to be a fly-fisherman's day. This was a day for spincasters. For dishwashers. For dogs with hemorrhoids. For those who travel the country in motorhomes with eight-by-ten frames they call their wife. This was a Bacon day.

The rainbow zigged and zagged, darting crazily around each corner of the pool. For over a full six minutes I battled, struggling to keep the line taut, but not too much so, maneuvering my rod in the bush, careful to prevent the zipping line from wrapping itself around any branches. Finally the big rainbow slowed to a cruising swirl, circling the perimeter of the pool, resting. Eventually it stopped completely, just below the tip of my rod. How I'd retrieve the great beast was another matter. I squeezed my arm into the branches, the jumble of twigs and thorns mashed against my face. Still, I pushed in further, shoving my arm down toward the water, hand open, ready to grip. With my other hand, I pulled back the rod, lifting the line, dragging the big rainbow up to the surface, just inches from the reach of my hand. It came smoothly without any kick or flinching, likely exhausted from the rabid fight. My open fingers carefully dipped into the water and slowly moved in around the fish. It lay still. I closed my fingers – slow and firm – around its thick frame, just behind the dorsal fin, and worried I couldn't even lift the thing. Then it fired off like a shot. The rainbow darted from my grip and around the pool like it had been zapped with a cattle prod.

213
≋

My line screamed and whirred, my rod nearly thrust from my hand. And then with remarkable speed and great strength, the trout launched itself at the dam, right up out of the water, slapping through two thin crossing branches, up over top of the fallen logs, and out from the hidden pool. The big fish almost seemed to pause there, suspended in mid-air above the dam, as if to flaunt its great strength and muscle and beauty. It had to be twenty inches long. It flexed and wagged and sparkled in the falling rain, and even before I felt the torturous whipping release of tension or heard the sad, crackling snap or witnessed the spiralling coil of thin, busted, clear nylon, I knew full well the six-pound test line would never hold.

The big rainbow splashed down into the creek with a great thud, fired itself like a cannon upstream, against the current, right past Kyle Cruikshank and around the bend. A sour and greasy smirk crawled up Cruikshank's face. The tip of his rod lifted slowly and deliberately, up from the water, rising high up above him.

"Doesn't count if you don't land him," Cruikshank shouted through the rain. His distorted voice oozed into my ears, filling up my head like a syrup. He tugged on the brim of his cap, turned, and followed the big trout upstream, into the open clearing of the creek ahead.

I didn't bother reeling in the nest of snapped line that lay piled atop the beaver dam. I simply collapsed apart the two pieces of my green and brown second-hand spincasting rod, gripped them together with the ball of line in one loosely closed hand, and walked through the rain back to my Firefly.

51. When I returned to the cabin,

I pushed open the door with my wet runner and sloshed inside. Poke, in his paint-splattered overalls, was leaving for his shift just as I was entering. "You got a guest," he yawned. Immediately I realized I'd forgotten to check out front for Laszlo's car. But when I lifted my eyes, I was shocked to see it wasn't Laszlo waiting for me. Planted on the couch in the living room, feet flat on the worn carpet, legs spread, a strong, meaty hand grasping each knee, small eyes frosted cold, a crooked snarl crinkled across her face, was Sara Mulligan.

"Hello, Bacon."

I ran.

I barrelled out into the driveway, hurled my green and brown second-hand spincasting rod with the thumb-button trigger into a hedge, and sprinted for my newly purchased Firefly. Sara was out the door behind me with the rumbling speed of a grizzly. Her fists pumped like pistons, her feet pounded into the driveway's gravel, mauling apart the distance between us. My shaking hand fumbled the key into the lock, and I threw myself into the Firefly. I slapped down the lock and wedged myself under the dashboard, down by the pedals. I heard a headlight shatter and peeked up to see Sara tugging her boot out of the front of the car. When she'd pulled herself free she used the same booted foot to hammer a mule kick into the driver's side door. I heard the side panel cave and fold inward. "Thought you didn't have a car?" Her face shoved up against the driver's side window. The outstretched fingers of both her hands were raking against the glass, trying to claw her way through. "You lied again!"

"No I didn't," I pleaded, hands cupped over my head. "I just bought it this morning."

Her snarling face ground itself up like she was trying to eat her own teeth. Then she eased off the window and stepped back. "So this shit box is yours?"

I nodded from under the steering column.

"Get out," she said.

I shook my head, not daring to look up.

"Bacon, get the fuck out or I'll punch through that window and chew your ears off." I tightened the hands overtop of my head and slammed closed my eyes.

Thud! Sara's fist hammered into the side window, rocking the entire vehicle. Somehow the glass managed to stay intact. "It'll give. So get the fuck out." And she was right. The glass would give. *Thud!* She hit it again. The glass was still there, but it would go. And likely with her next punch. Sara was going to get at me either way, it was just matter of how much of the Firefly she destroyed in the process.

"ok, ok." I threw up an arm. "Stop it. I'll come out."

Sara backed off a few steps. I lifted up into the seat, opened the door, but before I got my second foot out of the car, Sara lunged for me, threw me down in a heap of dust on the gravel drive, wrestled the keys from my hand, and leapt into the Firefly. She fired it up but paused – for just a moment – rolled down the window, and said, "You stupid asshole. I loved you." She stomped on the gas and pulled the Firefly out of the driveway, hopping off the curb and clipping a hedge on the way.

My guess was she was headed to Vancouver. She'd said it was wild there.

It's strange what fumbles through your mind at different times. I was lying there in the dust and gravel, the weight of my awkwardly crumpled body pressing my cheek into the tiny pebbles and stones of the driveway, watching the tail lights of my Firefly disappear down the road in a gust of hedge leaves. I wasn't thinking about the car I'd just bought and now no longer possessed, or whether I was a university man or college man, or whether it even mattered now that I could no longer drive to either institution. Instead the thought that formed in my mind was the large rainbow that had heaved on my line that morning. Not about the fact that the line had snapped and the fish had broken free, darting away upstream to another pool, and not about the fact that perhaps that pool was a pool Kyle Cruikshank had conquered shortly after I left. Instead I was simply remembering how it felt to have that big fish on my line. The great heave and pull I'd felt. That was the only part of the day worth remembering, the only part of the story worth telling. And what a great part it had been. It was the song in the story. How the big fish had chosen the Kamlooper I'd laid out for it, and for that short minute – a thrilling minute or so – we were connected. Even if only by a small, thin, translucent line.

52.

"**Bacon!**" Grandma's voice crackled through the phone. "Are you coming home soon?"

"I think so, yes."

"Thank goodness. When?"

"Soon. This is my last night in Waterton. I'm leaving here tomorrow. But I have some things to tell you, Grandma."

"What is it, dear?"

"I don't have the Lancer anymore."

"What?" She coughed twice. "Why not?"

"I hit a moose. So I bought a Firefly."

"A Firefly?"

"Yes, but it got stolen. But that's not what I wanted to tell you."

"Good gracious, what then?"

"I want to tell you about the fish I caught today."

"You did? What did you catch?"

"A rainbow. A great big rainbow."

"Bacon, that's great!"

"I know. But Grandma I'd rather tell you about it in person. At home. It'll be a great story."

"Bacon, if you don't have a car, how will you get here?"

"I don't know yet. Don't worry, Grandma. I'll find a way. There's always another way."

53.

Other than microwaving a frozen four-bean burrito as my homemade meal of the day, and making a quick visit with Poke to the maintenance shop for my fridge idea, I spent the afternoon preparing for, instead of hiding out from, Laszlo. I was through running.

It's an interesting feeling when a whole town of people is preparing to leave each other. It doesn't feel so much like getting left behind when everybody is doing the leaving. There was a definite change in current that day. A shift in the flow of the feel of the town. It reminded me of a last cast on a day of fishing when you'll throw out a lousy neon-yellow jig or a clunky, oversized old number nine muskill lure just for the hell of it. Maybe even splash yourself out right into the middle of the creek and start grabbing at the water, things you'd never normally do, but because you're leaving, you'll try anything and could just about care less what happens.

That night my roommates hosted the final party of the season. People arrived as early as three o'clock. They carried with them cases of Pilsner and Black Label and Club and bottles of Potters rum and Highwood rye and Alberta vodka. If you climbed to the top of a mountain shelf they called Bear's Hump and peered down on the town below, you'd see streams of people trickling out of their places, dribbling down the quiet streets into our cabin. It would look like the entire flood plain had been lifted, tilted, and all the townspeople had been shaken from their homes.

Some people, wired up in the excitement, cracked beers while they walked, unable to hold out the two- or three-block stroll. Others cracked their first beers even earlier, taking bottles into their morning showers. Some – those few who bothered to show up for work at all that day – were topping up their colas with rum or rye at that very moment, desperate to hasten their final shifts, furious at themselves for honouring their employment obligations.

People carried styrofoam containers stuffed with staff meal clubhouse sandwiches or buffalo burgers or mozza sticks. Each container overloaded with thick-cut fries so fresh they made the rest of their meals, their hands, and our entire cabin smell oily. Others brought striped bags of buttery popcorn from the garage across the street, most of it snatched up in unpaid dash-bys. Eventually, the entire popcorn machine was dislodged from its spot behind the counter and hauled across the street into our cabin.

The bingo girls arrived armed with apple vodka ciderjacks and a rainbow of ink daubers. They huddled in the corner, comparing bingo cards and pointing at the crowd with their little fingers. I avoided direct eye contact like I would a family of wolverines.

I seized a spot on the couch, throwing a leg up across a second cushion to hold for Woodrat, keeping a fish eye's periphery on the bingo girls, looking for Woodrat, and watching out for Laszlo.

By seven o'clock, every summer employee from every business in town packed our cabin. Every server, salad chopper, dishpig, food runner, room booker, flower finder, ice cream scooper, popcorn bagger, shooter girl, trinket teller, toilet scraper, and scooter rental sales assistant all stuffed into our musty cabin. I thought if I could make it through to the far corner of the living room I'd probably find a good portion of the park's wildlife, too. I was sure somewhere in the kitchen I'd heard the shrill whistle of a hoary marmot.

People drank on the roof, resting back against the mossy shingles. Down in the kitchen a lineup had organized itself of women looking to recover missing appliances. Not the refrigerator, though; it was disguised. And covered in blankets. Everyone in the living room moved in a swarm as if the mass of them were a whole, the entire room a great pot of slowly stirring stew. As the people shuffled around, they cautiously stepped over bottles and cans and other people who'd decided, or whose buckling knees had decided, to lie themselves down. Those on the floor stared up at those still standing through reddened and cracked-windshield eyes. Some reached up, asking for a hand, or for more mix, or for a blanket, or simply inquired as to their whereabouts.

The one brief moment I lifted my glance up, I spotted – and was spotted by – the tank-top girl and her three friends. Whispering together, their pale eyes fixed on me. The tank-top girl's fair-skinned friend with the thick mass of hair lifted a bingo card, tapping the row of unblotted Bs. I quickly turned away. That's when Woodrat finally arrived. She glided through the stew of people, her arms locked around a four-litre box of Entre Lac red.

As she sat, I caught a glimpse of a bra, stuffed into the back pocket of her green cargo pants, bulging out and adding a fresh fullness to her bum that caused me to hold my breath.

We talked about her upcoming flights to the Bahamas and Indonesia and Thailand and Sri Lanka. I didn't bother telling her about the Firefly or Sara or that I now had no way of getting her to the airport or me to college or university or back home or anywhere for that matter.

I kept the glass Woodrat had poured me sheltered in my hand, warm and full, not so much as even sipping a drop while she guzzled from the spigot. I needed full lucidity for when Laszlo showed.

Even in the bunched up clumps of what appeared to be several, perhaps her entire collection, of stolen bras, layered one over the other, lumped under her T-shirt, Woodrat radiated confidence. Her long, thick lips clamped into a wide, self-assured grin, stretching out behind the slick brown hair that swung in her face.

Sneaking glimpses of her clumpy chest, I felt the familiar blood rush as my "problem" began to fill, kinking and stretching out from its folded, sweaty position. It's likely the closest a man can get to knowing what it's like to carry a baby – the shifting, kicking motion of something inside you, nudging for space, wanting only out.

I couldn't imagine how such a girl was willing to sit there on that couch next to me, spending her last night in Waterton with me. It made me think of what Karla had said about girls that spend time with me. "Do you want something from me?" I asked.

Woodrat's round eyes blinked. "You mean like a snack cracker or some juice?"

"No, I mean in general." I crossed my hands over my rising lap. "Somebody once told me the only reasons a girl like you – not specifically you, but girls like you – would have anything to do with me is because they want something."

"Well that's bleak." Woodrat hiccuped. "But I suppose, in the end, everybody does *want* something. Nobody's entirely charitable." Woodrat stuffed her hand into her open collar and pulled out a bra. The garment couldn't have been fastened or even looped around an arm. She tossed it onto the coffee table. "One too many," she explained. "Well, I'll be blatantly honest with you, Bacon. I suppose one of the reasons I've spent time with you is because I enjoy your attention. Everybody likes to be admired. But the other reason is because I enjoy your company. I really do. You're a whole lot of goodness, Bacon. I trust you. That's nice to be around. I haven't seen a lot of goodness."

I don't know if it was her words or her sandy-coloured bra draped over the edge of the coffee table, but I felt my gut pinch with an expanding pressure in my intestine and I knew right then I was feeling more than just the need for a bathroom – though I did need a bathroom – but I also knew that my "problem" was preparing to fight for a way out.

After downing another glass of wine, Woodrat yawned and commented on how wiped she felt from the summer, how it was all catching up to her. I agreed to be agreeable but I didn't feel the least bit tired, in fact I had about as much energy as that big rainbow from Cameron Creek. And I may as well have had that big fish thrashing around inside me for all the rumbling I could feel.

I stood and excused myself, explaining I needed the washroom. Woodrat told me to hurry as she was just about ready for bed. "Bed?" I stopped and spun back around. "It's not even ten," I said, squeezing my legs together. "You can't leave now." How could she even think of leaving? Our last night together and she wanted to get to bed before ten? My throat tightened until it felt like I was breathing through a straw.

"What I mean is it's going to be an early morning. I've got to be on the road by seven to make my flight."

My bad timing remained faithful. Facing the threat of never seeing Woodrat again, in desperate need of convincing her to stay longer, my bladder and bowels chose that moment to nearly rupture. "It's our last night." I swung my squeezed knees from side to side in a crouched position. "You can't just go to bed."

"Bacon, I'm just saying I need to be in bed at a reasonable hour –"

"Just hold on." I grabbed two fistfuls of my jeans. "I'll be right back." I darted for the bathroom.

"Hurry," she called after me.

I flew into the bathroom, threw down my jeans, and only just got started when the bathroom lock popped – picked from the outside – and the door swung open. Laszlo Maximilian Mursky stepped in, relocked the door, and sat his heavy self on my lap.

"Were you actually expecting I'd not return?" Laszlo said.

I felt the first prickling of a headache wash over my brain.

Laszlo sat perfectly aligned on my lap, staring ahead to the same damp and chipping drywall I'd been glaring at while trying to hurry my business. "Surely you were expecting me," he said.

"Not specifically here," I said. "Look, Laszlo, I –"

"Hup, hup, hup." He folded his arms, crossed one leg over the other. "I know, I know. You sleep with my wife. You ditch us in Calgary. You leave behind a large, unpaid bill. Why was I surprised I had to come all the way down here to collect? It really is my fault. I'm a fool."

"Laszlo," I said to the back of his head, "could you lift up off my lap? Maybe let me finish up here –"

"I actually thought you might seek me out before today. You know, to pay off the rest as, I don't know, a of show of good faith?"

"Look, I'm sorry Laszlo, but Woodrat's going to leave. Can we finish this conversation out –"

"I guess I just naturally assume people are generally sincere. Can you imagine?"

"Laszlo!" I tapped his shoulder. "This is tremendously awkward. I'm in mid-stool, I desperately need to get back to Woodrat before she leaves, and you're sitting on my undressed lap."

"Oh, my apologies!" Laszlo threw his arms up. "Don't let me inconvenience you. Why don't I get up so you can finish. I'm sure you'll come find me out there. You're a man of your word. Or wait ..." He made a stop motion with his hand. "*Or* you could pay me now so I can go back to Calgary and be with my wife – the one you stole intercourse from. Now that sounds better. Yes." He refolded his arms and sighed, shifting his weight on my lap.

I cut off my business as quickly and dignified as I could, flushed, then squeezed myself out from under Laszlo. He scurried over to the door, cutting off my exit, still refusing to look my way. His pursed lips bulged as his tongue rolled over his teeth.

"Laszlo, please." I bent to meet his eyes, but he turned away. "You'll be reimbursed. Tonight. But right now I really need to get back to Woodrat. Soon. She likes her sleep. I'm afraid she'll leave. It's our last night together."

Laszlo pretended to pick something from his shirt then rubbed it away between his fingers. "Bacony Boy, you need to pay me now and you have two options to do that. You can pay by cash or by credit card. I won't take a cheque from you. Forgive my splintered trust. Cash or credit card. There are only two options, those are them."

The pain in my head was spreading lower, gripping my eyes, clenching down my spine, and moving into my stomach. To ease the growing intensity of the ache I imagined myself standing in water, calf deep in Cameron Creek, strolling up the easy current. Immediately I felt the throbbing slow to a dull, heavy pinch. Again, the thought of the big fish from this morning came back to me. The sudden tug of the line, the twitching arch of the bending rod, the explosion of water as the big fish burst free from the pool.

I wiped my fists over my eyes, locked my glance onto Laszlo's pupils, and said firmly, "No, there isn't."

"You mind your aggressive tone —"

"There's always another way," I said.

He scratched a puffed cheek. "Come again now?"

"Fine. We'll do it now. But hurry." I blew out a heavy sigh. "Follow me outside."

Laszlo cocked his head like a puppy. "I'm not following you anywhere, Bacony Boy. Look, the only thing I need to hear from you is 'cash' or 'credit card.'"

I hooked up Laszlo's fat pinky in mine, squeezing it tight, lifting it up with my fist, right up close to his bubbled eyes. "Touch pinkies, Laszlo. You will be reimbursed. That reimbursement is outside. Now follow me."

I led a wide-eyed Laszlo by the pinky out of the bathroom, through the stew of people, across the living room, out the side door, and under the driveway carport where a large, rectangular object sat draped under a blanket. I pulled free the blanket and unveiled a refrigerator freezer. The same refrigerator freezer I'd accumulated in the deal with Poke. Except now it was pink.

"It's ... *pink*." Laszlo said.

"It's pink," I confirmed.

"Pink!"

"Yes."

"Karla likes pink," he said.

"Karla *loves* pink."

Poke's maintenance shed had contained a stunning variety of paints, including, as I'd gambled, appliance paint. I had to mix red and white to get the appropriate shade of pink, but it worked. And now the large luxury refrigerator freezer was pink.

"Oh, yes, my Karly-fry loves pink," Laszlo whispered to nobody in particular, his mouth slung open. "She doesn't have a pink refrigerator. She has a pink toaster. A blender. A microwave. But no refrigerator."

"She does now."

"Hot mustard on a spicy sausage," he giggled. "Karla *loves* pink."

"Look, Laszlo, this beast is worth far more than the seventeen hundred you claim I owe. And it's pink. Whatever value it holds over and above what you think I owe, you can consider a gift. An apology. A peace offering."

Laszlo considered me long and hard. "It's brilliant," he finally said.

"So, are we square?"

"It's pink." He ran a hand down the side of the appliance like it was Karla's own pink flesh.

"Laszlo, are we good?"

He faced me. "Yeah, Bacony Boy. We're good. You're good." He held up the small finger of his right hand. I wrapped my own around his.

"Touch pinkies," we both said.

I bolted back inside, but the couch was empty. I fought through the stew of people, searching each face for the one I wanted.

"Woodrat!" I called out over the crowd like I was hollering into a sprawling forest. "Woodrat!" Stretching up on my toes, I couldn't find her. I shoved my way through the stew, around the entire living room. Nothing. I dodged into the bathroom. Nothing. I wedged myself through the crowd into the kitchen, out onto the porch. Nothing. I pushed back into the kitchen where I spotted Kyle Cruikshank.

"Did you lose your girlfriend?" Cruikshank laughed, mostly through his nose. "Woodrat said goodbye fifteen minutes ago. Said she needed to get some zz Tops."

"What do you mean she said goodbye?" I said, barely audible.

"What? No kiss goodbye?" Kyle Cruikshank's jaw wiggled with a smirk. "Have you considered you're fishing with the wrong gear?" The stew of people, which had started to thin, carried me out into the living room. Nothing Kyle Cruikshank said ever made sense. I collapsed onto the couch.

Woodrat, it seemed, knew the first rule about never getting left behind: doing the leaving first.

Part of me wanted to leap from the couch, chase her to her tent, demand to know if that's the way limited liability partners are supposed to spend their last night. But I guess another part of me knew that was the *limited* part.

I don't know what I'd expected. Maybe I'd just done too much imagining. If Kenny Rogers had been there in our cabin at that moment I'm sure he would've started singing something about Woodrat being right for not falling for a dreamer. He should've written a song about love being a load of peanut-packed crap. If I'd had a car I would've driven home to Bellevue right then and there. My mother would just be getting home from bingo. I could just see the pale concrete wash of her face and the contrasting black gloss in her eyes that said *I told you so.* Maybe she was right about repairing the barn when you lose a cow.

The cabin's air was still thick with the smell of French fries, spilled liquor, and sweat. At my feet, Woodrat's abandoned box of wine sat on its side next to the coffee table. It too had been left behind, knocked over in the commotion of the party. On the table sat a glass with a few splashes of mixed colour in it. I filled the rest of the glass with wine and downed it. I poured myself another glass, then another. I drank two more, then lifted the box above my thrown-back face, pinched the spigot, and let the wine run down into my mouth, over my chin, and across my cheeks.

"Whooa," a voice said. "You're well on your way." I rolled my head over to see the tank-top girl, setting herself on the couch beside me.

I lifted the wine box over my head and tipped another splash over my face, some of it reaching my mouth. The tank-top girl's head split into three heads, and those three heads swayed in and out of each other. My body slipped, sliding down a touch on the couch. One of my legs lifted, coming to rest partly on her lap.

"Bacon, I know you're enamoured with that laundry girl."

She dropped her eyes to her lap. "It's no secret. And don't get me wrong, she's certainly a ... a ... person." Hearing Woodrat's name I glanced around again, suddenly surprised it wasn't Woodrat sitting there talking to me. "But she's not here now. You're alone. And you don't have to be." I noticed my leg sitting on the tank-top girl's lap and attempted to kick it free. But that leg wouldn't move. I lifted the box and poured another trail of wine down my throat. It barely found my mouth.

"Woodrat left," was all I could slur.

The tank-top girl's fingertips gently stroked my forearm. She had fifteen fingers on that one hand. I saw her wince at my dripping face. "You look like you're about ready for bed," she said. I think I felt myself nod. "Would you like some company?"

I smeared the back of my wrist across my face. Her hard, green eyes reached out at me. All six of them. For a second I almost smiled to myself, afraid to check, but wondering if she might have six breasts, too. Six nipples.

"Let's look at it from your perspective. You're what? Eighteen? Nineteen? Almost done with your teens. You don't get these summers back." She touched her hand to my cheek as if to reassure me I was still a good man. "And from my perspective," she laughed three laughs from her three mouths, "You're the only B in town. I need that B."

I focused on the middle mouth and squinted. Despite the people all around us the cabin seemed strangely quiet and cold. We needed to remain on the couch, I told myself. As long as we stayed there, everything would be fine.

"You've wasted a whole summer here fishing for something that didn't want to get caught. The way I see it, you can either sulk about it, tormenting yourself, wondering if you said the wrong thing, or did the wrong thing, frantically speculate where she's gone, what she's thinking, submerge yourself into the terror that you'll never meet anyone like her again. Or we could go have sex. You choose."

The tank-top girl pulled herself to her feet. I watched her help me to my own feet. I knew I shouldn't leave the couch, but as long as we kept clear of the stairs, I was sure we'd be fine. I just needed to stretch my legs. The box of wine dropped from my hand and burped out a red splash across the floor.

The thin fingers locked around mine were soft and small. Gentle and comforting. I knew I needed to shake loose from that soft grip. But I didn't.

I caught my foot on the first step and stumbled down to one knee; the tank-top girl helped me back to my feet. I clung to the handrail, holding myself steady. As we climbed up the stairs, the cabin sloped and seemed to list or ebb. Each step up the staircase felt more like a descent, heading down instead of up. My feet continued to climb, waiting for something to stop me, to speak up.

At the top step, the tank-top girl's smile looked almost smug, her thin nose — noses, three of them — slid down, leading my eyes over the rest of her bodies.

In the morning Woodrat would be on her way to the Bahamas. The tank-top girl would be off to whatever school or job or life she was headed to. Everyone would be leaving. Except me. I'd be doing the staying because I had no way to leave.

I reached for the doorknob and held its coldness in my limp hand. It was a struggle to turn it just the slightest. I must've been holding on to that door for close to a minute; I think I may have even briefly drifted off into something of a sleep. The doorknob slid back through my flopping hand.

The tank-top girl lifted my chin, tried to shake my glance back into focus, to get my eyes to meet hers. "Are you going to open the door?" I had to check to see what door she was talking about. I was genuinely surprised to find a doorknob in my hand.

I wondered how long my father had stared at our door before he finally opened it and walked through. Before he left Bellevue. I wondered how long or how often my mother sat in the old recliner of our living room, staring at that same door, cussing the rusted hinges, cursing the crack in the door's window that had started to spider, or sighing about the draft that blew in from underneath.

I stood holding that doorknob, staring at the tank-top girl for what seemed like hours. Her smugness faded, turned to impatience. Several more moments passed and I swayed heavily back and forth on my bent ankles, not even attempting to reach out to steady myself.

All night the thunderous music rattled paint chips from the walls, and people cried out, trying to be heard overtop of each other. The laughter and shrieking must've carried clear across the lake, but you could've heard a pin drop when I stopped swaying and let go of that door.

"What are you doing?"

I couldn't find the words to explain. I couldn't even find the letters to make up a word.

"Don't tell me you're choosing to *sulk*."

Kenny Rogers would've described the tank-top girl as a beauty if he'd seen her come to me. And maybe he would've said I'd lost my mind, but there was no way I could hold her because Woodrat's words kept coming back time after time. "I have a limited liability partner," I managed to slur.

"I have no idea what that means but I think it probably means sulk," she sighed. "This isn't going to happen, is it?" She dropped her hand from my chin.

I shook my head at my shoes.

"You're a weird guy, Bacon," she said. "I'm not sure what to make of the fact that *you're* turning *me* down. In any case, I'm *not* going to lose that bingo game. You hear me? If anyone asks, tell them we *did*. OK? I really need that B." She turned and clopped down the stairs.

I wanted to apologize. I wanted to stop her. To reconsider. But I said nothing. I stood there for probably ten minutes. Teetering and staring at my feet, waiting for them to explain to me why they had — at this moment, of all times — gotten so cold. My feet, like every other part of me, had bad timing.

But I hadn't chosen sulk. Not at all. My problemed pecker would never let me. Besides, I had my word to keep. And something to finish.

Eventually my hand found the doorknob again, twisted it, and my hanging head pushed open the door. As the hinges creaked I looked through the darkness, toward the open window, where the breeze-blown curtains flapped at me like a hand saying, "to hell with you," and a nub of moon, like a finger tip, pointed tauntingly at me.

I sighed and pushed the door closed with my leaning weight. But I had no intention of brooding. I hadn't chosen to sulk. I unbuttoned my jeans, let them slide down my legs to the floor. A rush of ease settled over me as my fingers slipped inside my underwear; my mind sank into the warm pool of imagining what it was I had chosen. There's a place between being left behind and doing the leaving. It's a place between holding on and letting go. A place where you don't have to brood and you don't have to run. I shook and wagged my sagging penis like I was waving a smelt over the water. Drawing to the surface the snapping images of my someone.

Just as the rhythm of my body's blood flow returned, a voice broke through the darkness. "What are you doing?" it said. I leapt like a brookie, buckled over in attempting to cover myself, collapsed against the door, and crumbled to the floor. The dim bedside lamp clicked on and, through the wash of Entre Lac, my eyes beheld Woodrat Lynn-Marie Seever, sitting up in my bed and holding the sheets against herself.

"Woodrat?" I squeezed all my focus into one eye, winking hard until there was only one face swaying, until I was certain it was Woodrat's face and not the door or a pillow or the lamp.

"Close your mouth," she said, brushing her hair back with a sleepy fist. "You'll swallow something."

But I couldn't close my mouth. I couldn't feel my mouth. And I wanted to swallow something – I wanted to swallow her, my room, the cabin, the whole moment. Keep it forever inside me. She hadn't left. Not yet. Not without saying goodbye. And good Lord, I'd almost walked in with the tank-top girl! Just a slight turn of the doorknob, a few more steps, a few seconds longer ... and the moment would have been so much different. I felt a tickling, like a million aphids scurrying down the back of my neck, swarming out across my back. This was the unfamiliar – the entirely unknown – feel of good timing.

Woodrat clicked off the light. In the moonlight I could just make out her silhouette crawling out from under the covers, stretching out on top of them. My eye traced the dark outline of her body. "Come here." I heard her pat the bed beside her. "You can finish that over here. You know, I wasn't sure what exactly we were going to be able to pull off with me coming up here. But, Bacon," she chuckled, "I think you've found the one thing that could happen. The Bacon way."

I pulled myself up the bed as steady as possible, keeping clear of the edge, frightened I'd fall off, perhaps fall right out of my room, out of that instant. Settling in alongside her, I watched in the darkness as she removed her clothes and began on herself what I had started on myself by the door. Both her hands dipped down in between her own legs. Her breathing softened and slowed.

We lay next to each other, both on our backs, both staring up at the ceiling. Islands in the stream, Kenny Rogers would've had said, no one in between. Only the skin of our shoulders and the outside of our arms occasionally brushed. My hands moved over myself, and hers moved over herself. We held firm, not swaying from our positions, not even turning in to face each other.

"What do you think about?" I whispered.

Her body squirmed and wriggled as though swaying to the rhythm of some song I couldn't hear. "Dependability," she whispered. "You?"

I turned my head to watch her breasts rise and fall, carrying out small, soft moans as she exhaled. "My someone," I said.

Only once did my eyes start to close, my head to drift off to the side, my mind cloud over, the wine reaching up through the veins of my eyelids. But Woodrat nudged me with her elbow and I was back in an instant—still sleepy, but more awake than maybe I've ever been.

That night, after I finished—after we'd each finished—we lay there on our own sides of the bed, limited liability partners. We slept just like trout in a dark mountain creek, under the safe shadow of a fallen log, not worried about anything. And we slept through that full night, just as peaceful as the soft dark sky above.

54. When my eyes creaked open the

next morning, I woke to an empty room. An empty cabin. Poke and Cruikshank and Gibson and Peritz and all my roommates were gone. Woodrat had left, too. I could hear the hush of breeze through the trees out back, the gentle lapping of the lake, and even the soft snap of the flag down by the docks. But there were no sounds coming from within the cabin, except maybe the occasional quiet groan of the old wood frame's morning stretch. In those first few sleepy moments of that morning I felt like I might be the last person left on the whole planet.

I collected up the few clothes I'd bought, along with my fishing gear, stuffed them into my backpack, and stumbled downstairs. I wasn't sure how I'd get home or if that was where I should be going anyway.

The cabin felt cooler than usual, perhaps because of the changing season or perhaps because I was the only source left to generate heat.

I wasn't bothered that Woodrat hadn't woken me to say goodbye. Or even left a note. That just seemed like her style. Besides, what was there to say? I imagined her at that moment, thinking of me, right as she boarded the plane headed to the Bahamas. I could see her meeting up with some stranger sitting next to her. My guess is she'd be too tired to even sleep. So she'd stare out the window, out into the daylight. Soon enough the boredom would overtake her and she'd likely begin to speak. She'd tell that somebody next to her all about me, and how even though she had to leave, nothing could change the fact that she'd met her someone.

I took one last glance around the empty cabin, at the stained and sticky furniture, at the half-empty bottles and cans strewn across the floor, at the mozza sticks dumped in empty glasses, and at the partially eaten buffalo burgers discarded on windowsills or stuffed between the cushions of the couch.

I stepped outside, not sure where to head or even which direction to face. It was a clear, calm day, not a cloud in sight. The sun pinched my eyes closed and, when I was finally able to adjust and squint my eyes back open, I saw a Hyundai Sonata sitting in the driveway. Beside it, dressed in black slacks and a grey short-sleeved dress shirt, was Mr. Kwon. Focusing his hard, serious face my way. He was holding a microwave.

"*Annyeong*," he said, nodding at me.

"Mr. Kwon?" I made a visor of my hand. "What are you doing here?"

"I guessed you might needed a ride somewhere," he said. "Did I guess right?"

I shrugged at first, then nodded. "I suppose. So you came all the way down here?"

"It's only one hour," he said. "We are family, Bacon. Family does like this."

A ground squirrel scurried across the gravel between us. It disappeared into the hedge. I nodded toward the microwave. "What's that for?"

"I don't know," Mr. Kwon said. "Somebody gave it to me while I waited for you. Said he have three. Bacon, are you wanting to come to home?"

"I don't really know where I should be going."

"Did you decide between the university and college?"

I shook my head.

"You have not decided yet, or you decided neither?"

"I don't know," I said. "I guess I didn't decide what to decide yet."

"Mm."

"I don't really have any money left."

"I see."

"I bought a car but somebody took it."

"Yes."

"What do you think I should do?"

"What you want to do."

"I don't think I'm smart enough for school."

"Nonsense."

"I don't have much for skills. And I'm not sure I know much about anything."

"Your grandmother says you know about the dishwashing."

"Right." I tried to laugh. "That's not gonna do me much good."

"It will get you a job."

"I'm not sure that's a job with much future."

"It's a job that gets you in a kitchen, where you can train to other jobs. Like serving. Or cooking." His voice softened. He seemed embarrassed of his exuberance. "If you were interested."

"Cooking?" I blurted, almost startled by the idea.

"You could work in my kitchen," he shrugged. "If you wanted. You could learn the Korean cooking. Continue learning Hangul. Those would be skills. At least until you decided about the university or college." I had to tilt my head and squint from the sun. I looked back into the cabin, not sure what I expected to see. Then I turned back to Mr. Kwon.

He really was going to get this restaurant going. He really was going to stay in Bellevue. Bellevue was going to get some culture.

"I'd like that," I smiled.

Mr. Kwon stared hard. Nodded. "*Kapsheda*, Bacon." He motioned to the car.

We headed back to the Crowsnest Pass and I watched Waterton disappear behind us. As we neared closer to Bellevue I felt strangely surprised by how close home had been all this time. We passed the familiar countryside where cottonwoods still stood in patches a few metres off the highway, the rows of barbed-wire fences still leaned on weathered rotting posts, and the dusty ranch road turnoffs still sat marked by sun-bleached cow skulls or wood slab signs seared with ranch brands. The wild grasses leaned and waved in the slapping breeze.

I wondered how soon it would be before I received a postcard from the Bahamas or India or Thailand or Sri Lanka. The postcards wouldn't say much. That wouldn't be her style. But I was sure one would come.

I looked forward to getting back on the Crow and imagining Woodrat lying on the bank next to me, spotting fish instead of catching them, summoning trout to the surface with the waving of a twig. I'd use the tip of my green and brown second-hand spincasting rod to point out Turtle Mountain and the limestone rubble of Frank Slide, and across the river where the fish like

233

to hide up under the lip of the opposite bank. I'd update her on how Mr. Kwon's restaurant was doing and what weeds Grandma Magic Can was picking, and how much money my mother won or spent at bingo.

As Mr. Kwon turned off the highway into Bellevue, I spotted the giant crow, still perched in her nest, staring down at us with her large, white eyes. Her beak still gaped open. Watching me and my green and brown second-hand spincasting rod with the closed-face reel and thumb-button trigger return to Bellevue.

I wondered if that big crow knew all along. And as I followed Mr. Kwon up our steps and through the front door, trying to imagine Woodrat smearing tea tree oil on some dog's anus, I smiled and thought to myself how true it was that Kenny Rogers sure as shit knows what's what.

Ah-ah.

Acknowledgements

Hearty thanks to Suzette Mayr, Nicole Markotić, and Rosemary Nixon
for their expertise.

Thanks is also due to Kari Strutt, Fran Kimmel, Lisa Willemse, Jon-Paul
Jepp, Kim Seok Hee, and Kim Sang Dong.

Special thanks to my wife, Shantael, for providing a level of inspiration
and support that makes creative endeavours like this not only possible
but inevitable.

While Michael Davie has lived in South Korea, it was his years spent in the Rocky Mountain towns of Waterton, Banff, Canmore, and Jasper, living immersed in an often eccentric resort subculture, that most influenced his creative output, first in publishing a cartoon series, *The Last Resort*, then in literature with his first novel, *Fishing for Bacon*.

Davie graduated from the University of Lethbridge with a Bachelor of Management and studied Creative Writing at the University of Calgary and the Victoria School of Writing. He now lives in Calgary with his wife, Shantael, and son, Samuell.

This book is set in the typeface Miller, which was designed by Matthew Carter from 1997 to 2000.